PRAISE FOR VICTOR

Evelyn, After

"Hands down, the best book I've read this year. Brilliant, compelling and haunting."

—Suzanne Brockmann, *New York Times* bestselling author

"Readers will cheer on Evelyn when the power dynamic with her lying, cheating husband shifts, even while they watch her flirting with disaster in her steamy affair with Noah. A solid choice for Liane Moriarty readers."

—*Library Journal*

"Stone (a nom de plume of romance writer Victoria Dahl) . . . ably switches to darker suspense in a compelling story exploring what lurks behind a seemingly perfect life."

—*Booklist*

"Stone pens a great story that will have readers wondering what will happen next to the characters involved in this mysterious tale . . . Fascinating tale told by a talented storyteller!"

—*RT Book Reviews*

"Victoria Helen Stone renders the obsessions and weaknesses of her characters with scorching insight. Her sterling prose creates a seamless atmosphere of anticipation and dread while delivering devastating truths about the nature of sex, relationships, and lies, often with a humor that's rapier-sharp. *Evelyn, After* reads like *Gone Girl* with a bigger heart and a stronger moral core."

—Christopher Rice, *New York Times* bestselling author

Half Past

"A gripping, haunting exploration of the lengths to which we'll go to belong, *Half Past* will hold you in its thrall until the very last page. Stone's expert storytelling, vivid characterizations, and tantalizing dropping of clues left me utterly breathless, longing for more—and a newly minted Victoria Helen Stone fan!"

—Emily Carpenter, bestselling author of *Burying the Honeysuckle Girls* and *The Weight of Lies*

"A captivating, suspenseful tale of love and lies, mystery and self-discovery, *Half Past* kept me flipping the pages through the final, startling twist."

—A. J. Banner, #1 Amazon and *USA Today* bestselling author of *The Good Neighbor* and *The Twilight Wife*

"What would you do if you found out that your mother wasn't your biological mother? Would you go looking for the answer to how that happened if she couldn't provide an explanation? That's the intriguing question at the heart of *Half Past*, Stone's strong follow-up to *Evelyn, After*. [It's] both a mystery and an exploration of what family really means. Fans of Jodi Picoult will race through this."

—Catherine McKenzie, bestselling author of *Hidden* and *The Good Liar*

Jane Doe

"Stone does a masterful job of creating in Jane a complex character, making her both scary and more than a little appealing . . . This beautifully balanced thriller will keep readers tense, surprised, pleased, and surprised again as a master manipulator unfolds her plan of revenge."

—*Kirkus Reviews* (starred review)

"Revenge drives this fascinating thriller . . . Stone keeps the suspense high throughout. Readers will relish Jane's Machiavellian maneuvers to even the score with the unlikable Steven."

—*Publishers Weekly*

"Crafty, interesting, and vengeful."

—*Novelgossip*

"Crazy great book!"

—*Good Life Family* magazine

"Stone skillfully, deviously, and gleefully leads the reader down a garden path to a knockout WHAM-O of an ending. *Jane Doe* will not disappoint."

—*New York Journal of Books*

"*Jane Doe* is a riveting, engrossing story about a man who screws over the wrong woman, with a picture-perfect ending that's the equivalent of a big red bow on a shiny new car. It's that good. Ladies, we finally have the revenge story we've always deserved."

—Criminal Element

"Jane, the self-described sociopath at the center of Victoria Helen Stone's novel, [is] filling a hole in storytelling that we've long been waiting for."

—Bitch Media

"We loved being propelled into the complicated mind of Jane, intrigued as she bobbed and weaved her way through life with the knowledge she's just a little bit different. Both incredibly insightful and tautly suspenseful, you'll be debating whether to make Jane your new best friend or lock your door and hide from her in fear. *Jane Doe* is a must-read!"

—Liz Fenton and Lisa Steinke, bestselling authors of *The Good Widow*

"With biting wit and a complete disregard for societal double standards, Victoria Helen Stone's antihero will slice a path through your expectations and leave you begging for more. Make room in the darkest corner of your heart for *Jane Doe*."

—Eliza Maxwell, bestselling author of *The Unremembered Girl*

"If revenge is a dish best served cold, Jane Doe is Julia Child. Though Jane's a heroine who claims to be a sociopath, Jane's heart and soul shine through in this addicting, suspenseful tale of love, loss, and justice."

—Wendy Webb, bestselling author of *The End of Temperance Dare*

"One word: wow. This novel is compelling from the first sentence. An emotional ride with a deliciously vengeful narrator, Jane's tale keeps readers on the edge without the security of knowing who the good guy really is. Honest, cutting, and at times even humorous, this is one powerhouse of a read!"

—Brandi Reeds, bestselling author of *Trespassing*

FALSE STEP

ALSO BY VICTORIA HELEN STONE

Evelyn, After
Half Past
Jane Doe

FALSE STEP

VICTORIA HELEN
STONE

This is a work of fiction. Names, characters, organizations, places, events, and incidents are either products of the author's imagination or are used fictitiously. Any resemblance to actual persons, living or dead, or actual events is purely coincidental.

Published by Lake Union Publishing, Seattle

www.apub.com

ISBN-13: 9781542093491 (hardcover)
ISBN-10: 154209349X (hardcover)
ISBN-13: 9781542041287 (paperback)
ISBN-10: 1542041287 (paperback)

Cover design by Faceout Studio, Derek Thornton

Cover photography by Chrissy Wiley

Printed in the United States of America

First edition

FALSE STEP

CHAPTER 1

The man jogged through the parking area of a mountain trailhead, his blond hair wild and disheveled, a dead leaf caught in the golden waves. The small body in his arms bounced with each step. A young child, two or three years old, pale limbs disturbingly limp. It was difficult to tell much more past the jittery movement of the camera and the shadows of pine trees cutting lines of darkness across the scene.

"He's okay," the man said to the cars he passed, then again and again as a couple of other people stepped into view. "He's okay, he's okay."

Tears streamed down his face, but the boy's face was hidden, turned away. Impossible to tell from the video whether he was awake or asleep or alive. His legs hung down in dirty sweatpants. His hands were lost in the sleeves of his stained gray hoodie.

A black dog barked excitedly, running forward and back, sniffing at the child's shoes.

"I found him!" the man yelled. Then the video, shot on someone's smartphone, froze and ended.

"That's Johnny, right?" Caitlyn was practically panting. "That's him! Johnny found the boy!"

Veronica nodded in silent shock. That was definitely her husband on the video. She checked her phone again to see whether he'd texted or called, but the screen showed no recent activity. She texted three question marks to him.

Caitlyn grabbed Veronica's arm and held tight as if they were close friends, though they weren't. They were only coworkers. Associates, actually. Veronica was an occupational therapist and Caitlyn worked in physical therapy, and they used the same rehab facility for their more mobile patients. It was good to get clients out of the house when possible.

She'd never thought Caitlyn liked her much. But everyone liked Johnny. Caitlyn had only met him once, but she'd recognized him on the news just fine. He had that effect on women, and on plenty of men too.

"I'm sorry," Veronica murmured to her patient, but the elderly woman waved her off.

"Are you kidding?" Mrs. Lee exclaimed. "This is the most exciting thing to happen to me since I thought Miles Probst was having a heart attack in my bed." The woman pointed at the muted TV in the corner of the therapy room, and Veronica looked up to see her husband again, trotting behind cars, his face a grimace of fear and relief.

He's okay. Johnny's mouth formed the words silently. Veronica watched the boy's pale hand bounce. Was the child really okay?

Tanner Holcomb had gone missing four days before. A three-year-old boy lost in the mountains outside Denver. The temperature had been 50 degrees that first night. Survivable. But it had dropped to 38 the second. The entire city had watched and waited and sent hordes of volunteers into the foothills.

The boy had worn only sweatpants and a hoodie when he'd wandered off. Icy streams snaked through the rocky terrain. Mountain lions prowled for prey. By the third night no one held out much hope that he'd be found alive. He might not be found at all. Anything could happen to a body in these hills. A slip in a stream and a small child could be swept along and wedged beneath a boulder until nothing was left of him to find. Or those mountain lions again. They didn't leave meals behind.

A tragedy. His family should have kept better track of him. This was what happened when you let children explore too far on their own. A three-year-old, no less!

But now there he was.

The news shot switched to a live view of a narrow road overhung with lodgepole pines. The swirling lights of police cars flashed against the green. A button-nosed reporter gestured somewhere to her left, but the police had cordoned off the area, and the cameras couldn't get closer. More trees filled the screen. More lights. The producer ran the footage of Johnny again.

Veronica felt frozen, her hands and feet going numb. Johnny—*her* Johnny, for better or worse—had found little Tanner Holcomb and would return him to his family. Johnny hadn't even been part of the search. He'd just gone out for one of his normal hikes, same as he did once or twice every week when there wasn't snow on the ground.

"I'm sorry, Mrs. Lee," she murmured. "I think I'd better go."

"Of course!" Mrs. Lee agreed. "Of course you'd better go."

But why? Veronica wasn't sure. She just knew that her body was shifting from cold to hot, and she could feel a dozen eyes on her face.

Mrs. Lee made a shooing motion. "Go to your husband. I can do these stupid exercises without you."

A common insult Veronica had long ago learned to ignore. Her job was to help people regain remedial skills, and very few clients were thrilled to have that opportunity. Still, her career was one of the few pieces of her life that felt just right. The rest of the puzzle no longer fit back together, the pieces bent or swollen out of shape.

She swallowed hard and swung around to leave.

This video of her husband was good news. The best possible news. This was amazing.

Sweat prickled her hairline.

She'd gathered her things and was nearly to the car when her cell finally rang. The cheerful jangle she'd chosen as a ringtone seemed insensitive and stupid now. She juggled her bags and yanked the phone from her pocket. "Johnny?" she said in a gasp.

"Veronica! Oh my God, I found him! I found that kid!" His first words had been exuberant, but his voice broke at the end as if splitting open with suppressed pain.

Tears filled her eyes. They seemed to fill her whole head, pressing from the inside and clogging her up. "I saw it on the news," she choked out. "Is he okay?"

Johnny heaved a breath, and when he exhaled it sounded like a sob of laughter. "He's cold and dehydrated. But they think that's it."

"Really?"

"Really. They think he's going to be all right."

"Jesus. How did he even survive? This is just crazy, Johnny."

"I know!" This time he really did laugh. "I was . . . I was hiking Flat Rock Trail. You know the one? A mile off the highway near Kittredge?"

She didn't know the one and he couldn't see her, but she nodded anyway.

"Old Man started going crazy, barking and running ahead." Their black Lab had been born with white whiskers around his muzzle that made him look elderly even as a puppy. Whatever name they'd initially chosen had been forgotten in their first few days of ownership. And now he was a hero.

"What a good boy."

"I'd never have found Tanner without him."

"I'll buy some marrow bones on the way home."

"Do it," Johnny said. "He saved that kid's life."

"*You* did," she corrected, happy to stroke his needy ego for once. "*You* did that."

"I can't believe it," Johnny whispered. A police radio squawked somewhere nearby.

"Do you need to go?"

"I don't know. I'm just sitting here on a rock. They brought me a blanket. The ambulance is leaving. I heard them say the parents are on the way to the hospital already. They'll meet him there." She heard tears in his voice again and had to blink back her own. "I'm not sure when I'll get home . . . ," he murmured.

"Don't worry about that. I'll pick up Sydney. I'm not going back to work." She glanced toward the rehab clinic and saw faces in the windows watching her. There were phones in front of some of the faces, and her mind flashed with those snapshots that she saw in the gossip magazines of celebrities in grocery store lots. *They're just like us! They talk on cell phones in the parking lot!* Only she wasn't a celebrity. Or she hadn't been.

The cold returned again. She didn't want any spying strangers in her life. "There are lots of reporters outside the trailhead, Johnny. You'll have to go right through them when you leave."

"I know. Crazy, huh? My phone is blowing up. This will be great for business."

It *would* be great for business, she realized. And God knew they needed the money. Johnny's billable hours really dropped off this time of year. Everybody wanted a personal trainer on January 1, but by the end of October only a few hardy souls—or slightly obsessed fanatics—remained dedicated to fitness. And half of them would be too busy to make it to the gym once the holidays commenced.

December was usually a long month of Johnny needing far too much attention from her, broken up only by his abrupt jogging trips around the neighborhood to use up his excess energy.

He was a simple enough man. He needed attention, sex, exercise, and something to watch on TV. But her well of attention had grown shallower with motherhood. And shallower still with the resentments that built up into huge rifts in a marriage. New clients would keep him busy and give her the breathing room she craved.

Some of the fear she'd felt at the sight of Johnny in the video began to loosen its stranglehold on her heart. Everything was fine. In fact, it was good. He'd saved a child's life and improved theirs at the same time.

The police radio squawked near Johnny again. "I'll let you go," she said, then added an "I love you" automatically.

"Love you too, babe."

Her initial shock was wearing off, and there was nothing wrong with her. She wasn't sick, and this emergency required none of her attention. She should return to work. But she didn't. She texted her last few clients and escaped to her car.

A stop at the local natural foods market provided a ready-made lunch for her and bones for Old Man. On her way out she remembered the wine store three doors down and headed over to buy a bottle of champagne. Johnny would love the gesture even if he preferred to drink beer. On impulse she grabbed a bottle of red too. She needed a glass, and she couldn't very well pop the cork on the champagne before Johnny got home. Outfitted for the afternoon ahead, she drove the last few miles home.

She slowed as she drove past their slightly run-down ranch house. They'd been able to afford it only because it needed updating and it bordered a main thoroughfare of their Lakewood neighborhood. They hadn't quite gotten around to renovating it yet, and the sound of traffic had only grown louder since they'd moved in eight years before. It was a house, though. Another little tick on the list that proved they were successful adults.

Johnny took good care of the lawn, at least. The house looked neat and trim, if a bit unadorned. She didn't have the patience for gardening.

She turned left and left again, and her car was swallowed by the alley. She shut the garage door behind her before she even got out of the car, and when she got inside she left the blinds closed as she sat in the breakfast nook with her salad and chile tofu bites.

The dim light felt comforting, and the last of her panic melted away, but the adrenaline left a lingering ache of fight or flight in her muscles to remind her that something dramatic had occurred. She opened the red and poured herself a generous glass, determined to chase the feeling away.

The first sip of wine was still pooled on her tongue when she picked up her phone. Did you see the news? she typed out. The text zoomed away, and her heart hitched a little at the sound.

She waited a moment, knowing she wouldn't wait nearly long enough. When no response arrived, she typed again. Johnny found that missing kid! The little Holcomb boy! He's ALIVE!

She took another sip of wine. Then another. Her phone stayed silent and she purposefully set it facedown on the table. She'd nearly finished the wine when the phone finally buzzed, and Veronica's fingers grazed the glass in her excitement. Thank goodness for her cheap stemless glassware or it would've tipped and shattered instead of just wobbling.

A smile spread over her face as she picked up the phone and realized it was still buzzing. Not a text. A call. But her mom's picture filled the screen when Veronica flipped it over. Her smile faded. "Hi, Mom," she answered.

"Veronica! Johnny is on the news!"

"I know."

"He found that little boy!"

A car pulled up outside. Hopeful again, Veronica pushed to her feet and rushed to the window to peek through the blinds. But there was no sleek silver car at the curb. Instead, a white van was parked on the street, its paint job bragging about being "the number one news network in Denver."

"Oh shit," she breathed.

"What is it?" her mom squawked. "What's wrong?"

"Nothing," Veronica said, but the panic was back, and she imagined it would hang on a little longer this time.

Johnny was going to love this.

CHAPTER 2

By three o'clock there were two news trucks on the street and a dozen of Johnny's friends in the living room. Veronica would be hard-pressed to name a dozen of her own friends in the whole world, but Johnny had at least that many who lived nearby and didn't have jobs, apparently, because how else would they be here in the middle of the day?

She knew most of them, but she only liked a few, and there were none she particularly wanted to leave alone in her house. She glanced around the crowd again, hoping to see someone she could put in charge while she went to get Sydney from school, but even the few she liked had beers in their hands. This was a party, after all. The kind of celebration Johnny's friends lay in perpetual wait for, as if they were all still in college. Someone got a new gig? Party. Someone broke an arm skiing? Party. Someone appeared on the news after rescuing a lost little boy? Oh, that was definitely cause for a party. They'd likely have a keg rolled in before the hour ended. The crowd would grow larger as those few friends with eight-to-five jobs showed up.

"Damn it," she muttered, finally reaching for the arm of the nearest man. "Terrance, I need to run and pick up Sydney. I'll be back in fifteen; can I put you in charge?"

"Sure," he said, barely looking at her. They were all waiting for Johnny.

With a glance at the front door and the craziness lurking beyond it, Veronica headed out the back and into the alley.

Johnny usually picked up their daughter on his way home from work. When things were busy for him, he'd head back to the gym after Veronica got home.

At ten years old, Sydney could walk the half mile on her own, but that hadn't been the plan today, and she didn't have a cell phone yet. Not until age twelve. They'd decided that. Well, Veronica had decided that. Johnny had gone along with her but rolled his eyes at the idea that early smartphone use might be bad for kids.

If they were divorced, it would be a different matter. There would be pickups to arrange, schedule changes, and confusion over who had Sydney on which day. But they weren't divorced.

Feet crunching on the gravel-littered cement, Veronica hurried through the old-fashioned alley. She imagined this was one of the last neighborhoods in the Denver area that had been built with alleys. They simply weren't an efficient use of land. But she liked being here. It felt like a secret world behind their houses, and their narrow streets looked so orderly with no driveways or front-facing garages.

The alley was also an easy way to spy on the neighbors. People left their blinds open in the back. They stood out on their decks to smoke cigarettes and have loud conversations on cell phones. None of them seemed to realize how their voices echoed down the cement lane. But Veronica realized. She never took a private call outside or anywhere near an open window. She kept her secrets close.

She cut through another alley the next block over, then turned up the street to the school. Like the surrounding houses, the school was low and long and vaguely ugly. If it were redbrick it might have had a certain charm, but its beige-blond color depressed her, especially when she noticed the way water had trailed rust lines down the bricks from the roof. Still, it was a decent enough school, and Sydney had always liked her teachers.

She would move on to the middle school next year, and then she'd be on a bus with all the bigger kids. Veronica was more worried about it than her daughter was.

Veronica heard the distant trill of the bell and picked up her pace. By the time she got to the school, dozens of kids were milling about on the front lawn. A few stragglers chased one another around the baseball field in back. Their screams and laughter rose above the rumble of the waiting line of cars.

Veronica hurried past the idling vehicles and kept her head low. She didn't want to speak to anyone about Johnny. She just wanted to find Sydney and get back to the safety of home.

She was trying to decide whether she'd look more conspicuous with the hood of her light jacket up or down when Sydney squealed out "Mom!"

Veronica braced herself in time to catch her daughter's wild hug. Closing her eyes, she pressed her cheek to Sydney's warm, tangled hair and breathed in the smell of her shampoo. In a few years these hugs would be few and far between. "Hey, sweetie!"

"What are you doing here? Where's Dad?"

"He got held up. I'll walk you home today."

Sydney waved at a friend and they set off, as easy as that. Veronica blew out a sigh of relief and laced her fingers through her daughter's. No drama. No attention. Just a normal after-school pickup. "How was art today? Did you finish the papier-mâché project?"

"Yes, but I didn't get to seal it. I took too long with the paint details. She said we'll have free time next week so I can—"

"Veronica!"

The loud call cut off her daughter's words. Veronica winced and briefly considered making a run for it. She wasn't the social butterfly in this community. That role was reserved for Johnny. Whichever woman was calling out to Veronica wasn't looking to get coffee or invite her to a party; this was an information hunt.

But the moment to escape had passed. Sydney stopped and tugged Veronica to a stop too, so she took a deep breath and turned to see who was hailing her.

She'd met Kay Ronsom plenty of times. In fact, the woman came to every one of Johnny's backyard barbecues even though her son and Sydney weren't friends. "Veronica, oh my gosh!" she said breathlessly as she hurried over. "I saw the video, I just can't believe it. Johnny is amazing!"

"He is. But we're all a little stressed right now, so . . ." She cut her eyes meaningfully toward Sydney. "Sydney just got out of school."

"Oh!" Kay yelped, her eyes widening. "Oh, of course! Just . . . Wow, please tell him how proud we are of him. Your daddy is a wonderful man, Sydney."

"Um, yeah," Sydney replied. "Thanks?"

Veronica swung her daughter around and stepped up the pace toward home.

"Tell him I promise to get back to the gym!" Kay called out, as if Johnny gave a damn what she did. Or perhaps he did. Maybe they had a weekly meet-up in the locked family restroom outside the lap pool. Kay was a bit old for Johnny's tastes, but she looked at him with big, admiring eyes, and maybe that was all he needed. "I'll stop by the house later!"

Veronica sighed and shook her head at her own bitter thoughts. She'd suspected Johnny of cheating plenty of times, but as far as she knew, it had only happened once. Just once.

Since then, there'd been no nights unaccounted for, no diminishing kindness to his wife, no STDs. Just Veronica's weary knowledge that her husband adored being admired and had a tarnished record.

As for that one time? Well, she'd forgiven him. Or she thought she had. It turned out that frantically gluing the broken pieces of a marriage back together didn't make for the tightest hold. The seams had eventually given way and left her sitting in a giant, messy pile of hurt and anger and memories.

But their trust issues couldn't eclipse the love Johnny gave Sydney. Whatever else he was, he was a great father, and their daughter glowed under his care. It kept Veronica holding on.

"What's going on, Mom?" Sydney asked. "Why are we walking so fast? Is something wrong?"

"Everything is fine, sweetie."

"What was Mrs. Ronsom talking about?"

"Well . . ." They'd crossed one of the school's driveways and were past the idling traffic now, so Veronica slowed her pace. "Honey, you know that little boy who went missing in the mountains last weekend? Tanner Holcomb?"

"Yeah. That's so sad. Wait! Did they find him?"

"Yes."

"That's great! I mean, he's okay, right? He's alive?"

"He is," she answered with relief, thinking for the first time what the conversation would have been like if Johnny had found the boy too late. "Not only is he fine, but . . . Well, Daddy is the one who found him."

"Daddy?" Her eyes widened and warmed until they glowed with joy. She was a daddy's girl through and through, and Veronica couldn't even summon parental jealousy, because Sydney's love for her father was the purest thing she'd ever seen. It was healthier than Veronica's adoration of her own father had been, because Johnny was present and attentive. He didn't flit in and out of his daughter's life like an impossible-to-capture butterfly. Sydney beamed with pride for her dad, but then the glow in her eyes turned to a shimmer, and she burst into tears and threw herself into her mother's arms.

"Oh, honey, it's okay. The boy's going to be fine. This is all good news."

"I know," Sydney sobbed. "I'm just so happy. Daddy found him!"

Veronica tried to blink back her own tears, but they spilled onto her cheeks. That poor little boy. He was only three years old, so hopefully he'd remember none of this experience in a few months. It must have been terrifying being cold and so alone. At that age he'd probably been utterly confused why no one was there to help him in the dark.

"I'm so proud of Dad," Sydney whispered.

"You should be. He's a good man." A decent man, at least. And a great father. The sum of that surely added up to good.

Conscious of the cars driving slowly by, Veronica kissed Sydney's head before easing her back. "Come on. Let's get home. All of Dad's friends are there."

Sydney brightened up and nodded. She was outgoing like Johnny. There was nothing she loved more than being surrounded by people. She was already excited about all the clubs she could join in middle school. Veronica, on the other hand, had been terrified of leaving the little pond of her elementary school and jumping into a treacherous ocean of teenagers. Syd couldn't wait.

Her daughter's tears dried almost immediately, and she skipped a few feet ahead. "Is Dad home yet?"

"I don't know! Let's find out." When Sydney kept gaining ground, Veronica called out her name. "Wait! We're taking the alley. There are reporters in front!"

"Reporters?" her daughter yelped. "Mom, this is so cool! Dad is going to be famous!"

Veronica sighed. Yeah. Yeah, he was going to be famous. But surely someone else would knock him off the screen within a few minutes. She just had to wait it out.

CHAPTER 3

A cheer went up as if a goal had been scored at a championship football game. Sydney paused her race from guest to guest, then sprinted toward the front window to push her way through the gathered crowd.

"Daddy's here!" she yelled over the noise.

"Thank God," Veronica muttered. It'd been a full hour since she'd picked up Sydney, and their tiny house was only getting more crowded.

She headed for the kitchen sink and the small window above it so she could peek through the blinds. The scene playing out wasn't shocking, of course. She'd known the reporters were there. But a groan still managed to leak from her throat at the sight of Johnny holding court in front of the television cameras.

He looked like a tanned, outdoorsy dream in hiking boots, worn khaki shorts, and a tight blue T-shirt. He shook his head in seeming disbelief at part of his own story and his white teeth flashed. They'd been together eleven years and, impossibly, he was more handsome now than he had been at the start.

When he knelt down to hug Old Man, cameras flashed like strobe lights, even in the afternoon sun. Most of the cameras belonged to the press, but a few belonged to neighbors who'd gathered with their phones held high.

Veronica caught movement outside at the edge of her vision and stiffened. When the blur of bright color solidified into her daughter running across the lawn, Veronica yelped and sprang into action. She dodged around the small kitchen island and shoved her way through the party. But it was too late. By the time she emerged onto the front stoop, Sydney was against her dad's side, arms clinging tight to his waist.

Shit. Cameras were flashing again. Veronica felt anxious, but why? Sydney was proud of her dad. This moment would be immortalized forever, and Syd wasn't exactly shy. She was going to show the videos and pictures to all of her friends as often as they'd agree to look at them. She wasn't allowed a Snapchat or Instagram account yet, but she'd be thrilled to start one and post every single picture from this day.

Someone asked a question Veronica didn't hear, but she heard her daughter's answer when the rest of the reporters quieted down. "My dad is the best dad in the world, and he'd save every kid in danger if he could. I'm so glad that little boy is safe, Daddy." She and her father hugged tightly, and Veronica heard a chorus of *Aw*s rise up from the reporters in front of her and the friends behind her.

Veronica pressed her lips tight together and nodded, blinking away more tears. This was good. This was worth anything. Almost anything.

"Mrs. Bradley!" someone called. "Mrs. Bradley!" And then everyone looked right at her. Veronica took a step back, intending to retreat into the house and close the door. They couldn't know who she was, could they? She might just be a guest at the party.

But then Johnny sealed the deal. "Babe, get over here!" He scooped his arm out in a welcoming wave.

She froze. Looked at Johnny. Then at the reporters. Back and forth. Finally she looked at Sydney, who grinned and wiped tears from her eyes. "Come on, Mom!"

She couldn't make herself deliberately move toward those people filming and snapping. She didn't want this. But somehow the reporters were getting closer. Somehow her legs were moving, taking her to them.

The black pupils of the video cameras glinted. They had already zoomed in. It was already too late.

When she reached Johnny, he pulled her close, Sydney sandwiched between them. Their nuclear family. A tight, beautiful core. They must look so happy. No hint of strain or betrayal between them. The perfect family she'd expected they'd eventually grow into.

Veronica buried her face in Johnny's shoulder as Old Man nudged the backs of her knees.

"Mrs. Bradley! Are you proud of your husband?"

She lifted her head and looked into Johnny's eyes. They crinkled charmingly at her. "This is crazy," she whispered.

"Yeah. It really is."

Brow crumpling in disbelief, she managed a smile, then made it stretch into a grin before she turned to the cameras. "Of course I'm proud of Johnny," she declared, "and I'm so, so relieved for that little boy. We've all been watching and worrying for him and now his parents have him back. What a wonderful day."

"Were you with your husband on the trail?"

"No, I heard about it the same way everyone else did. I guess I can't ever tell him there's no time for one of his hikes now!"

There was far more laughter than the joke deserved, but everyone was giddy. Jubilant. They posed for some family pictures, and then Veronica led Sydney back to the house so Johnny could answer more questions. Fifteen minutes later he popped inside and was met with a wall of sound as his friends went wild. Even Sydney clapped her hands over her ears, and she was used to hanging with ten-year-olds all day.

Someone pressed a beer into his hand and Veronica suddenly remembered the champagne. She'd forgotten to put it in the fridge. But it didn't matter. Several other corks popped and the crowd began chanting *"Speech, speech, speech!"* Johnny glowed.

She'd loved his confidence when they'd met. She'd loved how comfortable he was with his own body and self. She'd felt blessed in that luminescence. Everyone did.

Johnny took a long draw from his beer and then held up his hands to quiet the room.

"I don't know what to say. I'm not really a big speech guy."

Chuckles rumbled through the house at that.

"I guess you guys want to hear the story."

"Hell yeah!" someone yelled, and everyone cheered in agreement.

For once, Veronica was in complete accord with his friends. She wanted to hear it all again too.

He rocked back on his heels and nodded. "Well, I was about a mile into a hike, and Old Man started going crazy. I thought he was just excited about a skunk or something, but he really took off. I followed him down a gully as quickly as I could and . . . wow. There he was. The kid."

"Hell yeah!" one of his friends screamed again.

"Hell yeah!" Johnny repeated, but he shook his head as the cheering resumed. "Seriously, nobody else would have done anything different. I scooped him right up and got back to the trailhead as quickly as I could. I hope the little guy will be okay. He was pretty shaken up and scared. I'm just glad I was in the right place at the right time."

He raised his beer, and bottles and glasses rose up everywhere. Two dozen arms, maybe? The crowd surged forward to grip his shoulder or offer tight, backslapping hugs. He'd been in a terrible mood for the past week or two, so it was nice to see him relaxed and happy. Things would be much less strained around the house now.

Still, the celebration was too much for Veronica. Far too many decibels of joy.

Overwhelmed by the press and noise, she found herself backing into the short hallway that led to their bedrooms. Someone had linked to their Bluetooth speakers and music started up. Veronica smiled at the few straggling guests she passed before she ducked into her room to shut the door. The cool air swept over her skin like physical relief. She yanked her phone from her pocket.

There were quite a few texts, but they were all disappointments to her. Multiple versions of "OMG Johnny is on TV!" There was also a missed call from her sister, Trish. Veronica clicked on that notification and called back.

"Jesus Christ!" her sister yelped when she picked up.

"My thoughts exactly."

"What the hell is going on?"

"All I know is what you see on TV. Johnny just got home, but the house is swarming with an impromptu celebration. Can you and Fitz come over and keep me company?"

"Yes. Absolutely. I assume you don't need us to pick up beer?"

Veronica snorted. Then she laughed. Then she positively guffawed. "Surprise," she finally managed to say. "They seem to have the beer covered."

"See you in a few," her sister said.

It would be more than a few. Trish and her wife, Fitz, lived down in Parker, a good forty-minute drive at this time of day.

They both taught at the same middle school, and the preteens loved that two of their favorite teachers were married. Trish taught science and Fitz—Ms. Zidan to her students—taught math. Sydney had been unable to say "Fatima" as a little girl, so Fitz had chosen the moniker "Auntie Fitz" herself. The memory of tiny Sydney curled up with her aunts still made Veronica smile. Both women were ridiculously cute nerds. Both were her best friends.

Or they had been. Things had been a little different lately. A little distant. That was Veronica's fault. But, distance or not, they would still drop everything to rush over when needed.

She checked her phone one more time for the message she was really waiting for. Still nothing.

After staring at the door for a few minutes, she sighed in resignation. She couldn't hide in the bedroom forever. *The street is a mess,* she texted her sister. *Come in the back way and park by the garage.*

Another cheer rose up from the living room. Veronica stood, squared her shoulders, and forced herself to walk into the fun.

CHAPTER 4

"This is insanity," Trish groaned.

"It's actually cleared out a little." Either that or the two glasses of champagne had made Veronica more tolerant of the crowd.

A few of Johnny's friends had left, probably for an evening shift at Dave & Buster's, but his core group of gym buddies remained, and a few neighbors had dropped by as well. Of course Kay Ronsom was right in the middle of them, laughing at all of Johnny's jokes.

Veronica and Trish and Fitz had retreated to the small dining room. They mostly had a view of male backs crowding the front rooms, but at least it was quiet enough that they could speak at an almost normal volume.

"The story is everywhere now," Fitz said, looking up from her phone. "But it's really just the first video of Johnny and the little boy. Nobody cares about you."

"Thanks," Veronica said, and she meant it. She'd stammered out the whole story of the news crews when her sister had arrived, explaining away her freak-out as general self-consciousness, but both of the other women had agreed that nobody gave a damn about her when they could watch video of the rescue itself. Still, her phone had blown up after the evening news. Every client she'd ever worked with had seemingly reached out. She'd eventually given up and turned off her phone.

"No word from the Holcomb family yet?" she asked for the third time in the past hour.

Fitz tossed her long black hair over her shoulder and scrolled through her feed. "Not that I've seen. Apparently they're still at the hospital. I bet once they leave, even Johnny will be off the front page."

"I doubt it," Trish said. "He's already got a fan page dedicated to him on Facebook."

Veronica groaned. "Twenty dollars says Neesa started it."

Trish rolled her eyes. "Stop it."

Veronica rolled her eyes right back. Johnny's business partner, Neesa Marin, had been a point of contention in her marriage for nearly two years. She was petite and ripped and she had flawless skin, and Veronica had been jealous of her from the moment they'd met. But they were just friends, Johnny promised. Just friends.

She'd tried to believe him two years ago when they'd started working out together. She'd ignored the hurt and fear and heartache that Neesa had brought back to the surface, but all those feelings had been simmering there the whole time, even with her back turned.

Last year, Neesa had proposed starting a personal-training company with Johnny, because she had lots of portable home equipment and he had more experience. As far as Veronica could tell, the business meant they had weekly meetings at a brewery and never made any progress. Luckily, Veronica now had another focus for her darker emotions, and her old heartbreak felt more like the annoying ache of a healing wound.

"Regardless," her sister said, "don't worry about all the attention. I'm sure it won't go to his head."

They all collapsed in laughter at that. Not that Trish didn't like Johnny. She liked him fine. Everybody did. But she'd been one of the few who'd urged Veronica not to marry him in the first place. *I'll help you raise this baby. You'll be okay. You're too young to get married.*

But if she hadn't been too young for a baby, she hadn't been too young for a husband. Right?

Sydney had been the nudge into adulthood she and Johnny had both needed. Finish college, get real jobs, get married, have the baby, buy a house! He'd brought up abortion, of course, but Veronica had convinced herself that it had been a halfhearted suggestion. They'd been wildly in love. Or blindly in love.

He'd been sweet and kind throughout the pregnancy, though he'd chafed a little under the constraints of caring for a newborn. Who didn't? But once the trips to the playground had started, Johnny had truly blossomed. A handsome young man with an adorable toddler? Good Lord, he'd been invited to every playgroup in the city. And maybe a few the next county over.

Veronica had been so lucky. Everyone had told her that constantly, and she'd known it too. So, so lucky. She'd had a gorgeous, adorable husband who helped with the child-rearing. The other moms had jokingly whispered their envy in her ear. Veronica had been determined to manage the dynamic better than her own mother had, but every year she'd felt more and more exhausted by the vigilance. Then she'd failed. She'd looked away. Lost her hold on him. And she'd paid the price.

Someone ordered pizza, and others volunteered to pay, thank God, because a giant stack of pizzas arrived, and Veronica could not afford to put anything else on their credit card. It wasn't maxed out, but the remaining balance was inching up each month as they awaited the windfall of New Year's resolutions that January would bring.

But they wouldn't have to wait for January this year. Johnny had already mentioned several times that his voice mail box was getting full.

He's going to leave me, she thought, then gulped down her last swig of wine, wondering how the idea could possibly still sting.

She was in pretty good shape, but she wasn't stacked or ripped or whatever the hottest women were these days. She wasn't Neesa. She was just . . . the breadwinner. That was what she brought to the relationship these days. Or it had been until tonight.

"Sydney!" Trish called out, and Syd raced over to give her a big hug despite the fact that she'd already hugged Fitz and Trish several times. She was too big to crawl into Trish's lap now, but she did it anyway.

Trish kissed her forehead. "Did you get some pizza?"

"Not yet. But I took Dad two big pieces."

"That's good. I'm sure he worked up quite an appetite today."

"I gave Old Man a piece too."

Veronica winced, hoping nobody else had done the same or she'd be cleaning up diarrhea in the morning. "I got him a bone, sweetie. I'll give that to him as a treat. No more people food."

Trish squeezed her niece tight. "Go get yourself some pizza, munchkin, okay? You don't want to run out of energy. And have a glass of milk."

"Okay."

After watching Sydney race away, Trish raised an eyebrow. "She's a daddy's girl just like you."

Veronica sighed as she nodded. "Yeah, but only in some ways." A daddy's girl, yes, but Sydney was more than that too. She was fearless and outgoing and confident. Maybe that would help her be more daring than Veronica had ever been. Someone had to break this cycle eventually.

Veronica would definitely have been the one to bring her dad a drink or food at a party, but she'd never have left his side to mingle with the other guests. She'd been too desperate to hoard all his attention for herself.

And then . . . Well, then she'd married a man just like dear old Dad. Surprise, surprise: she'd also managed to turn into her mother along the way. Or maybe she'd turned into Johnny's mother, taking care of his bills and laundry and all the responsibilities that were too boring to hold his attention.

Stop it, she scolded herself. *Your husband is a hero.*

As if on cue, the sound of the TV blared to life with a news report. Whoever was holding the remote turned it up loud so everyone could hear it over the music. Veronica squeezed her eyes shut at the racket.

"We want to thank all of the searchers, everyone who put their hearts and souls into finding our little Tanner—"

Veronica lurched to her feet and moved toward the living room.

"And the police, who never gave up looking for my grandson. And all the thanks in the world to Mr. Bradley. Thank you. Thank you so much."

Her home exploded with cheers again. Veronica could just make out Johnny's head above the crowd.

"He's fine," she heard Hank Holcomb say through her living room speakers. It sounded as if he were in the room with them. "Tanner is really doing great. Thank you."

By the time she'd pushed her way to the front, hoping to get a glimpse of the Holcombs, reporters were shouting questions, but the patriarch of the family was turning away with a wave. None of the other family members, whose faces had become so familiar in the past few days, appeared anywhere on-screen.

Veronica had desperately wanted to see Tanner's mother, to see the relief and joy on her face. The boy had looked so limp in Johnny's arms, and Veronica needed proof that he was truly okay.

A small man wearing square glasses stepped into place before the countless microphones. He offered nothing interesting, only more assurances that Tanner would be fine, along with a plea to treat the Holcombs with respect as they spent time with their cherished child.

"As you can imagine, the Holcomb family is eager to get little Tanner home and comfortable, so they'll be answering questions at a later date. Thank you for respecting their privacy. God bless you and have a great night."

The gaggle of reporters exploded into shouting again, but the man just waved and smiled before walking away.

The Holcombs had been famous in Colorado long before this story. Hank Holcomb's father had started out in ranching in the mountains of central Colorado, but Hank had one day realized that the true value of his family's acreage was a natural spring that cascaded straight out of the rock a mile from the homestead. Pure Rocky Mountain spring water. It marketed itself. And so a fortune had been born.

It didn't hurt his reputation that Hank was a tall and hardy cowboy with sparkling green eyes and a chiseled jaw. He'd starred in his own commercials and charmed the whole country as a good-hearted outdoorsman who loved to gaze out benevolently over his lands. He'd graced half the young women of Colorado with that good-heartedness in the eighties if the rumors were to be believed, but he'd finally settled down with a beautiful blonde who'd given birth to four sons. Four blond, chiseled chips off the old block.

Those sons had grown up as Colorado icons. All handsome. All athletic. Two of them were champion downhill skiers. Then they'd all married and had kids, and married again sometimes. Now there were dozens of grandkids constantly scrambling over a massive compound in the mountains above Denver, which was how little Tanner had come to wander away from luxury into the wilds of the Rocky Mountains.

The camera cut to a young male reporter, who recapped the evening, but the sound was interrupted by a booming knock on Veronica's front door.

She froze at the alarming sound, picturing a squad of stone-faced police come to convey the horrible news that there had been a mistake. The boy was not fine at all. He was dead or damaged beyond repair and the celebration needed to end.

A web of muscles beneath Veronica's skin tightened, raising all the hairs on her body. What was that? A leftover gene from primate ancestors who could puff up their fur to look more dangerous when threatened? Her whole body prickled.

Then Johnny opened the door, and it was a far less menacing threat than the police. A mere annoyance, really. Trey Swallow with his bleach-blond flattop and his two beefy sidekicks.

The hairs on her body lay down, but her lip lifted in a sneer instead. God, she hated these men. In fact, Trey Swallow had inspired one of the only ultimatums she'd ever issued in her marriage: if Johnny wanted to hang out with Trey and his boys, it wouldn't ever be in her house. But here they were again, walking in as if they were welcome.

It was Johnny's big night. Veronica wouldn't cause trouble. She wouldn't kick Trey out. But God, how had this become her crowd?

It was Johnny's big night. Veronica wouldn't cause trouble. She wouldn't kick Trey out. But God, how had this become her crowd?

Shaking her head, she made her way back toward the dining room and the waiting bottle of champagne. She knew exactly how it had become her crowd. The same way she'd become one of those women who regarded every other nearby female as a threat: she'd married Johnny.

Just as she reached the hand-me-down hutch that marked the imaginary boundary of the dining room, the front door opened again. She glanced back to see another group of arrivals. The man in the doorway was one of Johnny's best friends, Micah. Unlike Trey, he was lean and smart and wore a starched button-down shirt and dark slacks instead of workout gear.

Micah looked over the room, scanning the other guests, and then his eyes met hers. She slipped back into the seat next to her sister and glanced at the floor, afraid someone would notice the way her gaze sharpened with attraction at the sight of him. He was nothing like the rest of Johnny's social circle. He'd moved to California after college and had returned to Denver two years earlier. He was sharp and ambitious and successful.

When she looked up again, she saw the other people who'd shown up behind Micah: Neesa and her big, tattooed husband.

Great.

Someone had helpfully refilled Veronica's glass. She drank half of the bubbly in one gulp as she watched the beautiful young black woman hurry across the room to throw herself into Johnny's arms.

"Maybe I should get you some pizza," Fitz offered.

"Sounds great, but it won't stop me from getting drunk."

"Girl, this has been a hell of a day. I wouldn't try to take away your right to get drunk tonight. But I would like to prevent a severe hangover."

"Thanks. Aren't you two eating?"

Trish leaned close and put her hand on Veronica's. "We ate right after work. We'll probably leave soon."

Veronica felt adrift at the idea, which was ridiculous. This was her own house and she knew most of the people here. "Yeah, I know you both have an early morning. And this isn't exactly your crowd. I'll probably head to bed myself as soon as I tuck Sydney in."

"The question is, will she stay tucked in?"

Veronica snorted. "I doubt it, but what I don't know won't hurt me. I'll be asleep before my head hits the pillow."

"Even with this noise?" Trish's tipped head and raised eyebrows hinted that she'd thought of a more colorful word than *noise*.

Veronica laughed. "Yes, I'm totally exhausted. I don't know why. It just felt like something . . . awful was happening. Or about to happen. Does that make sense? Maybe just because it was such a near miss for that boy. I don't know. It's all been so bizarre."

"You just became a main feature in a missing-child case. Of course you're freaking out a little."

"Just a little." She rubbed her forehead. "I should probably call Mom."

"I already texted and let her know your phone was off. She's fine. Dad is too."

"Right. Thank you." Their mom had always been the point of communication in the family. The touchstone. It had been two years since the split, but Veronica still wasn't used to having to reach out to Dad too. Or maybe she just didn't want to bother.

Fitz slid two slices of supreme pizza onto the table and nudged the plate toward Veronica.

"Thank you," Veronica said in as cheery a voice as she could manage. "You're always taking care of me. But I'm fine. I swear. You two get home and relax. Nobody else here has to be to work at seven thirty."

"Are you sure?" Fitz asked.

"Of course. I'm fine. We're celebrating!"

"What if people just start . . . spontaneously working out? Then what will you do?"

Veronica giggled and reached for the pizza. "I'll throw a smoke bomb and make my escape. Go on. They're not that bad."

"I know," Fitz said, but she still glanced toward the bulging necks and wide shoulders that crowded the front room. "They're great."

"Okay, so they're not *your* type."

"Oh, I don't know. A few of them are pretty to look at."

"True." They were all fine specimens of fitness, but it was beginning to smell as if some of them had come straight from the gym, no doubt because they had.

Her sister kissed her cheek and stood. "Just get through the next few hours. Things will quiet down by tomorrow. Life will be boring again before you know it. You'll see."

"God, I hope so. Could you tell Mom I'll drop by at my normal time tomorrow?"

"No problem. Love you, sis."

~

She was sound asleep when her bedroom door opened with a slash of light, then closed quietly again. For a split second she couldn't quite remember what was off, but something was wrong, and she sat up with a gasp of terror. Who was in her room? Why did she feel like she was in danger?

"Hey, it's just me," Johnny whispered.

"Jesus, you scared me." She'd been too tense when she'd gone to bed, and the stress had brought on strange dreams. "What time is it?" she asked.

"Just past midnight." He smelled like beer and whiskey as the air shifted around him.

"Did you check on Sydney?"

"Yeah. She's asleep." She heard his clothing sliding over his skin and then he dropped onto the mattress like a boulder. "Man, what a frickin' day, huh?"

"Crazy. Are you doing okay?"

"I'm great. Just tired." He settled under the covers with a sigh that was more like a groan.

"I bet you are." She waited a few moments before pressing. "Were you . . . God, Johnny, we haven't even had a chance to talk! Were you scared? You must have been."

"When I found Tanner?" He sounded wary, as if he had to approach the idea of being afraid of something carefully.

"Yes. I think I'd have been at least a little freaked out, if not outright terrified."

"At first I was just worried Old Man was chasing after a skunk or, worse, a mountain lion. I was screaming for him to come back. But once I got into that gulley, I saw him whining and sniffing at something. When I realized it was a kid . . . Jesus, I was in shock."

"God. I can't imagine."

"At first I thought I was seeing things. Then I was trying to be quiet and soothing for him even though I was losing it inside, you know?"

"Did you know it was Tanner?"

"He was scared and wouldn't look up at me, but after the first few seconds I saw the clothes he was wearing and I knew it was him. The news kept repeating that he was wearing a gray hoodie, remember? So I scooped him right up. He started crying. He was scared, I think. But once we got on the trail and I was making steady progress, he fell asleep almost immediately. Little guy was exhausted."

"Wow. How the hell did he survive out there?"

"Jeez, I have no idea." He paused and she heard the sheets rustle beneath his shoulders as he shrugged. "Just pure luck, I guess."

"I guess."

"Weirder things have happened."

She nodded into the darkness, picturing the little boy all alone amid the tall trees. "How far is that trailhead from the Holcomb estate?"

"I'm not sure."

"It must be at least fifteen miles. How in the world did he make it? And what were the chances of you hiking out in Kittredge? We haven't been there in years."

"Ha!" His loud burst of laughter made her cringe in the quiet darkness. "Who knows. I just wanted to get someplace peaceful."

"Well, thank God."

Johnny shrugged; then he laughed again. "Funny, I would have thought he'd be happy to see me, but I guess kids learn about 'stranger danger.' Or maybe he was just in shock? He held on to Old Man, though. I asked him if he was Tanner, and he didn't answer. He just buried his face in Old Man's fur. But I knew."

"How far out were you?"

"Less than an hour. He slept almost the whole hike back."

"I thought he was dead. When I saw the video, he was so limp. I thought he was dead."

"He was fine," Johnny said soothingly. He reached out as if to comfort her, but when he pulled her close, his hand slid down her back to her ass. He nuzzled her neck. Then he kept nuzzling until he pressed himself against her, his erection poking her hip.

She didn't want to. She never wanted to anymore, unlike the first years of their marriage when she'd craved the reassurance of his hands on her. Tonight she was exhausted and he reeked of liquor. But this was his big day, and he wanted to celebrate, so Veronica just sighed. He groaned against her skin, mistaking her sigh for arousal.

"God, that was crazy," he murmured as he pushed her pajama pants off. "So fucking crazy. Can you believe the news was here?"

"It was definitely crazy." She just wanted to go back to sleep, so she took him in hand and spread her knees.

"God, yes," he groaned as she shifted onto her back and he settled between her legs. "That's it, baby."

She felt the familiar slide of his body, smelled the familiar scent of his skin. But tonight wasn't just a standard marital evening. Tonight he was pumped up, and he quickly settled into an eager rhythm inside her, murmuring *"Yeah, yeah, yeah,"* getting himself even more excited.

"I did it, babe," he muttered. "I did it. Fuck, I did it."

"Yes," she murmured.

"I fucking did it."

She rolled her eyes, confident he couldn't see her. But her sarcastic expression twisted when she heard a burst of male laughter from the living room. "Johnny! What the hell!" She shoved her hands against his shoulders, pausing his motion but not shifting his body at all. "Who's in the house?"

"Trey and a couple of guys were too drunk to drive home."

"So call them a ride!"

"Nah, I told them they could crash in the living room." He started moving inside her again, and Veronica slapped his shoulder.

"What are you *doing*? Not with them here. He's not even supposed to be in my home!"

"Shhh." He thrust once. "It's fine."

"They'll *hear* us!" And she'd never hear the end of their ridiculous junior-high-level humor. They'd probably make squeaking noises like bedsprings whenever she walked in the room.

"Come on. I'm almost done. They won't hear anything." He started again. Veronica lay tense beneath him, unwilling to push the argument so far that one of his friends might hear. Johnny didn't seem to notice. He was back in his own head, celebrating his heroism with her body, stroking himself with her flesh.

She could practically hear him replaying his heroics in his mind. She'd been his biggest fan when they'd first married, but, since the affair, her appreciation for him had receded, exposing the evidence of his narcissism it had helped to shield.

He started murmuring *"Yeah, yeah, yeah"* again. Veronica winced at the slight creak of the old box spring beneath them, but, true to his word, he soon grunted and finished, shuddering above her.

He collapsed heavily onto her body. She stared into the black hole of the ceiling and wished to God she were somewhere else. Johnny seemed perfectly content where he was, though. Her hands hovered over his shoulders. She told herself to lay them down. To touch his skin. Offer love and intimacy. Hold him. But her hands clenched into fists instead. She closed her eyes and waited until his breathing grew deep and regular before she pushed him off her. *Out* of her.

Shifting her feet, she finally found her pajama pants and slid them from under the covers to carry to the tiny bath attached to their room. She cleaned up, got dressed, and washed her hands, then stared at herself in the mirror until she couldn't take it anymore and shut off the light. On her way back to bed, she cracked their door open to keep an eye on Sydney's room.

An hour later she finally fell asleep again. When she woke at eight the next morning, Johnny was gone and the house was blissfully quiet around her.

It was over. Life could get back to normal.

CHAPTER 5

"All right, Mr. Padilla. Two more repetitions and you'll be done."

"If you're going to make me step in and out of my own shower like an idiot, the least you can do is scrub my back while you're here."

"And what would Mrs. Padilla have to say about that?"

Mrs. Padilla snorted from the hallway. "I'd say take this old man off my hands with my blessing. You can have him. He eats too much and he snores like a machine."

Veronica winked at her patient. "You're getting stronger and steadier. One more visit and I don't think I can come up with more excuses for rehab."

"Really? It's only been four weeks since the surgery."

"I know, but look at you. You don't even need help getting your foot over the edge of the tub anymore."

"I can fake it if you want."

She laughed. "No, what I want is you one hundred percent independent again, and you're almost there."

"Spoilsport."

Mrs. Padilla snorted. "Leave the girl alone. She has a big strapping man waiting for her at home; she doesn't need to put up with your bull, Juan." She grinned when Veronica glanced toward her. "We saw your husband on the news last night. And your sweet little girl. What a beautiful family you make. You must be so proud."

"I am," she confirmed, wondering how many times she'd hear that today. Mr. Padilla was only her second client. Then she'd stop by her mom's house for lunch before heading into the rehab center for the rest of the day.

"Thank God he was there," Mrs. Padilla continued. "They say that boy was just a little cold and dehydrated."

Veronica tucked a hand under Mr. Padilla's elbow as he stepped over the edge of the tub one last time. "I keep thinking about every tiny little thing that could have changed yesterday. Just the chances that he would have been on that trail . . . We haven't been there in years. Or if Johnny had taken a different branch from the trailhead or left the house an hour earlier. If he'd decided to leave the dog home. If there'd been a deer carcass nearby to distract Old Man. It's amazing he found him."

"All those prayers must have worked," her patient said as he straightened his sweater and wiped a hand over his brow. The men she helped with rehabilitation always thought the exercises were stupid. Of course they could maneuver around their own bathrooms. Of course they could move from a chair to their beds. Even when such a simple act made their brows sweat and their muscles tremble, they pretended not to understand their own frailty.

"You look so steady today," she said.

"Is there a gold medal for climbing over the edge of the tub?"

"No, but I did bring some gummy worms." She raised her eyebrows, well aware of his weakness for candy.

He snorted. "I'm not a little kid learning to use the potty."

His wife snorted in return. "Don't listen to him. He's easier to bribe with sweets than any of our kids ever were."

Veronica guided him over to the counter so he could put a hand down for support if needed. "Have you spoken to your son about installing a railing in here?"

"I don't need a railing," Mr. Padilla scoffed.

His wife ignored him. "He came by this weekend and finally measured. He just needs to get to the home improvement place."

"Great. I'd feel better if there was a handhold for a little extra help."

She left a few more instructions and a bag of gummy worms before saying goodbye and hugging both of them. The entire point of her job was to get people functional enough not to need her help. But it was a strange goal, at least with the patients she liked. *Trust me and I'll help you improve and then you'll never see me again.*

Still, it was better than the alternative. When she had to return to patients who'd worsened, it broke her heart. And it wasn't uncommon to lose a patient altogether. But patients like Mr. Padilla made up for that. He'd recover from his knee surgery and be back to normal in a few months. Better than normal, actually. That was the point of the procedure.

Her favorite days were Fridays and the Saturday afternoons she worked at senior centers. She didn't get more time with her patients there, but she did get the chance to see former patients who'd improved. And she almost always got invited to a dozen holiday celebrations. Those kinds of parties were more her speed than keggers and loud music. She'd done her fair share of partying in college, her introversion drowned by alcohol, but then she'd grown up. Or maybe she'd just grown tired.

Veronica huffed out a humorless laugh at her socializing preferences. As negative as she could be about Johnny's friends, at least he was normal. He liked hanging out with peers. She preferred patients in their eighties. *Or maybe*, a little voice whispered inside her, *you just want different peers.*

She shook off the useless thought with a sigh. It didn't matter what she wanted.

Her parents' place—her *mom's* place—was only a ten-minute drive from the Padillas', so she'd started dropping by for lunch when she'd taken Juan on as a client five weeks earlier.

A deep wave of nostalgia swamped her as she drove the familiar streets. This neighborhood had been her world for eighteen years. Now it was just a source of more adult anxiety.

Funny how the lens of childhood always cast adults with so much freedom and strength. She'd been far freer as a child. Happier too. And she'd damn sure been more determined. Now it felt as if all her strength went into making it through the day. Just one more day. They added up eventually, or so she kept telling herself.

Seven days meant she'd made it through a week. Fifty-two weeks made a year. Sydney was ten now, so in eight more years or . . . maybe sooner. Maybe Syd just needed two or three years to mature past her fears.

Speaking of her daughter's fears . . . Veronica pulled into the driveway of her childhood home, the split-level so familiar that she could've navigated up the front stairs in the pitch-black night. And had done on several occasions in high school.

Her mom was opening the front door before Veronica was even out of the car. "Hey, sweetie! You won't believe how many people have called me today. And Facebook! Oh my Lord, I can't keep up on a regular day. Now it's a hopeless mess! Everyone keeps sending me the same three articles."

"I bet." She stepped into her mom's open arms and hugged her.

"My word, this has all been exciting."

"It sure has. But I'm not sure I'll ever be able to turn on my phone again."

"Just ignore it. All that matters is that little boy is fine. Because of Johnny! How is he doing?"

"Johnny's great. He was at the gym bright and early to meet a new client. He texted to say he wouldn't be home until eight tonight. He's too booked up. So that's good news. But would you be able to get Sydney? I've got a full day too."

"You know I'm always happy to."

"Thanks, Mom. This is his slow period, so all this exposure is really going to help make ends meet." She followed her mom into the kitchen, though it wasn't as familiar to her as the rest of the house now. Renovating the eighties kitchen had been her mom's first big act of freedom or rebellion or whatever it had been.

Well, not the first big act. That had been kicking Dad out of the house. The kitchen had been number two. And then a three-week cruise through the Panama Canal. Two years after the divorce things had settled down, and her mom looked peaceful. In fact, she looked deeply content and happy. Veronica was painfully jealous.

"Your father called. Did you ever get in touch with him?"

Veronica kept her voice light. "No. It's been crazy. I'll call tonight."

"He just wants to hear from you."

"Sure. I'll call him."

"Veronica."

She rolled her eyes at her mom's skeptical tone. "I will!"

"He's still your father."

"Yeah, Mom, I'm not twelve. I get that." It wasn't that she never spoke to him. They talked every few weeks. The divorce hadn't been a revelation. Nothing as dramatic as that. It had been more of a bright halogen light shining unforgivingly on their past. And the past was supposed to stay warm and fuzzy and slightly out of focus. "He has another daughter to keep him in the loop."

"But you two used to be so close."

"Let's just have lunch. What culinary fabulousness have you made today?"

That got her mom off the topic of her ex-husband. She grinned and gestured Veronica toward the small table in the kitchen nook. "I made pad thai! Rice noodles with peanuts and chicken and all kinds of good stuff. Have you ever had it? I think it turned out great."

Janet Wroth had spent her whole life cooking pot roasts and meat loaf, but now that she lived alone, she'd become adventurous. She'd signed up for two separate meal services and texted Veronica the dinners she made for herself every night—the pictures and the descriptions and her final review of the recipe. Now she was a fan of foods from all over the world.

But one thing hadn't changed: the leftovers she froze were all neatly labeled and lined up in the deep freeze like little Tupperware soldiers.

On Wednesday afternoons, instead of waiting for dinner, she cooked up one of her meal kits to share with Veronica for lunch.

Veronica didn't mention that her visits to Juan Padilla were nearly over. She'd see if she could sign up a new client nearby so she and her mom could continue their weekly tradition. She and her mother hadn't been particularly close through Veronica's teen years, so this was a nice way to build bonds. She felt so lonely for female companionship these days.

Her mom patted her hand. "Sydney looked so pretty on TV. So did you, honey," she added hastily.

"It's okay, Mom. I know you only have eyes for your granddaughter now."

"She needs a haircut, though. That hair!"

"She likes it curly."

"Well, she's definitely got what she likes, then." She set two plates of noodles down, then hurried back to the counter. "I forgot the chopped peanuts. Don't start yet!"

Veronica waited for her mom to return to sprinkle a few peanuts on top of the dish, then dug in. "Mm. It's really good." It *was* really good. Not quite as spicy as she'd order at a restaurant, but she couldn't expect a woman of Danish heritage to add a Thai amount of pepper.

"This one might be my new favorite," her mother said. "Not good for freezing, though, I'd think. Rice noodles . . ." She frowned as if she'd never considered such a thing. "They seem quite delicate."

"I've been thinking, Mom . . . Maybe you should invite someone over for a few of these meals."

"I invite *you* over."

"That's not what I mean."

"And Sydney."

"Mom."

Her mom waved a hand and tossed back her silver-and-brown bob. "Don't be silly."

"Why is it silly? Dad is dating."

"Well, Dad was always dating, wasn't he?"

Oh.

There it was. The topic she tried so hard to avoid. Her father and his outgoing, attention-loving, philandering personality. She hoped to God her mom wasn't actually asking that question. "Mom . . ."

"Oh, come on. It doesn't matter. I'm done with all that now. Why the heck would I want to go back to it?"

"You'll get lonely."

"No. No, I don't think I will. I have everything I want here and no one I have to cater to. I don't have to pretend about . . . well, *anything*. It's not even worth talking about, sweetheart. I'm not lonely. At all. I'm just relieved. And I like cooking for myself. I make whatever I want."

Veronica swallowed her bite of noodles and maybe some of the lump in her throat too. Her parents had always seemed like the perfect couple. Dad the successful, world-traveling analysis system salesman; Mom the perfect stay-at-home housewife and substitute teacher. She'd hosted dinner parties and potlucks and barbecues. He'd brought all the friends. She'd never given a hint that she'd needed any more than that in life.

Was that the world Veronica had been trying to set up for her own life? Had she honestly thought her mother had been happy despite what Veronica herself had known about Dad? Or had she just thought that was the way it was supposed to be?

Whatever her reasoning, she'd jumped into the deep end and let herself sink. She hadn't realized the rest of her family was getting out of the pool and she'd be in it alone.

"It's really good, Mom," she said again, as if she needed to make her feel better. But her mother had moved on. She'd quietly put up with her husband's cheating for however long she'd known, and then she'd quietly said, "No more," and walked away.

It was Veronica who'd been left reeling. Mostly because her mother's choice had devastated Sydney and therefore removed Veronica's own option to divorce. She tried her best not to resent her mom. It wasn't her fault, and she'd put in her time. It was Veronica's turn to sacrifice.

"You're sure you don't mind getting Sydney tonight? I've got my support group, and Johnny won't be by until after eight."

"We'll be fine. In fact, I have just the dinner to make tonight: chicken with mushrooms in puff pastry! I was saving it for Friday, but Sydney will love it."

"Thanks. She loves cooking with you. And I like knowing you're building such wonderful memories together."

Maybe Veronica had built those memories with her mom too, but they'd long ago faded in the bright light of her father's charisma. He'd been the star, her mother the moon. Just like her and Johnny.

But that was fine. Veronica was fine. Five hours of work and then she would go home and shower and be out of the house by six thirty for the one night a week that meant something to her. The one night getting her through. Then six more days of waiting and another week would pass.

CHAPTER 6

Normally she felt anonymous in downtown Denver. Even on a cool October evening there were crowds of people on the streets walking to restaurants or breweries or theaters. Denver was young and hip and outdoorsy, and Veronica was just one woman among many, slipping through busy intersections, unremarkable.

But tonight she was acutely aware that her face had been all over TVs and phones for the past twenty-four hours. Hopefully people had barely glanced at her, their attention caught by Johnny and Sydney, or Johnny and the dog, or Johnny and the little boy in his arms.

And her sister had been right: already there was new video posted by the Holcombs. Why would anyone want to look at pictures of the Bradley family when they could watch little Tanner smiling brightly from the cocoon of his favorite blanket?

He'd looked so happy. Just utterly . . . invincible. Veronica had cried in the shower after seeing it. Hopefully her eyes had lost all their redness by now.

Her quest for anonymity was helped by the fluffy blue scarf she'd wrapped around the lower half of her face. The amber sunglasses added a nice touch too, as if even the fading dusk were too much for her sensitive eyes or ego. Her parking space was only two blocks from her destination, but it felt as if she held her breath until she spotted the familiar façade.

She slipped through the glass doors of the high-rise and headed toward the lobby attendant's desk. Her step hitched when she suddenly realized that her name could actually mean something to a stranger today. She'd been signing it for months and thinking nothing of it, but now she felt totally exposed despite her hidden face.

The man behind the desk glanced up at her hesitation. Or maybe he was a boy. He looked barely eighteen, brown skinned and baby faced, his uniform shirt too loose around his neck. Veronica forced herself to move forward and even managed a smile.

"Hi." She wrote down *1505*, her mind racing. If she wrote a fake name and the guy asked for ID, she'd be busted. They normally didn't, but he looked new, so maybe he was still paranoid about being thorough. Panicked and too aware of his attention, she scrawled her own name in deliberately sloppy script; then she spun and moved toward the elevators.

Back stiff, she waited for him to call out and stop her, but she pushed the button and the doors opened. She knew from experience that the lobby attendants were basically glorified package collectors until 10:00 p.m., when the building was locked up tight, but she still felt as if she'd run a gauntlet.

A middle-aged woman coming up from the parking garage was already on the elevator, so Veronica kept her face averted as she waited for floor fifteen. Had anyone from this building recognized her from the news? Had anyone wondered what she did here every Wednesday night?

She stepped out on the fifteenth floor, sure that she could feel the other woman's gaze burning into her neck despite the coils of the scarf. Once the doors closed, she slipped off the glasses and knocked on door 1505.

Veronica's tension rose, turning her jaw to stone as she waited. It wasn't fear any longer. It was hurt. Frustration. Anger. The tips of her ears burned with it.

The door opened. She pushed words past her teeth. "Last week you promised to stop ignoring my texts."

He sighed and swung the door wide to let her walk past. "I wasn't ignoring them."

"Oh really? Because you sure didn't respond."

"I responded later."

"Well, I turned my phone off after three hours of waiting, so yeah. *Later.*"

"Veronica, I was busy."

She glared at Micah. She wanted to tell him he couldn't treat her that way. That she wouldn't put up with it. But they both knew she would.

"I'm sorry," Micah said, approaching her slowly as if she might snap and attack at any moment. "I was in the middle of a job."

"I just . . . I . . ." *I just needed you.* That was what she meant to say. That was the betrayal burning inside her. *I needed you and you weren't there.* But she didn't say it. This wasn't love. It wasn't a *relationship.* It was only sex. Sex with her husband's best friend.

And she needed this more than Micah did. They both knew it. Micah was single, after all. He could have illicit sex in this gorgeous downtown condo anytime he wanted. He probably did. Veronica didn't ask. After all, she was having sex with someone else too, even if it was only with her husband on a sagging queen mattress in an unremodeled 1970s ranch home.

Micah's hands touched her elbows, then slid up her arms. When he cupped her shoulders, she closed her eyes and shivered, hating her weakness for this man. Hating that he could *see* it when she swayed closer to him.

"I wanted to talk to you last night," he murmured.

She shook her head.

"I hoped we'd get a moment alone."

"There were thirty people there."

"You know what I mean." His voice dropped lower. "Don't be mad."

"I *am* mad." She heard the pouty whine in her own voice as her muscles softened under his touch.

"I only came over so I could see you. I didn't do it for Johnny. You know I hate those gym rats he hangs around these days."

Veronica laughed and let herself meet Micah's dark, beautiful eyes. "How did you two ever end up friends?"

"The vagaries of college roommate assignments."

"Yes, *then*. But now?"

"Now? Opposites attract, I guess. He makes me laugh. He's easy to be around."

She let him pull her into his arms. Opposites indeed. Micah was dark and lean compared to Johnny's golden strength. Only an inch taller than her, he somehow filled her vision far more completely than Johnny did. He filled her thoughts with the same overwhelming ease. Micah was a deep, cool river of complicated nuance punctuated with little eddies and rapids that kept her head spinning. And Johnny was . . . not.

She tucked her face against his neck. "I worried someone would see me."

"Here?"

"Yes. I was all over the news yesterday."

"No one cares. They're all too involved with their own problems."

"Yeah. Maybe."

He tugged at her scarf. "Is it cold out?"

"No. I was hiding."

"Well, there's no need to hide in here."

She raised her head and smiled at him. "Are you trying to get me more naked?"

"I'm trying to get you all the way naked, V."

Grinning, she lifted her chin so he could unwind the scarf, but when his mouth finally found her bare skin, her smile gave way to a groan. Her skin was hot where the scarf had covered her, and his mouth felt cool against it. Until he parted his lips and touched his tongue to her pulse.

It wasn't love. She knew it couldn't be love. But it was *life*, and she craved this knowledge that she was still alive. Still vibrant. Still a risk worth taking.

With Micah she wasn't a mom or a wife. She wasn't the responsible one in the relationship. It wasn't a relationship at all. It was just . . . *this*.

For a little while, at the beginning, she'd worried he was using her. That she was just a stupid, easy, desperate lay. But she'd long ago dropped that fear.

She was the one using *him*, surely. He was her drug, the antidepressant that stopped her from breaking apart and running away forever. Every week, if she was patient enough, Wednesday would come around again, and she'd get her fix, and she'd be fine for a little while.

His teeth pressed into her skin just the way he knew she liked it. They'd been doing this for months now, and it never got old. It felt new every time. New but somehow better as they learned each other's bodies.

She unbuttoned his shirt. He pulled up her dress. They stumbled blindly toward the couch.

Sometimes they made love for an hour, but not tonight. Tonight it was wild and frantic and over in minutes, both of them desperate for something.

The bone-deep satisfaction that followed wasn't only due to her climax. She loved these wild nights the best because it meant nearly two hours of lying with him after. Talking. Joking. Stroking his skin. He always asked her to stay longer and she never could, but on nights when they moved slowly, leaving felt torturous. She wasn't done. She needed more.

Tonight she could have more. She stretched out next to him to absorb him into her skin.

"Did you finish that book?" she asked.

"Not yet. I've been working a lot."

"Slacker. Try to finish by next week. I'm dying to talk to you about it."

"I will. I'm sorry I've been so busy." She sighed at the way he pressed a kiss to her head.

It had all begun with a book. Micah had been at their house for dinner and he'd mentioned a book he wanted to read. Veronica had just started it. A few days later he'd texted her about a plot point, and they'd exchanged messages for days. She'd forced herself to read more slowly, trying to synchronize her consumption of words with his. A strange bit of intimacy, but a powerful one, it turned out. It was a secret. Something to steal her thoughts from work and home. She'd loved every moment.

When they'd finished that book, Micah had asked, "What should we read next?" And Veronica had been hopelessly, happily gone. Two books later they'd met for a drink near his place. The rest had taken no persuasion on his part.

But now ten months had passed, and he wasn't quite as quick with reading. He'd been stuck on their latest book for a month. Because he was busy with work. Or busy not caring quite as much what Veronica thought. Or maybe busy discussing books with someone else.

"Did you ever watch that documentary?" she tried.

"No, not yet. It's in my queue, though." Another way they stole time together when they were apart. Another way he was too busy for her these days.

She didn't ask him what he'd done over the weekend. She didn't want to know. Closing her eyes, she listened to his heartbeat. She breathed in his scent. It had all been so strange at first, after being with the same man for so long, but she was used to Micah now.

No, not *used* to him. She knew him, but she would never get used to this.

His breathing evened out, and she realized he'd fallen asleep. She spread her fingers wider to touch more of his chest. She wouldn't fall asleep. She never did. She wouldn't waste her time with him that way.

I'm not in love with him, she told herself.

She didn't want to be his wife. And he had zero interest in being a husband—or stepfather—to anyone. She'd never spent the night with him. Never tended him through illness or disappointment. This affair was a fantasy. She *couldn't* love him. Not really. But she still turned her head and brushed her lips over his shoulder with a sigh.

Tears gathered in her eyes, and it was safe to let them fall. He wouldn't notice. She never let him see her cry, because this was supposed to be fun. It had to be fun, because it couldn't be anything more.

His heart thumped against her ear, and she steadied her breathing to try to force her own pulse to keep time with his. Stupid. It wouldn't bring them closer. She'd given her child her own blood and oxygen and nutrients, and now Sydney was closer to Johnny than Veronica.

A little flare of resentment tweaked her languid mood, but it passed in an instant, barely even noticeable. It was good for a girl to feel that kind of love from a father. Sydney would grow up brave and strong. Then again, Veronica hadn't grown up strong at all.

Two years ago she'd planned to leave Johnny. Not in a wild, dramatic rage at his betrayal but a full three years after the affair when she'd realized she couldn't recover from it. She'd married a man too much like her father, and those lifelong issues couldn't be overcome. She'd grown exhausted by the idea of decades of vigilance and trying to keep Johnny's attention. Or worse, of ignoring his worst qualities just as her mom had ignored her husband's fickle ways.

She and Johnny had married so young. She'd still been a child, really, acting out her childhood all over again. Doomed to repeat the same dynamic. And Johnny hadn't exactly been mature.

She'd convinced herself that Johnny would be fine with a divorce too. It might have even been true. They would separate. He'd get a place close by. Close enough that Syd could walk back and forth between their two homes. They could both work a little more on the days they didn't have custody. They'd be friendly. Maybe they'd even get together as one big happy family for holidays. It wouldn't be bitter or ugly at all.

Veronica had meticulously planned it out. She'd obsessed over it. She'd practiced a speech for Johnny and imagined what they would say to their daughter.

But then she'd had to stay. For Sydney's sake.

She must have dug her fingers too hard against his chest, because Micah stirred and murmured, then pressed his lips to her head before settling back into sleep. Veronica swallowed as many tears as she could and stroked a comforting hand over his skin.

For an hour she lay there, her head rising and falling with each of his breaths. She let him sleep. It was easier than confronting the fact that he was losing interest in their little rituals and delicate ties. If he slept, she could pretend everything was the same as it had been ten months earlier, the first time she'd come here.

Had she realized she'd made a conscious switch then from being her mother to being her father? To being the betrayer instead of the betrayed? She shoved the thought away and breathed Micah in.

When it was time to leave, Veronica rose and stretched. Her dress was hopelessly wrinkled, but Johnny wouldn't notice. He'd be too busy watching a game. Or tonight he'd be too busy reading internet comments about himself. She wasn't above suspicion so much as below notice, and these days that was just fine with her.

She adjusted the skirt of her dress, then paused to stare down at Micah. He looked young and vulnerable like this, curled on the couch, his face soft with sleep. She'd only met him a few times before she and Johnny had married, and she'd barely noticed him then. But she pretended she remembered him and this was what he had looked like at twenty-two, before life had made him cynical. Still . . . maybe it was herself she was thinking of.

For the first time, she left without saying goodbye. Let Micah wonder for once. Let him worry that things were changing. She lifted her chin as she quietly shut his door, reveling in her pitiful scrap of power.

The lobby was quiet when the elevator doors opened. She tugged up her scarf and made a beeline for the entrance.

"Hey!" the lobby attendant called from behind his desk.

Veronica jerked to a stop and glanced carefully over her shoulder.

He was coming around the desk, moving toward her.

"Is everything okay?" she asked, palms instantly damp with sweat.

"Yeah, it's fine." Walking closer, he smiled and held up his phone. "I saw you online yesterday. Right? The kid? The one in the mountains? Your husband found him!"

The phone's screen glowed with a picture of her family standing on their browning lawn behind a gaggle of microphones. Veronica's stomach dropped. Her head went hot and dizzy. "I . . . I . . ."

"That's so cool."

"Yes," she managed to croak.

"Can I get a picture with you?"

The heat was spreading all over her body now. Her armpits grew slick with sweat. Her hairline itched with it. "I . . . I'd rather not. I'm sorry. It's kind of a sensitive issue. Privacy . . . I work in health care."

He frowned in confusion. He held the lie about her privacy right in his hand.

"I'm going to be late," she blurted out, swinging around to rush toward the doors. "Sorry! But thank you!"

Luckily the door pushed out or she might have broken her wrists slamming into the glass. She burst into the night air and rushed toward the corner. As soon as she reached it, she ducked around the wall and pressed herself against the stone, gulping in cool oxygen.

"Oh God," she whispered. "Oh God, oh God." Was he going to mention her online? On Twitter or Facebook or wherever kids hung out now? He was. That was what people did these days. She'd done it herself when she'd seen a reality TV star at the airport last year. *Guess who I spotted???*

And she'd been rude to him, so he'd be happy to post her private information online. Why not? But would he remember how many times he'd seen her before? Would he look through the book for her name and discover the truth? That she visited number 1505 every single week? Over and over, her name signed as if she were proud of it, as if she were bragging. Because maybe she had been until now. She'd felt wild and free and cocky, taking what she wanted. But now all she felt was dry-mouthed terror.

She shook her head, trying to deny the danger. "It's no big deal," she murmured. "You're being paranoid."

There was no reason for him to suspect an affair. It wasn't written on her skin, was it? On her wrinkled clothes and languid muscles? Surely the smell of sex and heartache must be muffled by her dress.

The crisp air finally began to work its magic, and she stopped panting. But the moment her body calmed, the damp sweat turned to ice, and she was shivering.

Everything was fine. It had to be. She couldn't give this up. And if it was a risk, it was worth it. She didn't want Micah exposed and she didn't want her daughter to know, but, other than that, what danger was there?

Veronica nodded to herself, pushed off the wall, and hit the crosswalk light just in time to make it to the other side safely. Teeth chattering, she ducked her head and hurried toward the side street where she'd parked her car. She was fine. She was good. As ready as she could be to return home to her hero and dutifully reflect his own light back at him. This was his moment to shine, after all. She couldn't deny him that.

CHAPTER 7

She expected to be greeted by a blaring television and bright kitchen lights when she walked in from the garage. Instead she stepped into a pool of quiet darkness no different from the night she'd driven through to get home. Old Man's nails clicked quickly across the kitchen floor. Veronica scratched his head. "Where is everyone?" she asked, the nape of her neck prickling with anxiety.

Old Man didn't answer, so she let him outside before phoning her mom. "Has Johnny not picked up Syd yet?"

"No, not yet. But we're fine. We had a lovely dinner."

"It's nine. Sydney has homework—"

"She did it already. She's good. We're eating ice cream now."

Veronica heard a cheerful "Hi, Mom!" in the background.

"I don't know where he could be. He didn't get in touch?"

"Not yet."

She frowned, glancing out the window as if the dark street beyond hid a secret. "That's really strange. I'd better come by. Maybe—"

"Wait," her mom interrupted. "I see headlights. Johnny just pulled up. No worries! They'll be home in a jiffy."

Veronica signed off with a sigh of relief. They were a fifteen-minute drive away. She just had time to rush through a shower and get into her pajamas. Tonight she felt jumpy and self-conscious, and washing the guilt off her skin helped calm her nerves immensely.

She stayed in the shower as long as she dared, until the steam cleansed even the memory of Micah's scent from her. She wouldn't be able to pretend she could still smell him on her skin tonight. Tonight was a time for caution.

When the door to the garage opened, she rushed toward the kitchen with a wide smile. "Hello!" she called out to both of them. "How was your day?"

Sydney was through the door first and she began chattering with excitement and probably a sugar high as Old Man trotted inside and circled her legs. "Mom, everyone saw the video of Dad. It was crazy. Oh my God, he's so famous at my school now. They want you to come speak, Dad. Like, maybe to my class or something?"

"Wow! Okay. Sure." Johnny tousled her curls and smiled, but his eyes looked tired.

"And I'm pretty famous too," she continued. "I mean, no one else at the school has ever been on the news. Well, there was that time when Bailey's Girl Scout troop got an award, but that was, like, fifteen of them, so it's not the same as—"

"Time to brush your teeth!" Veronica cut in. "You and Grandma partied way too late tonight. Tell me the rest of it when I'm tucking you in."

Sydney bounded down the hall, more cheerful than she usually was about bed as Old Man scrabbled after her. "Five minutes!" Veronica called before turning back to Johnny. "Hey," she said more quietly. "How are you doing? Long day?"

"God, yeah. It was crazy. So many people stopped by. I signed six new clients."

"That's great."

"Yeah." He nodded and scrubbed a hand over his face. "And a couple of reporters came by the gym too."

"Reporters?"

"Yes. Everyone wants the story."

She clenched her jaw, trying and failing to hold back that old anxiety about what Johnny was really up to. "So that's why you were so late? Reporters?"

"Yeah. But not really, I guess." He opened the fridge and peered in. "The police asked me to stop in to answer a few more questions."

"The police?" She froze in the act of hanging Sydney's backpack on its hook next to the back door. "Why?"

"Just clearing up some details about where I found the boy. Whether I could tell which direction he'd come from. Who else I saw on the trail. That kind of thing. You know how it is."

"I mean . . . I guess. Were you able to help?"

"Not sure," he said, head still in the fridge. "They said they'd be in touch again."

"Wow."

"It was no big deal," he snapped.

"Okay. Fine." She honestly had no idea what they could learn from a man who'd just stumbled across this child, but maybe it was the kind of information that would help with future searches. "Did they say anything more about him? He wasn't injured or anything?"

"They didn't say much. We should probably watch the news. I'm sure there'll be an update soon."

"Let me get Syd ready for bed. Maybe you could take Old Man for a walk."

"Sure. Great." He finally grabbed a beer and slammed the fridge door. Then he was lost in his phone before she left the room. No different from any other night, really, though he seemed to be bouncing from excitement to grumpiness more quickly than normal. She told herself he was exhausted. Anyone would be.

Sydney was still high on ice cream and happiness, and Veronica had to redirect her three times to keep brushing her teeth. "Do you have that spelling test tomorrow?" she asked.

"Yes." She wiped her face on a towel. "Grandma helped, though. I've got it all down pat."

Veronica smiled at hearing her mom's words come from her daughter's mouth. "Great. Do you want to read on your own for a few minutes, or do you want me to read to you?"

"Read to me," she answered, not surprising Veronica in the least. Sydney only very rarely chose reading on her own. She was a good reader, but interacting with people was so much more fun for her.

"Okay. We're already on chapter twelve! Ready?"

Fifteen minutes later she looked up from the story to see that Syd was asleep, and she closed the book and slipped her phone from her pocket.

You snuck out, a text read, and Veronica caught herself smiling slyly in response. In fact, she was so pleased that she didn't even text back. Let him be the one left wondering about their status for once.

A hollow victory, of course. He wouldn't stay up late waiting for a message that wouldn't come. He wouldn't obsessively check his texts and then emails and then back to texts again. That was strictly Veronica's domain. He didn't have to worry about her at all. Not unless she forced him to.

She checked her email in spite of herself, but her box was full of spam and one email from work. She made note of a schedule change for the next day, then locked her phone and spent a few minutes straightening one corner of Sydney's hopelessly messy room before shutting off the light and closing the door.

Johnny was just where she'd left him, drinking a beer and staring raptly at whatever social media he'd logged into.

"Any news?" she asked.

"Channel two posted a story that mentioned where I train, so that's good."

"I meant about the boy."

"Oh. No. The family hasn't said anything else." He cleared his throat and shifted on his feet. "Maybe they're trying to protect his privacy or something."

"Are you worried?"

He looked up sharply. "No. About what? Why would I be worried?"

"I just thought maybe you were concerned for his health."

"They say he's fine," he snapped.

She held up her hands at his snippy tone. He was probably concerned it would tarnish his image as the hero if the boy turned out to be ill or injured. Still, she'd hoped his weeks-long bad mood had ended with the uptick in clients.

He tossed the beer bottle in the recycling bin and got another, sighing as if he were trying to let go of his stress. "I'm still getting lots of calls. This is all so crazy."

"I bet. You should come to bed. You look tired." She only made the offer because she knew he'd say no, and, sure enough, he shook his head. "The news is almost on."

"Right." She glanced at the muted TV screen and held back a sigh. "I think I'll get some sleep. It's been a crazy couple of days. There's still leftover stir-fry in the fridge if you want it. I'm sure there are a few pieces of pizza too."

His head tipped down toward his phone again. "Yeah. Thanks."

"And could you take Old Man out for a quick walk?"

He grunted.

Veronica retreated to the bedroom and the new book awaiting her. She'd been trying to slow her reading to wait for Micah to catch up, but she felt too pitiful putting it off for him. And if she were being honest with herself, she was worried she'd have to put off her reading forever.

She was three pages in when she tossed the book down and picked up her phone. I didn't want to wake you, she typed. You looked so peaceful.

Minutes dragged past with no response until she finally turned her phone facedown and retrieved the book, determined to put him from her mind. Her efforts were as successful as they ever were, and she dreamed of him again. They were the only dreams she remembered anymore.

CHAPTER 8

One more day at the rehab center, and then she could retreat to her rounds of senior-living facilities and the sweet escape of gossip. There was always so much gossip. They should really do a *Real Housewives of Sunset Village* television show. Once the ratio got to one man to five women, things got vicious real quick.

Idly wondering whether Bess from the third floor had confronted her boyfriend about his indiscreet cheating, Veronica stowed her purse in a locker tucked into the break room of the small center. When a hand wrapped around her elbow, she jumped in shock and glanced back to see who'd grabbed her.

Caitlyn's face loomed. "It's weird that I've never heard about this support group, isn't it?" she asked.

Veronica shot an irritated glare at the woman's pale hand. "What?"

Caitlyn tightened her hold for a quick moment before Veronica turned around, jerking her arm away.

"The rehab support group," the other woman said.

A prickle of alarm ran up Veronica's neck, her primal instincts reacting more quickly than her brain.

The rehab support group. Oh no.

Her mouth twisted into a grimace of sheer panic she hoped to disguise as irritation. "I have no idea what you're talking about."

"Johnny told the paper you lead a support group for the rehab center. Which is kind of strange, since I haven't heard of it."

The prickle spread up Veronica's scalp and down her spine. This was exactly what she'd feared and it was happening right here, right now. "What? What paper? He was talking about *me*?"

Caitlyn smirked, triumph flaring in her eyes. "The *Post* did a little profile of him because he's a local hero. Isn't that sweet? He talked about you and your daughter. He's very proud of you both. So cute. But we don't have a support group, so I thought that was so odd. I even asked around. No one knows what he's talking about."

This was the cloud that had clung to her from the first moment she'd seen Johnny in that video. This publicity. This *exposure*. Because that was what this was. She was *exposed*. Not by the lobby attendant at Micah's building, but by her own husband.

There was no support group on Wednesday nights. There never had been.

Her panic had released a burst of adrenaline into her blood and now Veronica's brain was working overtime, analyzing escapes and attacks. "I . . . Um . . . I guess Johnny phrased it badly."

"Phrased what badly? There is no support group, Veronica. I already corrected him on Facebook."

Jesus. This woman was going to ruin her. Ruin her marriage. Ruin her reputation.

Okay, if Veronica were being fair, she'd admit she was ruining all of it just fine on her own, but she wasn't feeling fair. She was feeling cornered.

"He misspoke, Caitlyn. I do host a support group. But it's not about the rehab center."

"Then why did he say that?"

She shrugged. "I have no idea what he said. Journalists screw up details all the time. Why are you so concerned?"

"I just thought it was so weird he would say that. What kind of support group is it? Maybe I could recommend it to some of my—"

Veronica leaned her face so close to Caitlyn's that the other woman jerked back. "That's none of your business," she hissed.

"My word!" Caitlyn gasped, feigning innocent offense as she raised a hand to her chest.

Veronica forced a tight smile, but she let her eyes stay hard. "You understand that support groups deal with extremely private, personal matters, right?"

"I suppose."

"Then please don't make me escalate this situation."

Caitlyn grimaced in confusion. "Oh, come on. What situation?"

"Exactly." Veronica dipped her chin in a nod. "I'm glad we can agree on that."

Caitlyn gaped at her as Veronica slammed her locker and stepped into the main rehab area to get ready for her first client. She kept her head high and settled a pleasant smile on her face, but her hands were trembling. She needed to get a look at that article. Why hadn't Johnny said anything about it?

She pulled her phone from her pocket and her irritation faded back to fear. Johnny had texted her about the paper that morning. In fact, he had sent six texts and she'd glanced at the last two and ignored the rest. Right there in the first one was a link to the *Denver Post* write-up.

She read through it quickly, and her shoulders relaxed a little. Johnny had mentioned the fictional support group in passing. He hadn't placed her there on Wednesday nights. Even if that lobby attendant saw this, he wouldn't leap to his feet and shout out her lies to the rest of the world. Her secret was safe. Probably. As long as Caitlyn hadn't stirred things up too much.

Most of the story had been a puff piece about Johnny's training business and outdoor habits. He'd even claimed that the Kittredge trails were some of his favorites, as if he were pumping up the little mountain town. The mention of Veronica's support group had been a tiny blip on the screen.

With a quick glance out the window to be sure her client wasn't on her way in, Veronica checked Johnny's Facebook page. Sure enough, he'd posted a link to the article. And, sure enough, Caitlyn had posted her correction in his comments, along with a shrugging emoji and four question marks.

Bitch.

But it hardly mattered. There were upward of a hundred comments, all of them praising Johnny. He probably wouldn't notice Caitlyn's. If he did, Veronica could play it off. *It's not associated with the rehab center. I organized it for some of my clients. Caitlyn is jealous that she isn't invited to participate. She's petty.*

She was tempted to post a clarification right now, but she was saved by her own impulse when her client's white Lexus pulled up outside. She knew it was better not to call attention to the question. Just let it go.

Everything is fine, she told her racing heart. *Everything is fine.*

And what was the worst that would happen anyway? She'd end up divorced and free?

The thought shocked a laugh from her, and her pulse finally began to slow. No one knew the truth. Sydney would continue living in a stable nuclear family for a couple more years, at least. Woohoo.

When Mrs. Washington entered, Veronica gave her a big hug, her sudden relief making her squeeze too hard. But the older woman didn't care. She didn't even need occupational therapy at this point, but she was wealthy and widowed, and she'd discovered a new world of socializing after her stroke last year. She'd made friends at the rehab center. She liked coming. She paid every bill without complaint.

She'd ignored her graduation from therapy and every gentle reminder since, so Veronica invented new tasks for Mrs. Washington to work on every week, each more intricate than the last. After her session today, the older woman would head out for a water exercise class at the local YMCA pool. It kept her active, and her left arm was nearly as strong as her right at this point.

Mrs. Washington pulled back from the hug and held Veronica at arm's length. "You're famous," she said calmly, as if imparting solemn news.

"That's a terrible exaggeration."

"Perhaps. But you're famous for today, and you're going to make me famous in swim class in about an hour!"

"So you're finally admitting you're just here for gossip, Mrs. Washington?"

"Yes. Absolutely yes. Now tell me all about this handsome husband of yours. He looks like he could pick you up and carry you right to the bedroom. A man hasn't done that for me in nearly thirty years!"

Veronica laughed. "Mr. Washington was a big man, huh?"

"Oh no. Not him."

"I thought you married him when you were twenty!"

The woman's grin spread slowly, crinkling her brown cheeks. "Well. A wedding isn't the end of life, is it? In some ways it's just the beginning."

Veronica pressed a hand to her mouth to cover her laughter.

"Now give me some details to pass on to my friends. And why haven't I ever been invited to your support group?"

Her gut twinged with faint alarm, but Veronica shook her head and ignored it. "That was a misquote. The group has nothing to do with this center."

"You're not just leaving me out?"

"No, I promise."

"Well, I suppose I'll have to believe you. Now tell me everything your husband knows about that little boy."

Nobody really cared what Veronica did with her time. For once, she was damn thankful to be the mousy-brown bookworm of her world.

~

By the time she left work, she'd been asked six times about the support group and had finally lost the fear response that came with the question. Now as she pulled into the garage, she wasn't worried whether Johnny would bring it up. She had a good answer ready for him. And frankly she was just too exhausted to be afraid. Too exhausted to care about anything but getting these damn bags of groceries into the house.

She hated grocery shopping more than any other chore. Something about it felt insulting. Probably because it was basically doing the same chore four times. First you moved the groceries into the cart, then onto the checkout belt, then into the car, and finally into the house. Hell, it was really a fifth time if you counted putting everything away once you got to the kitchen.

She just . . . hated it. But when Johnny went, he came home with ground beef and protein powder and fruit and that was about it. So she did the shopping and half of the cooking, and he did all the dishes. That was the deal. One of the little, everyday deals that kept their lives moving smoothly. Sex on Saturdays. Laundry on Sundays. Grocery shopping twice a week. An occasional date night. And for her, Wednesday nights in a sleek fifteenth-floor condo downtown.

Maybe Johnny had a special day of the week just for himself too. She wouldn't ever know. She hadn't suspected the first time, after all. He worked at gyms and parks and occasionally in people's homes. Hell, his job was to make his clients sweat, to get close and work their bodies, to shape them into people who felt more alive and attractive. He could come home reeking of another woman and she'd never be able to prove anything.

Had she ever even expected he'd be faithful when she'd picked him? Or had she wanted to remove the suspense of it so she wouldn't spend her whole life wondering whether he was like her father? After all, she'd married a man a little out of her league who liked attention from women. It must have been purposeful.

Not that it mattered anymore. She'd given up on the fantasy of "till death do us part." Now she was just trying to get through the work of it all.

She hooked as many bags on her arms as she could lift and pushed through the back door. "I hope you're okay with sandwiches tonight," she said. "I'm not up for cook—" The last syllable faded out to a soft breath when she glanced up and saw Micah sitting at the kitchen counter. She gasped before she could stop herself.

"Hey, babe," Johnny said. He grabbed the bags and gave her a kiss, but her eyes were still locked on Micah.

"Hey," she murmured. "I didn't . . ." She couldn't quite think what she meant to say. Micah's lips lifted in a small, secret smile. Her pulse tripped and she wanted to slap him. Kiss him. Run away. Scream.

He was out of place, and she desperately needed things in their places right now.

"Are we having another party?" she finally asked, the words strange and high as they left her mouth.

"Nah. Micah just dropped by."

He'd dropped by? Why would he do that?

Johnny took the bags to the counter and she narrowed her eyes at Micah. He winked and sipped his beer, his shoulders slouched in relaxation. Did he think this was a game? What the hell was he doing here?

"Just in the neighborhood, Micah?" she asked in that same odd tone.

"Something like that."

Johnny cleared his throat. "We hardly got to talk the other night. Too many people around."

"Yeah," Micah agreed.

She stood frozen in the doorway until she realized they were both watching her. "I'll get the other bags," she finally said, then closed the back door too hard behind her. Neither of them offered to help. And that was a good thing, she told herself. She needed a moment alone.

It wasn't that she never saw Micah with Johnny. He was one of Johnny's best friends. They hung out together. Went to movies. Trained for marathons. It was just that she always had time to prepare herself. Micah couldn't just show up like this, popping into her kitchen like some illicit genie here to tease her with guilt and wishes.

She paced outside, sucking in the fresh air, then returned to the trunk of her car. But she couldn't go back in quite yet. This was too much. It was all too much.

Instead of returning to the kitchen, she wandered back out the garage bay door and let dusk settle over her. The night was dark blue and lovely, but her eyes were still drawn to the bright-yellow square of the kitchen window. And beyond it, to the two men who faced each other. They stood close, talking, both of the men she took to her bed. Both of the men in her life.

Did Micah feel guilty? He didn't look guilty. Johnny was the one who seemed tense. Micah looked like all was right with the world, and she wished like hell she could shake him up a little. Ruin a little of that confidence she found so sexy. It made her feel small sometimes. Insignificant.

At least if he's here, he's not with someone else.

She hated the pitiful thought. Hated it with all her soul. But hateful as it was, it soothed her. She watched him for a few more minutes, grabbing this chance to spy. But Johnny broke the spell by glancing out the window toward the garage.

Veronica gathered the last few bags and slammed the trunk shut.

After twisting the knob, she kicked the door open. This time she was ready. This time she didn't look at either man as she set the bags on the counter next to the fridge.

They both stopped talking, as if they were waiting for her to say something.

They could keep waiting. She put away the groceries quickly, though it still took nearly five minutes. The last step in this stupid chore she'd have to repeat again in a few days. They'd run out of something. Dinner plans would change.

"Where's Sydney?" she finally asked.

"Online," Johnny answered, the sound of his voice facing her even as she stayed turned away.

She should ask him about his day. Ask him about the article. The boy. The police. Instead she took out the bread she'd just put away, slapped some ham and cheese between two slices, and dropped it on a plate along with an orange.

"Going to take a shower," she said as she took a Capri Sun from the fridge. "I'm tense."

With that, she finally glanced up to find Micah watching her. Let him think of her pissed off and naked just a few feet away. Maybe he wouldn't be so relaxed.

She forced her gaze to move to her husband. "I'll take this to Sydney."

He wasn't looking at her. He was scrolling through his phone again. "Great."

Screw both of them. She stalked out of the room to find her daughter. Their only computer was in Sydney's room, just where a ten-year-old girl's computer shouldn't be, but there was no place anywhere else in the cramped house. Still, Veronica made sure the monitor was visible from the doorway, and Sydney wasn't allowed to close the door while she used it. She was totally absorbed in a world-building game when Veronica walked in.

"Hey, sweetie. All done with homework?"

"Yep."

"How did you do on the spelling test?"

"A-minus."

"That's great! Good job. Maybe you should always study with Grandma."

"Maybe. Hey, Grandma reminded me that Grandpa's birthday is next week. I made him a card. Can we go see him for his birthday? I don't want him to be lonely."

Veronica winced, but her daughter was still staring at the computer screen and didn't notice. "He won't be lonely, Syd. I'm sure he's going out with his friends."

"That's not the same as family, Mom."

No, it wasn't. Friends were more important. Especially pretty young friends who lived in Las Vegas. Or LA. Or London. Anywhere but here in the boring suburbs of the high plains.

"I'll see if he'll be in town," Veronica offered, though she hadn't decided whether she would. "Here's your dinner." She set the plate on Sydney's desk and retreated to the master bedroom.

She knew she was being hypocritical about her father, treating him like he was beneath her for his transgressions. After all, she was a cheater too.

And it was more hypocritical than that, because she'd known who he was since she was fourteen, and she'd ignored it all those years. A woman had called the house. She'd thought Veronica was the wife instead of the daughter. She'd wept and yelled and confessed her love.

"I just want you to know who your husband is," she'd sobbed. And so Janet hadn't known what her jet-setting husband was up to, but Veronica had. And she'd still loved him.

In fact, maybe she'd loved him more. His love and attention had become a prize to her. Something to compete for. And her mother . . . her mother had just seemed pitiful.

So she'd kept her father's secrets. She'd been his accomplice. And now she gave him the cold shoulder.

Not because he'd cheated. That was the worst part of all. At fourteen, her child's heart had learned to accommodate his flaws and make excuses. He was successful and handsome, and life in Lakewood, Colorado, was just so boring.

No, the wandering eye she'd learned to accept. Now she gave him the cold shoulder because he'd cheated too much with too many, and he'd forced his wife to leave, and that had ruined Veronica's plans to leave her own spouse. That was the reason she couldn't look at her father anymore. Not because he disgusted her, but because she disgusted herself.

So she didn't want to see her father or see herself in him. The wound was too deep. Maybe she could drop Sydney at his place for an hour and drive away without interacting.

Too exhausted to deal with washing and drying her hair, Veronica pinned it up in a clip and jumped in the shower to stand under the hot spray. Steam filled the tiny shower stall, fogging the glass until she was completely cocooned from the world. Once she was hidden, Veronica let her head fall until her forehead touched the cool tile. Her face crumpled. She wept. She wept until she had to cover her face with her hands to hide the sound.

She was so tired. So goddamn tired.

And she didn't even have any real problems, did she? She had a job and a home. Her child had love and food and friends. Everyone was healthy. She was *fine*. This was a life others dreamed of.

Her own selfishness just made her cry harder. All those years of thinking her mother was a fool and her father a wicked sinner and she'd become both of them somehow. Her only chance at redemption now was keeping everything steady for Sydney. So she wept quietly and stuffed the remaining scraps of emotion back down.

By the time their old water heater's effort began to fade, she felt spent and almost relaxed. She washed up quickly in the lukewarm water and wondered whether anyone would notice if she just crawled into bed and slept for twelve hours.

Probably not. They'd all be happy she wasn't there to remind them of tomorrow's appointments or tonight's obligations.

By the time she'd dried off and brushed her hair, her eyes looked almost normal, though they still felt sandpapery and overworked. She ran her fingertips under cold water and pressed them to her abused eyelids for a moment. She'd cried more this week than she had in the past six months.

What physical purpose did crying serve? Was there an evolutionary explanation? What weird mutation caused humans to release liquid from their eyes in response to stress? It must work, though. It must have made people healthier and able to deal with challenges more efficiently because our bodies wouldn't bother funneling energy into a useless function.

Her strange turn of thoughts brought her all the way back to calm by the time she tucked her towel more tightly around her and stepped out to the cool, dry square of their little bedroom. It was a master bedroom in name only, a credit to the tiny attached bath. Otherwise the room was nearly the same size as Sydney's. It had been all they'd needed when they bought it. And even now it felt more than big enough when she was alone.

As she opened a dresser drawer to dig out a T-shirt, she realized the bursts of male voices from the front of the house were too chaotic. Too layered. She stood and frowned, trying to puzzle out the sound. Just as she was tipping her head in an attempt to hear better, the bedroom door opened and the sound rolled in.

"Who's here?" she asked as the door shut quickly again.

"Trey and his asshole friends," Micah answered.

She gasped so deeply that she almost lost her balance as she turned, clutching her towel to her breasts. "What are you doing in here?"

"Shh."

He ignored her shock and took a step that covered half the distance between them.

"Micah!"

"I excused myself to use the restroom."

"What if he—?"

"He's drunk and regaling Trey with the story again." He said *the story* like it had quotes around it. "Why would he follow me to the bathroom? That would be really strange."

"Micah . . . ," she tried again, but another step brought him to her, and he slid his hands around her waist.

"Mm. You smell good." One of his hands slipped under the towel and she was somehow paralyzed and helpless.

"Don't," she murmured. "You need to get out of here."

"I never get to see you like this," he whispered as he ducked his head to kiss her neck. "We're always in such a hurry."

"Oh," she sighed. She raised her hands to his chest as if she'd push him away, but her head tilted to give him better access to her favorite spot.

"God, I want you," he growled, sliding one of her hands down to the front of his pants. She felt stupidly, embarrassingly pleased that she affected him this way. She'd wanted to make him crazy and she had.

"There's no lock," she groaned.

"We'll be quick."

"No." She was panting now, panting and rubbing him. "We can't. Sydney is here. And Johnny."

Her towel fell away, and her body surged with alarm at her own nakedness, but when he stroked a hand between her legs she could barely stifle a moan.

"Seems like we can," he murmured. "Seems like you like this. A lot."

She did. She more than liked it. She was already trembling with lust. But they couldn't. They couldn't take this chance. She was about to open her mouth to tell him no, but instead her hands were unbuttoning his jeans. Her legs were leading him toward the bathroom and a door that could lock behind them.

He sat her on the bathroom counter, and he was right: it was quick. And she liked it. She loved it. Pride surged through her when he choked out her name past gritted teeth and finished in a frantic surge of lust.

Because at least he was here and not with someone else.

She should have felt used when he adjusted his clothing and slipped back out as quietly as he'd snuck in, but all she felt was triumph. She let her head fall back to rest on the steam-fogged mirror. The counter burned ice-cold under her naked skin. She felt decadent and wrong as she pressed a hand between her legs, and that was so much better than weary and old.

This was what her father had chased all those years. The difference for him was that he'd wanted it all. The wife at home waiting. The loving daughters. The many chaotic pleasures of the road. All of it separated in ways that made his life as easy as pie.

As a woman, she'd been taught by the world that she couldn't have it all no matter how hard she tried. And she'd finally come to believe it. So she kept her life in little compartments. Everything in its place. At least until Micah had mixed her world up tonight.

She closed her eyes and listened to the faint rumble of male voices in the other room. It was less a sound than a steady vibration. A low roll that barely managed to penetrate the walls that hid her.

She should take another quick shower. Instead she stayed sprawled on the icy tile and smiled. Maybe Micah's feelings for her weren't fading after all. Maybe the passion would keep them going another year. Two years. However long she needed it.

"Please," she whispered to whatever god of infidelity might be listening.

When her neck began to ache, she stretched hard and forced herself to stand and get back into the shower. She cleaned up quickly, then dried with her damp towel before rubbing lotion into her skin with a secret smile.

Was Micah gone now or was he lingering? It didn't matter. She wasn't going back out to the living room, not with those assholes there. She wanted to stay hidden and secret. Alone with the blur of what had just happened, the feel of him still on her skin.

But she loved the thought of Micah on the couch, ears straining for the sound of her coming down the hall as his mind flashed with images of what they'd just done.

She loved having secrets. She loved that no one in her life knew everything about her. She was a puzzle, and only she had all the pieces.

The bedroom felt cool and crisp, a different ecosystem from the humid pool of the bathroom, and a little of her dreaminess faded as she finally slipped on the T-shirt she'd dropped on the bed.

When her head popped through the fabric, an unexpected square of light caught her gaze: her phone screen glowing on the dresser when it should have been asleep. She leaned closer to read the alert. She'd missed a call while in the bathroom, but whoever it was had just wrapped up a message. Not a number she recognized, so she had no idea what to expect when she played it, but as the words tumbled into her ear, she realized she never could have braced herself for this.

Veronica's legs, still a little weak from the latest illicit activity, gave out and dropped her onto the mattress with a whoosh.

Maybe her secrets wouldn't stay secret for much longer.

CHAPTER 9

"At your convenience," the woman on the voice mail had said. But not quite at her convenience. "Before ten a.m. would be grcat."

And so Veronica was walking into a police station for the very first time in her life at eight thirty in the morning. Another secret. She didn't even know why she was keeping this one. Why she hadn't told Johnny.

Still, it was only a quick stop before work; no big deal. Except it must be a big deal, because she could smell her own panicked sweat as a slim African-American woman strode forward with her hand outstretched.

"Hi, I'm Detective Reed. It's great to meet you." She said it so casually. As if they were friends. But then she added, "Thank you for coming in. We'd like to establish all the facts up front so no one has any questions later."

Her tone was cool and she kept her expression very blank and careful. It was the exact same sentence she'd said when Veronica had returned her call the night before. It seemed to be a reasonable explanation. She shouldn't be feeling so afraid. Should she?

Veronica followed the detective to her cubicle, then waited for her to begin, studying her broad brown face, her high cheekbones, the short natural curls tipped with auburn. Her straight spine and set shoulders gave a promise that she could see through crap to the dirty truth beneath. Veronica desperately wanted to keep all of her dirtiness deeply buried.

Unable to stand the silence a moment longer, Veronica cleared her throat. "I'll answer any questions I can," she said. "But of course I wasn't there. When he found the little boy."

"Right." Reed picked up a pen. "Where were you, exactly?"

"I was working. Someone posted the video online, I guess. The video of Johnny carrying him. One of my coworkers recognized my husband and played it for me. I tried to call him right away, but I think he was busy talking to you. I mean the police. Not you personally, probably. Or maybe. I'm not really sure . . . ," she trailed off, worried that even the simplest question was sending her scrambling for the right words.

Detective Reed wrote in tight blue script on a notebook for a few moments before looking up.

"Did he call you back?"

"Johnny? Yes. He called back later to tell me he'd found him."

"'Him'?"

"Tanner Holcomb."

"What else did he say?"

"Just . . . just that he was hiking near Kittredge. He mentioned a trailhead. I can't remember the name. He said he was hiking and Old Man—that's our dog—Old Man started going crazy. That's how Johnny found the boy."

"On the trail?"

"Yes. Or not exactly. Not on the trail. Off the trail somewhere, I think. He said he'd never have found him if Old Man hadn't started barking. He had to walk down into a little gully, maybe?"

Detective Reed kept writing.

Veronica clenched and unclenched her hands. "Is everything okay?"

"Everything is fine," Reed responded, still writing.

"Is this normal? These kinds of questions? Because he found that boy in the woods and that's a good thing, and it feels like . . ."

Reed looked up, her eyes sharp as onyx, but deep and liquid. Endless pools. "Feels like what?"

Veronica shifted. She swallowed. She felt glad she wasn't a criminal, because this woman would immediately intimidate a confession out of her. But what Veronica was hiding wasn't a crime, so she forced her body to still and made her eyes meet the other woman's gaze as steadily as she could. "It feels like you're spending a lot of time asking questions about a happy accident."

"That's our job."

"Okay, but . . ." *But you're supposed to investigate crimes.* That was what she wanted to say. *You're supposed to investigate crimes, and this was just a lost child who was found.* But she didn't say that. She didn't say anything, because she was too anxious and paranoid about her own sins.

Reed nodded as if they'd reached an agreement. "What can you tell me about Friday? The day the boy disappeared."

"Friday?" She shrugged. "It was a normal day. I work half days every other Friday, and that was one of those days, actually. I get off early and then I work a few hours on Saturday with the new intakes—"

"So you were home when on Friday?"

"In the afternoon. I came home before noon, and Johnny made lunch. Then he picked up Sydney at school."

"What time?"

"Three."

She wrote for quite a while before nodding. "Tell me, were you following the story on the news?" she asked.

"On Friday?"

"Last week in general."

"Not closely, but sure. I saw it all over local news feeds. Not on TV, I mean. I can't remember the last time we watched the ten o'clock news. Well, we watched it after all this happened . . ." She felt herself babbling and couldn't stop it. It felt like she was about to blurt out the truth about Micah at any moment, unprompted.

"So you and your husband were following the story?"

"Yes. I mean, I don't know. I'm sure we mentioned it to each other at some point."

"What did he say about it?"

"About Tanner?"

"Yes."

Veronica shrugged. "I can't remember. We talked about how awful it was, I think. We've hiked all over the foothills. We used to take Sydney along in a pack when she was little. When she got older, we talked to her about what to do if she ever got lost or . . ." Her words trailed off under Detective Reed's steady gaze. "I remember now. I said, 'I hope they told that little guy to stay put if he got lost.' But he was only three. That's so young."

"Did your husband help with the search?"

"No."

"You said he was familiar with the area. But he didn't offer to help in the search?"

Veronica felt her face snap to a frown despite her efforts to remain serene. "I don't know that he's *familiar* with the area. I mean, I don't know. He hikes a lot."

"But he didn't join the search."

"Johnny works most weekends and he doesn't get sick days. He's paid by the appointment. On school days he has to be home by three to pick up our daughter."

"But on Tuesday he was free. He was hiking right there."

"Sure. I guess."

"He said he's hiked the Kittredge area a lot."

Veronica paused. What did *a lot* mean? As far as she knew, he hadn't been there for years, but they'd gone once or twice when Sydney was younger. She finally settled on "I can't really say where he hikes when he's on his own."

"So you've never been there together?"

"No, I've been there."

"Often?"

"No."

Detective Reed jotted down another note.

"These seem like strange questions . . . ," Veronica tried again.

"Sometimes people try to insert themselves into a case. These are standard inquiries after an incident like this."

"Oh. I see. He definitely didn't try to insert himself. We hardly talked about it. And no, he didn't volunteer to search. I don't know why. He gets a little distracted this time of year because it's his slow season. He worries."

"About money?"

"Yes."

"So he's been acting worried lately? Stressed?"

"I don't . . . I mean, yes, he's been stressed, but just the normal amount." But had it been the normal amount? He'd been grumpy because money was tight. A little snippy, sure. But nothing worth even starting a fight over.

The detective began writing again and her left hand spread out a little on the desk. Veronica noticed she was wearing a wedding ring. Did she have kids? Or was she too dedicated to this job to carve out time for a family? Veronica squirmed again, not sure why. When she noticed her own shifting, she took a deep breath and forced her body to stillness. Looking up, she found Reed watching closely.

"I hope I've been able to help," Veronica offered, trying to prompt an ending.

"He's done quite a few news interviews."

Her throat clenched. Her stomach burned. Yes, Johnny would keep himself in the press as long as possible. She nodded. Then shook her head. "Maybe. I don't know. They wouldn't leave him alone. Reporters were camped outside our house."

"Yeah. They like to do that."

"I had to sneak out the back door to get my daughter from school."

"You said your husband normally picks her up?"

"Yes. He said he was still answering police questions. I left work early. Everything was crazy."

Reed nodded and her cutting eyes finally softened a little before drifting down to her notes. "What time did he get home the day he found Tanner?"

The burning rose to her throat. Acid from her stomach, eating away at soft linings. Another nonsensical biological response. What purpose could this possibly serve in stressful situations? A reminder that things that were bad could always get worse? "On Tuesday? I think he came home around four thirty. It wasn't late."

The detective made another note. "Any strange behavior?"

This time what rose up in her throat was a wild bark of laughter. She slapped her fingers to her own mouth in shock. Reed's eyebrows rose in surprise. "Sorry. I just . . . It was a very weird day for all of us. Obviously. So everything was strange. But no, there was nothing in particular. Johnny was excited and relieved and happy. That was all."

"And in the days before?"

Her body could sustain tension for only so long, and it was beginning to evaporate, leaving a gritty coating of anger in its wake. Johnny had been stressed. Most people were stressed about something. "Okay, this is getting ridiculous. Everything was normal 'in the days before.' My husband found a little boy in the woods and helped him. The media mobbed us afterward. That's it. What the heck do you want from us?"

The detective only nodded again, her lips pressed tight together in something that wasn't a grimace or a smile. It was more like . . . cynicism.

Veronica felt immediately guilty. This woman dealt with horrible crap all day, every day. That was her job. She probably felt more stress on her best day than Veronica had felt in all of this week.

"I'm sorry," she offered.

Detective Reed held up a hand. "I get it. I think we're done here. But if you think of anything you forgot to mention, give me a call, all right?"

"Sure," Veronica said in a voice that wasn't sure at all. What could she have possibly forgotten? There hadn't been much to remember in the first place, but she took the card Reed offered. "Thanks."

She rose, and Reed stayed at her desk, turning to her computer. She started typing before Veronica even walked away. She'd been dismissed.

But not quite. "Oh, Mrs. Bradley?" Reed called when Veronica was only three steps toward freedom.

"Yes?"

"Who were you with when the child was found?"

"I was at work. I was with a client."

"Can I get her name, please?"

By the time Veronica walked out of the station, she was sweating again. Not a healthy kind of perspiration, but the pungent sweat of fear that chilled your whole body into shivers, because you hadn't been warm enough to need cooling in the first place.

Fear of what, though? Something felt so strange, but nothing she could put her finger on. Her own guilt was stirring up paranoia.

But why hadn't she told Johnny about the call from the detective?

When she reached her car, she got in and sat there, keys in her hand. Her first appointment at the care center began in fifteen minutes. She needed to get on the road. But she didn't move.

Last night she'd frozen up. She'd stood in the hallway and listened to Johnny and his friends, their laughter and the low words she couldn't quite make out. If they hadn't been there, she would have marched right out and told Johnny about the detective. But she'd felt too vulnerable to walk into that den of artificially enhanced testosterone. Or too resentful of their presence. Which was it?

Johnny had agreed that he wouldn't invite Trey over anymore. The guy had given Veronica a bad vibe from day one. He and his friends treated women like crap and bragged about it constantly. She suspected having the last name Swallow had scarred Trey and he'd spent his whole life overcompensating for the homophobia that had been bullied into him.

She'd disliked Trey from the moment she'd met him. She'd made her irritation clear every time he dropped by the house or invited Johnny out for a drink. But when she discovered Trey was dealing steroids at the gym, she'd put her foot down. Not hard enough, apparently. He was back. Because Johnny was back in his prime. He felt powerful and triumphant. He was the man of the house again, and he could invite whomever he wanted into his castle.

So last night she'd stood there and let resentment build in her, and she'd decided Johnny didn't deserve to know what was going on in her life. But now, in the bright light of day, should she tell him?

She should. If only to let him know that the detective was still checking up on him.

After taking a deep breath, she touched his name on her phone and let it ring. And ring and ring. He was with a client. Or a journalist. Or the police. Or maybe a woman. She cleared her throat and left a message.

"Hey. The cops wanted to talk to me. Detective Reed? Maybe you know her? So they asked me to come in and answer some questions about when I heard from you on Tuesday and if we were following the case. I don't know. It was weird. I dropped in on my way to work. Everything went fine, I think. I guess some people get involved in these kinds of things for attention. I'm not sure. Anyway, I'm on my way to my first appointment."

Once she ended the call, there was nothing to do but drive to work. She put on music to distract herself, loud music that reminded her of dancing in clubs during college. Before she'd met Johnny, but after too. She'd been an introvert, but she'd had good friends. Friends who'd dragged her out of the house for a night of fun once or twice or three times a week.

Johnny had loved going out with her and her friends. She'd never met a man like that. Someone who liked her friends as much as she did. He'd been so much *fun*. Everyone had adored him.

It had felt damn special to be chosen by Johnny Bradley. After all, she hadn't been a sorority girl or a homecoming queen or anything more than a slightly nerdy student who had to be talked into putting down her textbooks for a night on the town. Johnny had liked that she was smart and "low-key." That was what he'd called her. Low-key.

She'd liked that he was . . . well, *Johnny*.

She knew she was the one who'd changed since then. Johnny was the same as he'd always been.

She'd isolated herself. She'd become smaller to make room for his presence. She'd given up her friends. It had been her own doing.

She'd told herself it was because she'd become a mom just when her friends were starting careers and moving away. They were still single and dating, and she was caring for a baby. Of course they'd grown apart.

But that had only been the beginning of it. Because then Johnny had screwed up. That's what he'd called it. "Screwing up." But he'd really screwed in, right into a little redhead he'd met at the gym. That was when women had become competition instead of allies. And now Veronica was just . . . lonely.

She indulged in one of her frequent fantasies about how happy they would be apart. They'd both date other people. They'd be civil and polite and supportive of Sydney. He'd have to get a roommate to afford a decent place, but he wouldn't mind that much. He liked being around people. She could see Micah even if it never got more serious.

She could fill her house with books and bright paintings. A cat that would've made Johnny sneeze. All her curtains would be sheer and light, puffs of useless fabric floating on the breeze, exactly the kind of fluffy crap he hated. She'd have family and girlfriends over and not care whether any of them were sleeping with Johnny. Sangrias in the summer. Book club in the winter. And when she was alone, she'd be truly, blessedly alone. It would be so much less lonely than living with someone who'd ruined the love you'd once had.

Half a mile from the senior center, she put her fantasy away and hit the Off button on the stereo. Fantasies were cheap and useless. This was real life. And she wasn't alone. She was married. She was a mother. And she couldn't go back to age twenty-two and tell herself that no man was ever a prize in life, much less Johnny Bradley.

Two years ago, when her mother had announced that she was filing for divorce, Veronica had been surprised but not shocked. Not really. Sydney, on the other hand, had been blindsided and devastated by her grandparents' split.

Veronica still wasn't sure why. Maybe they'd sheltered her too much. Maybe she'd seen a friend's parents going through an ugly breakup. Maybe she just adored her grandfather the same way she did her dad. Whatever the reason, she'd cried uncontrollably. She'd begged Grandma not to kick Grandpa out. She'd started wetting her bed and coming home sick from school. And she'd sobbed and pleaded with her mom and dad, begging them to promise they'd never divorce.

Veronica had promised. She'd had no choice. Her little girl had been anxious and weepy for months. Veronica would have said anything to stop her tears.

So she'd promised. And here she was.

"Here I am," she said aloud to her quiet car as she pulled into a parking space. She squeezed the steering wheel and stared blindly at the welcoming redbrick of the senior-living facility. "Here I am."

Her phone buzzed. She picked it up to find a text from Johnny. Ok no biggie. See u tonite.

No biggie? Really?

She rolled her eyes and grabbed her purse. Whatever. She'd told him, so she was done with it. If *he* wasn't worried, then what the hell was *she* stressed about?

She stretched her stiff back and headed inside to deal with other people's problems instead of her own, but before she reached the wide front doors, her phone buzzed again.

What did they ask?

Her muscles hardened into painful knots again. I already told you, she sent back.

They were acting weird?

I don't know. The whole thing is weird.

Yeah.

She frowned at the screen. You told them you've hiked in Kittredge a lot?

Went twice this summer.

Oh. I didn't know that.

She paused, waiting for another text. She was about to sign off and slip her phone into her purse when he texted one more time. Let me know if they call u again.

Of course. Sure.

Hey can your mom get Syd? I booked a full day.

Veronica nodded, but she frowned as she typed. I'll check but she probably can.

Great. Home around 8.

She tucked her phone away and reached for the glass door. The woman in the reflection glared at her, accusing her of something. But Veronica had no idea what it was.

CHAPTER 10

She tried not to think about it. Tried to put the whole situation out of her mind for the day. She laughed at all of her clients' jokes. She comforted the ones who seemed anxious. And she confirmed that Bess from the third floor had indeed confronted her lover about the rumors, and he'd admitted he was cheating before breaking up with her.

Poor Bess was devastated, and her friend Sunny claimed that now Bess regretted confronting him about it at all. "Can you believe that? She wishes she'd just let him keep cheating! I've told her to have a little pride, but I guess you can't find it if you don't have it."

"She's lonely," Veronica had countered, trying to hide a little jolt of guilt as she watched Sunny do her finger stretches. "You're at repetition fifteen," she murmured. "Ten more."

"Well, don't spread this around, but Bess told me she . . ." Sunny let her fingers relax and leaned forward. "She messed around a little with another girl in college. What was that, fifty-five years ago? I told her she should try it again. There aren't enough men around here."

Veronica grinned. "All right. Other hand." Gossip was the best way to keep her clients distracted from exercises that worked their stiff joints, but she had to keep things moving. "And what did Bess say to that?"

"She just sniffed like I was ridiculous, but maybe she'll consider it now if she hasn't already. These men are no good anyway. And they can't keep it up with condoms, so God knows what they have."

Veronica decided to let that one drop. "What about you? Are you dating any of these no-good men?"

Sunny blew air through her teeth. "Never. I had two husbands. That was at least one too many."

That was a refrain she'd heard many times from many patients, but it still made her laugh. Sunny finished the last of her stretches and sat back with a groan.

"You're doing great," Veronica said. "Which is good, because this is our last visit."

"No, don't say that! My hands are still stiff."

"I know, but look how much improvement you've made since last month. Your range of motion is fifty percent better and I'll leave instructions on doing these exercises on your own."

"But I still have arthritis."

"You'll always have arthritis, but now you know how to manage it better. You can slow the progress. Keep things moving."

Sunny blew air through her teeth again. Veronica patted her arm. The men were often happy to be done with her and her instructions, but many of the women seemed to regard her as a friend, which was nice. Nicer than not having any female friends at all. "I'm not going anywhere, you know. I just had lunch here with one of my previous clients today. I'm around every week, and every other Saturday I'm in the memory unit."

"Fine. But you'd better stop by for gossip. You're the only one I can trust not to rat me out."

"Deal."

Sunny was her last client of the day. It was only five thirty. Her mom had picked up Sydney from school, and for a brief moment Veronica considered walking to the old dive bar across the street for a bacon cheeseburger and an ice-cold beer. Her mouth watered. Her heart yearned.

She'd missed out on solitary adventures in her younger, single years, but now she was older and less self-conscious. Now she could walk into a place alone and order a drink with a wink for the cute bartender. She could flirt. Let loose. Live in her own skin with no shame.

She let herself take a long look at the bar and its flashing "Famous Cheeseburgers!" sign, but looking was all she'd do tonight. She couldn't leave Syd at her grandmother's for so long again. This week had already been too upside down.

Sighing, Veronica packed her therapy equipment into her car and got behind the wheel with only one more wistful look at the burger joint.

If she hadn't settled down so young, maybe she'd have had enough one-night stands that she wouldn't fantasize about the kind of crazy mistakes people made at a dive bar. If she'd waited until thirty-five, she'd have slept around and traveled alone and gone to weddings and yearned for comfortable companionship. Or maybe she was just her father's daughter and fidelity had never been in the cards.

For the first time it occurred to her to wonder whether her mother had ever felt the same. She'd married young and had Trish a few years later. Then Veronica a few years after that. Veronica had always thought of her mom as the boring one. The constant. The default parent who cooked and cleaned and laid down ground rules. But had she wanted more? Had she ever *taken* more?

"No," she said aloud, unable to imagine it even as an adult, though she was beginning to wonder how much of an adult she'd become. Maybe she was still stuck at twenty-two, stunted and selfish.

She was halfway home when she reached the intersection of South Street. The light turned red. She slowed. Stopped. Then, without even pausing to consider it, she signaled a right and slipped into the turn lane. Johnny's gym was a mile to the east, and she headed in that direction. Each tenth of a mile ticked her jaw tighter.

She knew what she was doing. She didn't have to delve deeper into her consciousness to figure out her impulse. Johnny was likely working late with new clients, but he was also strangely distracted. Maybe it was just the newfound fame. Maybe it was more than that. Checking up on him would cost her nothing. Frankly, it was the smart thing to do.

She spotted his truck as soon as she pulled into the lot, and she breathed a sigh of relief. He really was at the gym. She almost drove past it to continue on home, but the empty space just a few yards past his truck beckoned to her. Did she really still care or was jealousy just a habit at this point? Sad that she couldn't find the answer even in her own heart.

Veronica didn't recognize the black-haired girl at the check-in desk. As she dug her membership card from her purse, she realized she hadn't been to the gym in months. She'd been going for long biweekly runs and occasionally stopping in at a yoga studio, but that was it. It was almost as if she'd been avoiding her husband.

"Surely not," she whispered to herself with a little smirk as she slid her card through the reader and got a green light.

"Have a great workout!" the girl called. Veronica waved in response, then ducked her head in the hopes no one she knew would recognize her as she crossed to the stairwell. Halfway up the stairs to the expansive workout room, she realized she should get an excuse ready. She could run right into Johnny as soon as she reached the second floor, and she wasn't wearing any workout gear.

She stopped, one foot perched on the next step as she breathed in the chlorine scent from the lap pool below.

She hadn't stopped in to say hi in years, and an explanation evaded her. Why in the world would she be coming by with no packed dinner or forgotten keys or . . . ?

She couldn't even conjure up a fake reason she'd want to see her husband. The misery of that knowledge swelled inside her like a black balloon. Her stomach ached with it. Her muscles burned.

"A massage," her mouth blurted out. The whir of machinery and the clank of weights drowned out her words, but she still glanced back in embarrassment at the man jogging up the stairs behind her. She smiled stiffly and he jerked his chin up in silent greeting.

She hadn't splurged on a massage in quite a while because they didn't have splurging money these days. But now that Johnny was earning big bucks, it was the perfect excuse. She didn't even need to check whether there was a massage therapist in residence today. Johnny wouldn't bother checking, after all.

A small smile tightened her lips as she bounced the rest of the way up the steps. When she reached the top, she eased toward the edge of the wall that hid most of the weight room from view.

The *thump thump thump* of runners on treadmills prompted a Pavlovian response of weary scorn, and she sneered a little. No wonder she hadn't come by in months. The gym filled her with all sorts of negative emotions, but the ball of knots inside her was far too tangled to pick apart quickly. Was it just because Johnny had wasted so many years here? Or did it remind her of the darkest days of their marriage, when she'd discovered that he'd cheated and that Trey and his buddies had talked him into using steroids?

She'd been too absorbed with Sydney's first year of kindergarten to notice any changes at first. She'd been annoyed at how much unbillable time her husband spent at the gym, but that hadn't exactly been a new fight. He'd gotten a little bulkier. Fine. She didn't care either way. He'd seemed happy with his new muscles.

Until he hadn't been happy. Until he'd gotten volatile and moody. Until the day he'd cornered her in the hall and screamed at her for five minutes about her leaving his favorite warm-up jacket in the washer until it smelled of mildew.

He'd never hit her. That would've been a deal breaker. But he'd scared the hell out of her and made her cower in her own home.

Scanning the weight room, Veronica told herself for the thousandth time that she should have left then, when she'd had an excuse. No one would have faulted her. But Sydney had been so little, and money had been so tight, and she'd told herself that they'd get back to trust and passion when Syd got older. They'd get through it. Grow closer after the struggle.

Plus, Johnny had addressed the issue. He really, truly had.

That fight in the hallway had scared him too. He'd admitted to taking some "questionable supplements." He'd promised to give them up. And he had. But in the interest of starting over, of being honest, he'd dropped another bombshell. In the depths of his drug use, pumped up on steroids and frustrated with his life, he'd cheated on her.

The suddenness of that revelation had thrown Veronica for a loop. He'd managed to frame it as something positive. "I'm being totally honest with you. I really screwed up and I don't want to lose you. I'm telling you so we can start fresh with no lies between us."

In that horrible, shocking crack of a moment, she'd barely let herself feel the heartbreak. It had been there. She'd glimpsed it. But she'd plastered over it immediately. Johnny had given her honesty when he hadn't needed to. He'd been terrified she might leave, and he'd begged her to stay. It was proof he really did love her. She hadn't lost. She'd *won*.

After all, he'd given her the power to leave or give him another chance. He'd left it up to her. So she'd forgiven him. She'd issued new ground rules that he'd followed. He was attentive again and cheerful.

Their life had returned to normal, and she'd been grateful. At that point, she'd still had a picture in her mind of a white picket fence and a growing family.

But the temporary plaster had eventually worn away, and she hadn't realized until it was too late. He'd broken something. Her trust or her image of herself. He'd turned her into her mother, and it seemed she couldn't forgive that after all.

Now she didn't love Johnny anymore, but somehow she still couldn't stop competing.

Veronica scanned the workout room again, but her husband wasn't around. She was wondering whether she needed to go downstairs and check out the locker area. Specifically the individual family restroom with the locking door and extra-deep countertop area, where people were known to hook up. Maybe he was there with that redhead he'd slept with five years before. Maybe he was there with Neesa . . . or someone else entirely.

Suddenly he stood up from behind a butterfly machine and she realized he'd been sitting on one of the low windowsills.

She jerked away automatically to hide behind the wall, but when she eased her head back around, she saw that he was looking down at his phone, probably checking for more news stories about himself.

As she watched, he tapped in a message with his thumbs, then waited. Veronica stared hard at his phone, wishing a giant text bubble would pop up and hover over the screen like it did in TV comedies. But nothing appeared and she realized she was being ridiculous, spying on her husband at work like a psycho.

Why the hell did she even care if he was cheating?

Glancing around to be sure she hadn't been seen, she started to ease back to leave. But at the last second Johnny's furtive movement caught her eye. He put the phone into the pocket of his very expensive Under Armour warm-up pants; then his eyes slid quickly over the room as he reached into the other pocket. Shoulders hunching a little, he lifted his hand and glanced around one more time.

Veronica flinched, afraid she'd be spotted, but he didn't look toward her hiding place as he palmed a phone. A different phone. A different phone he kept in his other pocket.

He typed in a passcode. He checked the screen for a few seconds, his mouth tight, brow puckered. Then he tucked that phone away as well.

"What the fuck?" Veronica whispered. She blinked several times as if she could reset her vision, but nothing changed. She watched Johnny walk to a shelf to grab a paper towel and cleaning spray. She turned and put her back to the wall just as he began wiping down a bench.

Her husband had two phones? What the hell did that mean?

No. That wasn't the right question. That was a stupid question. She knew exactly what it meant. Bad things. Really bad things. Cheating or lying or breaking the law. The real question wasn't "What does it mean?" The real question was "How bad is it?"

That black balloon swelled inside her again. It choked up her throat and hardened her muscles and seized up her joints. The wall behind her refused to soften and swallow her up no matter how hard she wished for it to melt.

CHAPTER 11

"Thanks, Mom," Sydney mumbled around the handful of fries she'd just stuffed into her mouth. She didn't get fast food very often, and she'd been glowing with excitement since Veronica had pulled into the drive-through.

Veronica didn't eat fast food often either and she should have been relishing it, but she could barely taste her burger as she chewed, slumped over her kitchen table.

Was her husband involved with steroids again? Had the police picked up on that? Maybe they'd found something in his car at the trailhead and that was why they were asking so many questions. Or maybe this had something to do with Tanner Holcomb himself?

No. She shook her head at that. What could Johnny possibly have done wrong with Tanner? Even if he'd screwed up evidence or accidentally destroyed something at the scene, he was just a civilian. This had something to do with Trey.

Or maybe the phone was about Neesa. *Or ten other women,* the competitive little lizard part of her brain suggested.

She shook her head.

"What?" Sydney asked.

Veronica jumped a little at being caught. "Nothing, honey. Hey, you promised to show me that history presentation you and Brian put together."

"It's not ready yet."

"It doesn't have to be perfect. I just want to see it. You made it sound so cool."

"Not yet," Sydney insisted. She got back to eating fries and browsing the internet on the family iPad, and Veronica got back to stewing about whatever the hell Johnny was doing wrong.

Well, screw him. If he was cheating, so was she. And if he was dabbling with Trey and his boys again, he deserved whatever he got.

He'd denied dealing last time around, and she'd let him get away with that little lie. He'd sworn he'd just been buying and helping with some of the logistics. But she knew the truth. He hadn't just been buff; he'd been flush with cash. She wasn't an idiot, but she'd pretended to be one to keep the peace. Just like her mother.

Veronica wiped her greasy fingers on a napkin and watched her daughter stare down at a frenetic YouTube video. Images danced in her eyes. Her lips froze in the tiniest half smile in response to the show she was watching.

She was such a good girl. Sweet and bold and smart. She loved life. She loved her family.

Johnny might deserve whatever trouble he'd cooked up for himself, but Sydney didn't. Their daughter couldn't even deal with the idea of her parents living in separate homes, much less her father somehow being removed from her completely.

Veronica ran the back of her hand over her sweaty forehead and took a deep breath. She was panicking and jumping to conclusions. Probably it was the lesser of two evils. He was just messing around and he needed the other phone for sexting.

Veronica choked on a bitter laugh, then turned it into a cough when Sydney looked up.

"Sorry," she managed. Her daughter narrowed her eyes in suspicion, but her attention was quickly drawn back to the screen as Veronica coughed a couple more times to hide her outburst. She was the only woman in the world who would sigh with relief that maybe it was just an affair.

But God, despite her habitual jealousy, it would be a relief, wouldn't it? She could do her thing, he could do his, they'd limp along for a few more years until Sydney was a little more mature and solid . . .

She'd seen an ad somewhere for a book about raising more resilient children, and she'd made a mental note to check into it. Maybe it was time to track down a copy. Not tonight, though. Tonight she had more important things to accomplish.

She dumped the last of her burger and fries into the trash and marched into the bedroom. The small room was crowded with secondhand furniture piled high with the miscellany of their lives. The mirrored dresser had been plucked from her old adolescent bedroom. It had once held her teenage makeup and perfume and hair scrunchies. Now it was piled with old bills and documents. Things that seemed important enough to keep but somehow not essential enough to be carefully stored.

The tall dresser had been inherited from one of Johnny's grandparents, and it was topped by various workout accessories, like exercise trackers and an old heart rate monitor.

The wardrobe they'd found at a garage sale, and that was where Johnny kept most of his clothes, because the closet wasn't nearly big enough to share.

She threw open the doors and began patting down every article of clothing hanging inside it. When she found nothing, she dropped to the floor and pawed through the drawers stuffed with shorts and socks and running tights. Nothing. No steroids or needles. No condoms or hotel key cards. Not even a stray bottle of cologne.

In desperation, she moved his pair of dress loafers that sat on the one shelf. When her fingers slipped inside the left shoe, she felt something stiff and rubbery. Pulling the object from the shadows of the black leather, she realized it was a charging cord. For a cell phone.

Veronica stared at the black cord in her hand for a long while as her mind flashed BINGO in bright colors. This was it. His hiding place. She dug her hand deep into the left shoe and then the right but found nothing else inside them.

Not at the moment, anyway.

After stuffing the charger back into its hiding place, she closed the doors of the wardrobe. If he hid the cord there, he likely hid the phone there as well. She'd check later, after he'd fallen asleep. He wouldn't hear her rustling around. A broken nose in high school had left him with a snoring problem that would keep him oblivious to any noise she might make. His snoring would also act as a low-tech alarm. If she woke him, he'd drop straight into silence, and she could freeze and wait for the noise to start again.

She checked a few other drawers in the room before satisfying herself that there was nothing left to find. This was a new era of lying, after all. All the evidence, all the notes or dirty pictures or receipts, showed up in only one place, and that place was currently in his pocket.

Veronica retreated to the bathroom. She stared at the countertop where Micah had taken her, where she'd spread for him and clutched him tighter, and she wished to God she could have him anytime she wanted. She wanted him now. She needed him.

Tears welled in her eyes and spilled onto her cheeks before she could blink them back. She kicked the door shut and buried her face in her cold hands. "I don't want this," she sobbed against her clammy palms.

This. Her husband, her life, her crowded old house, and the borrowed furniture they could never get rid of because their credit cards were maxed out on groceries and car repairs and school supplies.

All the lies between them, accumulating over the years like rocks at the ocean's edge, collecting barnacles and a crust of old salt. His first lie that he'd support whatever decision she made about the pregnancy. The desperate panic in his eyes when she'd rejected the idea of an abortion. The way she'd told him over and over that it would be fine. *They'd* be fine. Nothing would change, really; it would just get *better*. How he'd finally proposed and promised forever.

The lies had grown like neglected children until they were too big and heartless to control. She wept for long minutes, her sobs receding into little hiccups and then pitiful sniffles. She was okay. She'd be okay. They all would be.

Thank God she hadn't kept up her ridiculous, choking self-pity, because just as her spigot of narcissism dried up, a quiet thud startled her into a yelp.

"Mom!" Sydney called too loudly through the cheap, hollow door. "Are we gonna watch *Survivor*?"

Veronica drew a deep breath, then blew it out as slowly as she could.

"Mom!"

"Yes, honey," she finally managed. "Did you do your math sheets yet?"

Sydney groaned, and the dull thump that echoed through the bathroom was no doubt her forehead hitting the wood.

"Come on. You know the rules. Homework first. Do you need help?"

"Nooo," she answered, managing to draw the one syllable out into an impressive whine.

"Get to work at the table then. I'll be there in a few minutes. We'll watch *Survivor* after I check the answers." Her voice sounded admirably steady, though it was clogged with snot and the abrasions the sobs had left in their wake. Her daughter didn't notice or didn't care, and that was a blessing. Children were naturally selfish. Their selfishness protected them from noticing the rough currents of life that pulled in all directions. But they noticed the rapids. They knew when they were being sucked under.

There had been fights between Veronica's parents. There had been shouted words late at night behind closed doors. Her mother had wept. Her father had blustered. But in the morning her mother had served breakfast and her dad had told jokes, and that had been the end of it. Veronica had put the arguments from her mind and gotten back to the selfish work of childhood.

But how many times had her mother sat like this, hiding her sobs behind closed doors? Even during the divorce, Veronica had never wondered. She'd chosen to believe her mother had just discovered the betrayals and decided to end it. But her mom must have been so lonely for so long. If a teenage Veronica had known about the infidelity, her mother had known too. But she'd set aside her own hurt for her children. That was what mothers did.

Veronica turned on the tap behind her, then caught the cold water in her cupped hands. She lowered her face into the icy pond she'd created and something like a sigh drifted through her whole body. She held the water to her skin as long as she could, then dropped it with a splash into the tub.

After drying her face, she blew her nose. The woman in the mirror looked like shit, blotchy and swollen, but Veronica turned the lights off on her and left her behind.

The sheet on the table in front of Sydney was still pristine, as Veronica had known it would be. She sat down across from her and stared until Syd picked up a pencil. As she began to scratch, Veronica opened her texts.

Do you know what's going on with Johnny? she asked.

Micah didn't reply.

CHAPTER 12

She waited for the snoring. Then she waited longer, watching the digital clock on her side of the bed as it ticked away the minutes in glaring red numbers. Once he'd been fully asleep for a quarter of an hour, Veronica eased out of bed like a snake, slithering her way from under the edge of the comforter.

Aware that the floor creaked near the window, she kept her feet as close to the bed as she could, paranoid that she'd stub her toe on the bedpost, but determined to keep her mouth shut if she did. Once she'd navigated past that disaster, she felt her way slowly across the thick rug to the cheap, rough carpet just past it. Hands out, she waved blindly in the dark until her fingers brushed the wardrobe.

Did these doors squeak? She'd never noticed if they did. None of her sneaking around had ever involved the wardrobe—just closing the bedroom door on prying eyes. And then the bathroom door. Her lips quirked in a bitter smile as she trailed her fingers down the cool wood to the ice-cold metal of the latch.

As if it could help her prepare, she squeezed her eyes tightly shut in a grimace before trying a gentle pull. Too gentle. Nothing happened. She tried again. And again. She should have practiced earlier, but opening the doors had seemed such a simple idea in the light.

Finally she clenched her teeth and tugged hard. The doors opened with a dull bonging sound as the wood vibrated. She grabbed both edges to still them and her fingers clunked far too loudly against the wood.

Jesus.

Veronica held her breath and waited for her husband to snort himself awake, but after what felt like a thousand heartbeats, he inhaled on a long snore that sounded the same as the last one. She exhaled into a slump and said a quick prayer to a god she didn't believe in.

The rest was easy. She reached blindly into the wardrobe, hands thrusting between his clothing before she slipped her way down to the shoes. Inside the left was the charger. Inside the right was a phone. She pulled it out, closed the doors without latching them, and tiptoed to the bathroom.

After locking the door behind her, she turned on the lights and collapsed onto the edge of the tub. The phone was designed to look like an iPhone but it felt cheaper and lighter in her hand, the edges thick and clumsy and the glass recessed a little beneath them. Veronica found the power button and pushed it. Her pulse sped as the screen turned from black to a fuzzy gray. A logo she didn't recognize appeared. A few seconds later the phone glowed with a request for a passcode.

She'd watched him unlock his real phone often enough. Heck, she'd unlocked it herself a few times in the distant past just to check up on him. Assuming he used the same code here—and suddenly terrified that he didn't—she typed in 0302, Sydney's birthdate. It worked. The code screen disappeared to show a generic blue background topped by a few icons.

This was it. The moment she found out the truth.

She tapped the icon that looked like a message bubble. The screen opened and invited her to input a phone number to start a text. She hit the contact icon instead. A blank screen opened. It said "Contacts" at the top, but there were no entries. She backed up to the message screen again and tried to find old messages. They didn't exist.

Frustrated, she backed out and hit the phone icon. Another dead end. There was nothing there. If he was calling or texting anyone, he was deleting all evidence afterward.

"Damn it," she whispered. She hadn't expected he'd be this careful. *She* wasn't this careful. Maybe Johnny had more to lose.

Oh, she deleted texts from Micah eventually. But not right away. She needed to savor them first. But whatever Johnny was doing, he wasn't sentimental about it, apparently.

"Wait," she muttered, then tried one last icon. Photos. She fully expected to find a few saved nudes of some gorgeous young woman or at least a dick pic of Johnny, but it was another dead end. One blank square of gray showed where a photo should've been if any had been taken. There was nothing.

The phone's clock said it was just after 11:00 p.m. Maybe if she waited here patiently the girl—or Trey—would send Johnny a late-night text. Veronica could pretend to be him. She couldn't exactly ask the person for a name, but she could probably tell if it was a man or a woman texting. If it was a woman, Veronica could pretend to be Johnny and ask her to send a cute picture.

Not that she cared. Did she?

A few minutes later, she was sleepy and bored, and the unforgiving edge of the tub felt like it was trying to drill a hole through the muscles of her butt. Veronica squirmed, trying to find a more comfortable spot. Then she heard a buzz. Like a text message.

Startled, she glared down at the phone in her hands. The message icon hadn't changed, but she touched it anyway. Still nothing. It took her a few sleepy moments to remember she'd tucked her own phone into the pocket of her sweatpants before getting into bed.

Micah. He'd finally texted back. But when she opened the message it wasn't him at all. It was her sister.

Are you still awake? Did you see the news?

No. What news?

That Holcomb boy was kidnapped!

WTH? What do you mean? Someone stole him???

No, he was kidnapped BEFORE. He didn't wander off. The family finally admitted they paid a ransom the day before Johnny found him! The police had no idea!!!

Veronica stared at her phone. She stared until the letters blurred into sickly green puddles of nothing.

Then she looked at the phone in her left hand. Its cool blue screen waited for something. Someone. But who exactly?

CHAPTER 13

What was she thinking here? What did she suspect? That Johnny had kidnapped that boy?

No. She wasn't thinking that, because he hadn't. It wasn't even in question. Johnny had been with her the day Tanner had gone missing. He'd kept his normal schedule. He'd been around.

Well, not all day, certainly, but she'd only worked a half day, so he'd cooked lunch on the grill and then he'd picked Syd up from school. He'd gone for a run later, sure, but his truck had stayed in the garage. She'd already recalled it all for the police. There was no big chunk of time he'd been away. No opportunity for him to drive to the mountains and kidnap a child.

Plus, he was *Johnny*. He wasn't a kidnapper. The very idea was ridiculous. He didn't even like it when Veronica put mousetraps in the pantry. He might be a narcissist, but he definitely wasn't a sociopath. Hell, he cried over Disney movies more often than his daughter did. It was one of their running jokes.

Okay, she told herself. *Okay, you're freaking out for no reason.*

Well, not *no* reason. Kidnapping was a pretty damn big deal.

Frantic, Veronica scrolled through news feeds on her phone, but the story had just broken, and everyone repeated the same scant details. *After consulting with attorneys, the Holcomb family admitted that they had received a ransom demand on Saturday night, and that they had paid the kidnapper without informing the police, according to the kidnapper's instructions. Police have scheduled a news conference for 9:00 a.m. Mountain Time.*

More than nine hours until she could find out more.

Veronica turned off Johnny's secret phone and slipped it back into its hiding place, but not until she'd compulsively wiped off the prints she'd left on the screen. But that was ridiculous. He was just having an affair. Or dealing drugs.

There were crimes anyone might commit, like jaywalking or smuggling a really cool rock home from a national park. Then there were certain crimes you could assign to people you knew well. Trish, for instance, might steal a campaign sign from a bigoted school board candidate and throw it in the trash if no one was looking. Veronica herself had once keyed a guy's car in high school because he'd lied to his friends about them hooking up. And Johnny might deal steroids; he had before. But he wouldn't hurt a child for any reason.

She slipped out of the bedroom and hurried to the living room to turn on the television. All her rushing was in vain: she'd missed the local news. She eventually found a local news story online, but everyone was using the same brief, useless source of information. There were no details to be had.

Veronica looked at the four messages she'd sent Micah in the past hour. He hadn't texted back. What the hell was he doing? Who was he with?

PLEASE CALL ME! she finally typed out in all caps, no longer caring that she was blaring her desperation out for him to see.

She stared at her phone, waiting, waiting, waiting for the moving dots that would signal his typing. Was she panicked over Johnny or panicked that Micah was probably with another woman? She couldn't process her anxiety well enough to even know.

Finally, an eternity later, the little dots appeared. Veronica pressed a shaking hand to her mouth in relief. She expected an apology or worry or something, but all she got was a query.

CALL you?

Screw this. Veronica hit the call button.

Her blood swirled through her body as if the steady beat had gotten pushed up against a ragged shore. Waves and spray and dangerous eddies everywhere. Teeth clenched, lip raised, she listened to each tinny ring, wondering whether Micah was excusing himself from the bed of some other woman to answer his phone.

The line clicked open. "Why are you calling?" he asked immediately.

Her mind blanked red at his greeting. Not *Are you okay?* Or *What's wrong?* Just alarm that she'd overstepped her place. Her place on her back beneath him.

"I've been texting you," she ground out.

"I just texted you back."

"You can't just—"

"How are you calling me?" he interrupted. "What if Johnny hears this?"

"I'm calling because I need you, obviously!" Her voice rose indiscreetly, but she didn't care. Let Johnny hear. Let him come out and explain himself and his choices.

Her rage spilled over and spread everywhere. "Have I ever called you at night? Have I ever asked you to call me? Who the hell do you think you are, treating me like I'm some idiotic piece of ass who can't use common sense?"

Silence on his end. She, on the other hand, was panting with fury. She knew he could hear it and she didn't care. Let him wonder if she'd completely lost her mind. Let him worry.

"I'm sorry," he finally said, and her heart clenched with one last spasm of rage before calming a little. Then a little more. Some drain had opened up to provide relief. "I'm sorry," he repeated. "You're right."

"It's not like . . . it's not like I text you all day, looking for attention. You keep ignoring me—"

"I'm not ignoring you. I've been putting together some designs and bids, catching up on emails. It's not like that."

"Are . . . ?" *Are you home?* That's what she wanted to ask. It croaked in her throat, looking for escape, but she swallowed it down. If he wasn't home, it couldn't mean anything to her. It couldn't.

"Something happened," she finally managed. "More than one thing, actually." She barked out a laugh at that.

"What's going on, V?"

"I told you things have been weird. With Johnny. With the police."

"Yeah."

"They're saying now that Tanner Holcomb wasn't lost. He didn't wander away. He was kidnapped."

"What?" His voice cracked out sharp and bright.

"He was kidnapped and the family paid a ransom without involving the cops. That's why the police have been asking so many questions."

"Well, that explains it, then." He said it so calmly.

"That explains *what*?"

Micah sighed. "It explains why the police have been bothering Johnny. They were suspicious about the whole thing, and he was the only person they could question. Well, him and a three-year-old kid."

She nodded. "Oh. Right. I guess that's right. He's their only reliable witness. It makes sense that they'd pump him for every detail."

"Exactly. So what are you freaking out about?"

"There's more."

He stayed quiet for a moment, and his voice came softer when he spoke, as if he'd finally decided to be patient with her. "What do you mean? More what?"

Veronica craned her neck to look down the hallway, but the bedroom doors remained closed.

"V?" he pressed.

She curled into herself, hunching around her connection to him. "He has another cell phone, Micah. An extra phone. One of those cheap throwaway ones you can buy at the gas station."

"Who? Johnny?"

"Yeah. I saw him checking it. He keeps it hidden in his armoire."

"Oh. I . . . That *is* strange."

"Yes. That's not normal. So what if he really is up to something? What if he . . . I don't know. Criminals have those kinds of phones. What if he did have something to do with this?"

Micah huffed out a chuckle and she could practically see him running a hand through his dark hair. "Come on, Veronica. *Johnny*?"

"I know. It's crazy. But the phone . . ."

"It could be anything," he countered.

"No, it couldn't be *anything*. It couldn't be something good. It's not good!"

Another pause. She heard a cabinet door close. The click of a glass being set on a counter. He was home. But that didn't mean there wasn't a closed bedroom door keeping someone in the dark just as there was at her house. Maybe she could sneak out and drive over there. Was she desperate enough to expose herself as a jealous psycho? Probably not.

"I don't know," he finally sighed, weary of this conversation or weary of her. "Maybe he's just doing the same thing you're doing, V."

"What?"

"Cheating."

Tears clogged her throat at the word. Tears? Why? She knew what she was doing. And hell, she knew she was doing it with Micah. But he'd never said it outright like that. He'd treated it as something harmless. A little fling no one would ever know about.

And sure, Micah was Johnny's friend. That was a betrayal. But Veronica was his wife. She'd made promises. They had a child. She was the cheater here, not him.

She swallowed her choking hurt and cleared her throat. "Is he?" she croaked.

"What?"

"Cheating?" The clink of ice. A pour of liquid. Silence. "He'd tell you," Veronica pressed.

"V. Come on. It's late."

It's late. As if she didn't know how late it was. As if she hadn't been tortured by both of these men for hours. "I know it's late," she snapped. "And I know he'd tell you if he was cheating. So tell me what you know, Micah. Is Johnny cheating on me or is this something bigger? If it's just a woman, *I need to know*."

"Fine." The word hitched as if he'd just dropped onto the couch. She pictured him in his dim apartment, staring out the tall windows at the lights of downtown Denver. Despite her anger, she wished she were there, lying on the couch again, his body impossibly warm against hers.

"Okay," he said, stalling, picking out which truths would be safest to hand to her. "There *is* a woman . . ."

Yes. Yes yes yes. She couldn't deny the relief that crashed over her in a dark, warm wave. Relief that she wasn't the only bad guy, relief that she had an out, relief that there was nothing more nefarious than sex here. Johnny was cheating on her. He had nothing to do with a kidnapping. The end.

God, all those years of trying to keep her prize away from other women, and now she was actually relieved.

"Who is she?" Veronica demanded. "Neesa?"

"I don't know."

"A client?"

"I don't know."

"Yes you do."

"No," he snapped. "I don't. I don't want to know. All of this is fucked-up, and I didn't want to hear his confession. Not under these circumstances. I'm sleeping with his wife, so I didn't want to know. Can you understand that?"

Some of her angry triumph cooled under the ice of his tone. He'd always seemed so cavalier about what they were doing, but apparently he felt some guilt too. "Okay. I get it." But she kept pressing. "So what did he tell you?"

"He said there's a woman, and she's . . . whatever. I don't know anything about her. There's a woman, and this sudden media coverage of your happy family has caused some tension between them."

"Good," Veronica snapped before she could stop herself. This wasn't the fun, sly side of her she offered Micah. This was the bitchy, cruel side she trotted out in arguments. *Good* that this other woman felt tension, because Veronica had been pretty damn tense for days, and why should she be the only one suffering? "So this isn't just quick sex in the locker room? They're . . . they're some kind of couple?"

"No idea."

"They must be. If she's upset about me, and it's serious enough that he got a phone to communicate with her . . . I bet it's Neesa. Though maybe he's always had a phone and there are lots of women. If I confront him—"

"Don't."

She blinked. "Don't? Why not?"

"If I'm the only one he's told, he'll know I told you."

"Okay, but I did find the phone. I can ask him about that."

"Why?"

She pulled her phone away from her face to frown at it before sliding it back to her ear. "*Why*? What do you mean, why? He's cheating on me and hiding a secret phone in our bedroom."

"So you want to call him out? Get it out in the open?"

"Yes!"

"You told me we were doing this because you couldn't leave him, Veronica."

"I . . ." Her outrage died in her chest and began to shrivel. She felt it drying out and curling in, drawing important bits of her with it.

"You said Sydney would be devastated, that you couldn't do that to her. That's why we're sneaking around like this. Lying to everyone."

Her chest felt hollow, her skull too light.

"If you confront him, you'll be dropping a bomb into this whole situation. If you want to blow up your family, you'd better be damn sure first. You can't just throw it in his face without thinking. You won't be able to control what happens afterward. You won't be able to protect Sydney."

She shook her head and pulled her body in close, wishing she could curl tight enough that she got smaller and smaller until she disappeared. "I . . . I . . ."

"Shh," he murmured.

She was crying now, high, strangled sobs she didn't want him to hear. "I can't . . ."

"I know. It's okay."

He was right. Confronting Johnny would open the teeth of this awful trap she was stuck in, but she'd be sacrificing her daughter to free herself.

"Listen," Micah said, "if Johnny has someone on the side, fine. How does that change anything? It doesn't."

She hiccupped in a breath.

"It just means you don't have to feel guilty, right?"

Right. Yes. She'd already thought of that herself. She was getting caught up in being right. In winning. When all she should really want was a truce.

"And it means you don't have to worry about what he's up to, because you *know* what he's up to. That's why he's been acting strange."

"Yeah," she managed. "I guess it is."

"Unless you're jealous?"

For a split second she thought of Micah and all the other women he could be seeing, but then she remembered he was talking about Johnny, and that chased the last of her tears away. "No. I'm not jealous."

But she'd felt a burn of delicious righteousness today, hadn't she? She'd loved that she might have a place to throw all her anger and frustration. Right into Johnny's face.

So she definitely felt *something*. But it was only residual. A memory of what she'd once wanted with Johnny. The hot, ridiculous love she'd once felt for him.

"If you're going to rock the boat, just let me know first, okay? I think I deserve a say in how this shakes out."

He did. He was a part of this too. He'd known Johnny even longer than she had. "Okay," she whispered.

"Are you going to be all right tonight?"

"Yeah. Yeah, I'm fine. Just . . ."

"Just what?"

"Micah . . ." She sighed his name. Not a sweet sigh. More of a growl, really. But then she shook her head. "Never mind."

"Come on," he said. "Don't do that. Don't play those games."

It wasn't a game. She shouldn't have to ask him to treat her nicely. He should *want* to. But if she didn't communicate her feelings, could she expect him to work it out on his own?

"Okay. I feel like I've been really respectful of what this is. I don't ask . . ." She wanted to say it. She wanted to tell him all the fears that crawled into her head when they weren't together. But if she spoke it aloud, he might answer questions she would never, ever be brave enough to ask.

"I don't think I ask for much," she finally said, downplaying her pain. "Not for anything, really."

"Veronica—"

"So when I text you, could you please just treat me like a person who . . . who you have some respect for? Or some *regard*, at least? I wouldn't ask for anything if it wasn't important. I don't . . . I never . . ."

"I'm sorry," he said on a sigh, cutting off her stammer. "I've been stressed about work with the season wrapping up, and I'm trying to get crap organized for my accountant, and . . . I'm truly sorry. I've been insensitive. I know I have."

She nodded, holding in the words she really wanted to say. That she needed him. That she was afraid he didn't need her. That he didn't even want her as much as he used to. That if he got tired of this, she'd have nothing good to look forward to, nothing to get her through.

"I'm sorry," she whispered instead. "This week has been crazy. *I've* been crazy."

"You're fine," he murmured. "You're fine, V. I'm glad you called."

"All of this has just been . . . I mean, things will calm down. Everything will get back to normal. Right?"

"Of course," he said, the words breezy with relief that this conversation was over.

She wanted to keep talking. They so rarely got to talk, but he let silence fill the seconds between them. "I'd better go," she muttered.

"Night, V. I'll see you soon."

The line went dead. She stared at the black rectangle of the narrow window next to the TV and whispered good night in return.

CHAPTER 14

This time the police came right to the front door. Veronica's nerves sizzled mildly as Detective Reed explained the reason for the visit, but it wasn't true fear this time. Of course they needed to question Johnny. Everything had changed, and they'd need to follow up on what they'd learned from the Holcombs.

Veronica was only a little surprised that they wanted to question her again as well, but they were covering all their bases. Perfectly logical in the midst of a kidnapping case.

In fact, she and Johnny had been discussing it before the police had knocked. He'd brushed his teeth and dressed early after Veronica had pointed out the cops would probably want to speak again soon.

Thank God Trish had already dropped by to pick up Sydney. She spent time with her aunties most Saturdays and they spoiled her rotten, so she didn't even mind waking up early and being ready to go at 9:00 a.m.

Johnny left the house to follow a male detective to the station, and Detective Reed stayed behind to sit at Veronica's kitchen table.

Did they do that on purpose? Have Veronica sit with another woman in the comfort of her own home while sending Johnny off with a man in a show of authority? Not a bad plan, but if they'd asked, she would have advised them to have Johnny speak to a woman as well. He liked to impress them. Liked to be pleasing.

"Let's go over last Friday again," Reed said in a voice that seemed cultivated to convey that any secrets spoken would fall onto a soft and understanding place. "That was the day the boy went missing. The last time we talked you said you were with your husband that afternoon."

"Yes. I worked in the morning and got home before noon."

"What time exactly?"

"Eleven fifty, I think. Maybe eleven forty-five. It's basically the same every other week." Tanner Holcomb had disappeared sometime around three, according to last week's news stories.

"And where was Johnny when you got home?"

"He was here. In the backyard. The grill was lit and ready." She watched Reed scratch away at her notebook, filling it with the details of Veronica's life.

She could offer up even more details if that was what Reed wanted. *I remember it all distinctly because I'd dreamed about having sex with my lover that night, and I'd been thinking about it all morning. I was annoyed at having to spend quality time with my spouse, because I wanted to lounge around and touch myself and think of Micah's fingers in me. His tongue. His body. I wanted to take a bath and stroke my hands down my skin and remember. Instead I had to chat about my husband's plans to fertilize the lawn for winter.*

Veronica kept her face placid and her mouth shut and waited for the next question.

"You made lunch?" Detective Reed asked.

"Johnny made lunch. Chicken breasts and grilled zucchini."

"And you ate together?"

"Yes."

"Then what?"

"I think I paid some bills. We watched a little news. He left around two forty-five to walk to the school and pick up Sydney just as he always does."

More pen scratching. "He brought her back here?"

"Yes. Everything was perfectly normal."

"So they got home around . . . ?"

"Three fifteen," Veronica answered easily. She'd hoped maybe they would stop at the park and she could sneak in that bath, but they'd walked through the door right on time.

"And after that?"

"Johnny went for a run. I helped my daughter research a topic for a history project. He was gone for about an hour."

Reed perked up at that, her eyebrows twitching higher for a split second. That was when Veronica felt a strange little zing down her neck. A tiny bolt of awareness. Because maybe he hadn't been running after all. Maybe he'd jogged a couple of blocks and then slipped into someone's house. A woman's. The woman he was texting on his secret phone or even another woman altogether. Maybe there were several in the neighborhood. He could have daily appointments.

"How do you know he went for a run?" Reed asked.

How indeed? He'd left on foot and he'd come back sweaty and gone straight to the shower. And what did that prove? He'd exerted himself. That was all. "I know because he goes for afternoon runs when things are slow at the gym. His truck was here. He took off jogging."

Did her voice sound warped and high, like she was lying? Were her words as doubtful as her soul? Reed wrote something down and then her dark-brown gaze rose to study Veronica. The detective's face was a blank, but her eyes blazed with a thousand thoughts.

"Ma'am," Veronica blurted out, then: "Detective. I saw the news. I know what you're asking."

"Is that right? What is it I'm asking?"

Veronica clenched her fingers tight together into fists, then regretted it immediately when Reed's gaze slipped down to light on them before darting back to her face.

"I know that . . ." She had to swallow against a suddenly dry mouth. "I know it takes thirty-five minutes to get from here to that area of the foothills. And another thirty-five minutes to get back. I assume kidnapping a child would add at least another thirty minutes—"

"Thirty minutes?" Reed interrupted sharply.

"I have no idea!" Veronica said in a rush. "Thirty minutes? Four hours? A whole day? Whatever it is, Johnny was gone for an hour or maybe an hour and fifteen minutes. That's it. He took a shower and he was playing video games with Sydney at five thirty. I remember the time because I told her she had to practice her ukulele for thirty minutes before dinner because she was the one who asked to take the class even though I warned her she wouldn't like practicing. And Sydney . . ."

She drew in a deep breath. Too deep. The sound of it filled the room, and Reed wasn't scratching anymore; she was just watching, eyes alive with intelligence and suspicion and something harder. Something that was always there or had arrived just for Veronica. She couldn't know, though she desperately wanted to.

"So what I'm saying is . . ." Another deep breath. "Johnny didn't kidnap that child on Friday afternoon. He wasn't involved. He just happened to find Tanner Holcomb off a trail while he was hiking. Any one of those people parked at that trailhead could have found him."

"But they didn't."

"Right. And Johnny wouldn't have either if he hadn't brought Old Man along. He was lucky." She said the word, but it was an out-and-out lie. The boy had been lucky, but Johnny hadn't. That fear she'd felt from the start had been the right thing to feel. This was dangerous. This was awful. "The boy was probably hiding," she said softly. "He was probably too scared to call for help. So it was lucky that Old Man was there to find him."

"And later in the evening?" Reed asked.

Veronica blinked and realized she'd let her head fall to stare at her hands. She forced herself to straighten. "Pardon?"

"Later in the evening, did your husband go anywhere? A trip to the store maybe? An appointment at the gym?"

"No. I'm pretty sure that was our whole day. He lifted weights in the basement around eight. He almost always does during the slow season. But he never went anywhere." She knew because she'd wanted him to leave, just leave, just leave her alone so she could think about Micah.

"He was in the basement?"

"Yes, but—"

Detective Reed stood and blocked out half the light in the room and all the air. "I'd like to see it."

"Oh. Sure. Of course." Veronica scrambled to her feet. "Yes." How many ways could she babble out an affirmative? Afraid to open her mouth again, she led the way to the hallway and the door halfway down that was always locked to stop Sydney from falling down the stairs. But Syd wasn't a baby anymore. They didn't have to lock it. Maybe Veronica was afraid of what was hiding down there.

Sweat prickled at her hairline as she thumbed the lock. She gestured toward the narrow stairs as she swung the door open. "Should I . . . ?"

"Please."

Veronica clicked on the bare bulb that lit the stairway, then led the way down toward the cement floor. She hit a second light switch and two more bare bulbs flared to life, exposing the whole length of the unfinished basement.

There wasn't much to see. The furnace. The water heater. A washer and dryer. Plus all the normal detritus of family life: two storage racks holding ancient paint cans and dusty Christmas decorations and God knew what else, a few stacks of boxes, one old twin mattress propped against a wall, stained with the results of her daughter's potty-training struggles. And of course, Johnny's weights and his ancient red weight bench. They'd had sex on that weight bench a few times early in their relationship. She hadn't even bothered glancing toward the cracked leather in years.

Reed walked the entire perimeter. She opened the lid of the washer and the door of the dryer. She lifted the flaps of a couple of the larger boxes. She looked behind the heater and under the lip of the shelves.

Goose bumps rose on Veronica's skin as Reed studied the dull cement floor. She'd never liked the basement, but now everything about it felt unfamiliar and ominous. Had that patch in the floor always been there? It looked shiny with a brownish patina, so it must be old. There probably wasn't a skeleton buried there.

Reed paused over a decrepit boom box that sat on the cement near Johnny's weights. She stared at it for a long while. What was she looking for?

"All right, Mrs. Bradley. I'll let you know if I have any further questions."

"Thank you," Veronica said quickly. She waited for Reed to start up the stairs, then turned off the lights and jogged quickly after her, relieved to leave the gray, cold basement behind.

Once she'd popped free of the claustrophobic stairwell, she slammed the door behind her with far too much force, then locked it automatically. Reed looked up from her notebook with that bright gaze again. Veronica smiled for no reason, then frowned to make up for it.

"Is he okay? The little boy?"

Three heartbeats boomed in her ears before Reed answered. "He's doing fine."

"Okay. Good. Thanks. I've been thinking about his poor parents. This is all just . . ." She waved a hand. "Do you know when my husband will be back?"

"No. But I'm sure he has quite a few more questions to answer than you."

"Yeah. Right. That makes sense. Do you have any leads? About the kidnapping, I mean. About who could have done it. That poor baby."

"I'm not at liberty to discuss the case."

"Oh, of course! I'm sorry! I shouldn't have asked."

"I'll be in touch, Mrs. Bradley."

"Okay. Sure. Thank you. And good luck out there."

Good luck out there? Her face burned as Reed glanced around one last time before taking her leave.

She'd started out calm, but every question had reminded her that she and Johnny had secrets to hide. Neither of them had kidnapped a child, but they weren't innocents. They were both liars and cheaters. They were both sneaking around. They were both hiding so many things. Surely cops could pick up on that?

She'd been so frazzled there at the end. Reed must know she was hiding something.

"Fuck," she whispered as Reed shut the door firmly behind her. Maybe she should just fess up. *If it seems like I'm hiding something, it's because I'm having an affair. That's all. It's not the kidnapping.* Maybe the other woman would be sympathetic. At the very least, she must have seen it all a hundred times before. It wouldn't shock her. She wouldn't even care.

Chewing on her bottom lip, she paced for a few minutes, hoping to burn off a little adrenaline. She could easily run ten miles right now, but her belly turned in warning. Running might take care of her anxiety, but most of that anxiety felt like it would immediately heave up from her stomach.

What if *she* was the problem here? What if Johnny was answering every question openly and honestly and Veronica's behavior was the reason the police kept coming back?

But there was something strange. Something that kept bobbing up in her thoughts. Had Johnny really been to Kittredge twice that summer? He usually told her where he was heading. She was sure he hadn't mentioned Kittredge. Or maybe she just hadn't been listening. Desperate to know more, she switched on the TV. It was just past the late-morning news hour, so she backed up the digital recorder until Hank Holcomb's face suddenly flashed on the screen. She tried to pause it and fumbled the remote. It clattered to the floor with a plastic bang loud enough that she worried she'd shattered it into a hundred pieces. But when she retrieved it, she found that only the battery cover had broken free. A tab had snapped off. She'd have to tape it back into place, but for now she straightened the half-escaped batteries and lined up the news story.

Hank Holcomb stared defiantly at the cameras, his green eyes steady, his wrinkled skin flushed above his strong jaw.

"On Saturday night, in the midst of the search for our grandson, we received a text message that included a picture of Tanner. He appeared to be sleeping unharmed, wrapped up in an old quilt. The monster who had kidnapped him demanded a million dollars in untraceable bills and promised to release Tanner uninjured as long as we never involved the police in the transaction. After consulting security experts in several countries, we agreed to comply. On Monday we left the cash at a highway rest stop, and on Tuesday the kidnapper released Tanner near a busy trailhead as promised. I regret that we had to lie to the authorities, but I do not regret the actions that brought my grandson back to us. Now that he is home safe and we have had time to consult with attorneys, we will fully cooperate with the police. Thank you."

The audio exploded into a maelstrom of shouted questions, but Mr. Holcomb simply folded a note back into his pocket and turned away.

Veronica collapsed onto the couch. That was it, then. The kidnapper had promised to release Tanner near a trailhead, obviously assuming someone would come across him. Johnny had simply been in the right place at the right time. Or the wrong place. She had no idea anymore.

Her hands shook. Her heart raced to an impossible speed. She had no idea what emotion prompted her response, but she knew who she needed.

Can you talk again? She sent the text without a second thought, but it was all she could think of after as the minutes dragged on and on. And in the end Micah failed her one more time.

Sorry. On a call.

This time she wasn't even surprised. At least he'd acknowledged her. Was that what she'd been reduced to? A woman relieved to be glanced at?

Yes, sadly. Absolutely yes.

CHAPTER 15

An hour later it was her husband who surprised her with a message.

Going straight to the gym.

Veronica stared at her phone in disbelief. That was all he had to say? *Going to the* gym? Johnny had been at the police station for two hours, and now he was just excusing himself to the fucking gym?

She didn't respond. She still had a couple more hours before she needed to pick up Sydney down in Parker, and if Johnny wanted to play the *Everything's cool* game, she could play it too.

But this was ridiculous. Yes, she'd known he was speaking to the police, but he still owed her the details. How could he just bow out for the day after an interview with the police about a goddamn kidnapping?

Flashes of movies were now playing in her head. Men in dark suits and black cars. Serious people wielding serious power.

This was a kidnapping now. That meant the FBI, didn't it?

"Jesus," she breathed. Surely Johnny would have told her if he'd met with the FBI. There was no way he would have left that out. Except that he'd left everything out. He'd told her nothing. He was so busy communicating with everyone else—the press, his girlfriend, his fanboys—that he couldn't bother communicating with his own wife.

Tears burned her eyes and clogged up her whole head. Just stress. Not grief. Not sorrow. She swallowed them down, tipping her head back in the hopes of stopping her eyes from watering. She was just so tired. So damn tired. All she wanted to do was crawl back into bed for the day.

No. That wasn't true. It was never true these days. What she really wanted was to crawl into another bed. But the owner of that bed was too busy for her. Or he claimed to be. An hour had passed and he hadn't even texted, much less called.

She glanced at the time on her phone. He often worked from home, but he also attended meetings with clients and did consultations. Would he invite her over if he was home? Did it matter?

Yes. Yes, it mattered. She couldn't go on like this. She'd made her expectations clear and Micah didn't give a damn. She was his whore. That was it. She was an easy piece of ass and he knew damn well he didn't have to treat her well to get what he wanted.

Screw this. Screw all of it. She couldn't keep living like this, uncertain of everything in her life.

Veronica marched to her car and zipped down the alley. Once she hit the main road, she sped toward the freeway, hands strangling the steering wheel like she wished she could strangle him. *How dare he? How fucking dare he?*

She'd made things as easy for him as she could, and that had been her mistake. At first she'd been something valuable. A prize he'd won through slow seduction. But she'd made herself cheap in the past months. Ubiquitously attainable. She was a piece of old hard candy in a dish on his table. Worthless and unwanted and barely noticed.

Her affair with Micah had started off as empowerment, or so she'd told herself. She'd felt as if she were taking action instead of idly waiting for her life to limp forward. She could improve her life a little without hurting anyone else. A victimless rebellion.

Not that she'd thought it was *right*. It had never been right even if Johnny had done it first. But if an affair kept her married and raising their daughter together for a few more years and no one found out, was it technically *wrong*?

When she spied the open parking space just a few feet from the front door of Micah's building, it struck Veronica as a sign that she was doing the right thing. This space was for her. It seemed to mutter *You go, girl* to her as she pulled next to it.

Her third attempt to parallel park was finally successful, but she didn't let that tiny humiliation slow her down. She strode through the doors and straight toward the female desk attendant to sign an illegible name. She nodded once, then stalked to the elevators, unworried about being recognized. Who the hell cared?

She willed more anger into her heart as she rode the elevator to his floor. She set her face in stern coldness as she knocked on his door. She waited, and she hated him. They'd had a friendship. This wasn't fair. She was going through all this insanity, and *it wasn't fair* that he was turning his back on her now.

The door swung open. The familiar scent of his apartment breathed over her. Micah's eyes looked heavy with sleep and bowed down with a frown as they focused on her. He blinked slowly a couple of times before shaking his head. "Veronica?"

"We need to talk," she bit out past her tight rage.

"Yeah." He looked even more confused. "Sure."

She brushed past him, resisting the need to tip closer for an embrace. He didn't reach out either, and her hatred tripped into pain. There was no purse on the table. No woman's coat slung over a chair. There was only a rumpled blanket on the couch.

Walking to the window, she kept her back to him and stared out at the view she'd looked at dozens of times before. The view she'd wished she could look out on a hundred times more. She dreamed of this view sometimes. Of staring out at rooftops and lights as his arms slipped around her and brought her closer to his heat.

"What's wrong?" he asked, giving her the prompt she was obviously waiting for.

"What do you *think* is wrong?"

He sighed. "I didn't have time for you?"

"Oh, you think that could be it?"

Another sigh, because her dignity was such a goddamn burden to accommodate. "I'm working my ass off, V. There are half a dozen projects to finish before winter. I have a lot going on here too."

She tossed a glance over her shoulder at the rumpled throw on the sofa. "Yeah, you're obviously blazing away today."

"I was up at six this morning to meet with a contractor in Centennial, okay? Then I needed a nap. What the hell do you want from me?"

She swung around, aware that her face had pulled into an ugly mask and unable to stop her snarl. "I told you what I wanted. I put my big-girl panties on and *asked* for it like an adult. And you agreed!"

He raised his hands in appeasement. "I know. I'm sorry. I'm frazzled and stressed, and . . ." His hands dropped. "Fuck. Look. Maybe if I—"

"It's over," she spat out. "I'm not a whore."

"Of course you're not a whore. Come on. What are you doing?"

"You were my friend. Not just . . . not just some guy I picked up at a bar. Or maybe you were just pretending to be my friend the whole time. Maybe this was all a stupid game to you."

"I wasn't pretending, V. Come on." He took her flailing hands between his and she let him. She let him, because his hands curling over hers felt better than anything in the world right now, even if she hated that she wanted it.

"You're not being a friend anymore, Micah. Everything has gone crazy, and . . . Hell, maybe I've gone crazy too. I can't do this. I can't." Her pride stirred, and she made a token effort to tug her hands away, but she felt nothing but gratitude when he held on.

"You're just stressed. Everything is fine."

She shook her head in denial, but the shake turned into a nod. "Maybe it is. But I feel so alone." Tears again. Pitiful. She didn't want them. She tried to swallow them down, will them away, but they forced their way free and spilled down her cheeks.

"Veronica, don't. I'm so sorry. Come here."

He pulled her to the couch, and she sank into the cushions, the leather still warm from his nap. She curled her body into his, all her anger burned away into a desperate, lonely ash.

"We were friends," she whispered. "I miss that."

"We're still friends."

"No. I'm just a dirty secret now. Or an old habit. I'm stress you don't need. I just want it to be the way it used to be, Micah."

"Hush." He kissed the top of her head. "You're not stress. My job is the stress. I took on too many projects this summer, that's all. That's all it is."

"I'm sorry," she managed to say. Her face twisted with more tears, so she buried it against his shirt and forced herself to breathe slowly. "This is supposed to be fun. I know that. I don't want this to be something you try to avoid."

"It's not."

"Just be honest with me, okay? If you don't want me anymore . . ."

He eased her off his chest and ducked his head to meet her watery eyes. "You know I want you, V."

She shrugged a shoulder and tried to tamp down the stupid happiness his words brought to life in her. "Maybe. But I know what this is. Don't worry that I want more than this. I'm not . . . I'm not trying to get more from you, okay, Micah? I just want what we've always had. That's all. Can't we get back to that?"

"Yes. Of course we can."

She snuggled back against him with a sigh.

"So you're not going to break up with me?" he asked, the words tipped with teasing.

"Shut up."

He laughed, his humor rumbling through her, and it was all she wanted. This closeness. This love, even if it wasn't love.

"I've got an idea. Want to go over some plans with me?"

"Really?" She grinned as the words sank in. "We haven't done that in months."

"I know. Come on. I've got work spread all over the table. Tell me what you think."

As giddy as if he'd offered to sail away with her on a private yacht, Veronica jumped up and grabbed his hand to tug him to the dining room table. As promised, the metal-framed mahogany slab was covered with files. She clasped her hands together with ridiculous delight. "What are you working on?"

"Well, let's see . . ." He grabbed the closest file and opened his laptop. "This place is way down near Castle Rock. I love the natural rock formations in the yard. I'm trying to incorporate them . . ."

A monitor that hung on the dining room wall flashed to life. The plot of land was mostly sagebrush and tufts of tall grasses, but red boulders thrust up in places in front of a four-foot-tall cliff of rock. "My plans are almost done."

A new image bloomed to life on the screen, this one a stylized drawing of the same plot of land with rock trails and strategic lighting framing an outdoor kitchen in the foreground of the picture.

"Wow," she breathed. "It's perfect. They must love it."

"They're a little persnickety, but I think we're working it out. They finally okayed the order of the stove and sink and the pizza oven. We picked out all the stone. But here's the question. What do you think of the water feature?"

Another picture appeared of a tiny stream cascading over rocks to a pond below. It was pretty, but a bit more refined than she would have chosen.

She glanced at Micah's face, but he only watched her carefully. "Where is it?" she asked.

"Here." He zoomed out to show the narrow waterfall next to a stone patio seating area.

Veronica tilted her head. "You know what? I thought it was a little boring, but I think the placement is nice. It would be really peaceful on a summer night."

Micah smiled. "I think it's boring too. But they think it will be peaceful on a summer night."

She laughed. "Well, the customer is always right. Maybe you could liven it up with some strobe lights or something."

"You're awful," he scolded.

"I know."

Laughing, he pulled her into his arms and kissed her softly. Slowly. She eased back a little and looked into his beautiful hazel eyes. "I'm sorry I've been so erratic, Micah. I'm feeling a little crazy lately. Forgive me?"

"I'll forgive you anything," he murmured. "Forgive me for letting you down?"

"Yes. Of course. You didn't do anything wrong."

"I did. I got distracted and I hurt you."

They kissed again, but her phone buzzed against her thigh and broke them apart. "I'm sorry," she murmured. "Let me see if it's Syd."

"No problem."

He closed the file as she dug the phone from her pocket. When she saw the text, she groaned. "It's Johnny. He's going to Trey's place for lunch. Why is he hanging out with that asshole all the time?"

Micah raised both eyebrows. "No idea. As long as he leaves me out of it. I hate that dumbass."

"Do you think . . . ?" She frowned and let the words fade away as she realized Micah might not know about Johnny's history with Trey. Micah had been living in California when all that had gone down.

"Think what?"

"Nothing," she said quickly.

"Come on, V. This isn't about the Holcomb boy again, is it?"

"No!" She thought of Kittredge again, but she flashed a smile. "No, of course not."

"You can't keep dwelling on that."

"Easy for you to say. You didn't have to talk to the police again this morning."

"So . . . what? You think Johnny and Trey were involved in a *kidnapping*?"

No. No, of course not. She shook her head. "Johnny was with me. And Trey is just . . ."

Micah raised an eyebrow. "An idiot?"

Veronica couldn't help but laugh. "Yes. That. No, it's not really that. But did Johnny tell you what happened with Trey a few years ago?"

His brow lowered and he went quiet, studying Veronica's face for a moment. "You're talking about the steroids?"

She slumped a little with relief that it wasn't her secret alone. "Yes. We had a deal after that. Trey and his boys weren't allowed in our house, and for a while Johnny avoided them entirely. Now they're everywhere. I guess I'll have to put my foot down and be the bitch again."

"They're trying to get a piece of Johnny's fame. That's all. Bugs attracted to light."

"Yeah. I guess you're right."

"But you know what the good news is, don't you?" His eyes sparkled at her, melting her heart.

"What?"

"You have a couple of free hours now. And here you are."

Now more than her heart was melting. She was a puddle of desire with just one mischievous tilt of his lips. And he knew it. He tugged her toward him and she let her body fall into his. His hands slid up and under her shirt, to spread over her back and up her spine.

"God," she groaned. "Micah. I can't."

"Oh, I bet you can."

A moaning laugh escaped her throat as she tipped her head back. "I have to pick up Sydney at my sister's. I can't stay."

"But you don't have to leave right this second?" he murmured against her neck.

"No," she breathed. "But soon."

"Good." He unfastened her bra.

"Your bed," she whispered. "I want to be in your bed."

"Anywhere you want, V."

They tumbled into sheets that smelled of him. There was no perfume here. No scent of another woman. Tears burned behind her closed eyelids even as she smiled into the crisp fabric of his shirt. Everything was fine. In fact, everything was *good*.

She stripped him naked and crawled down his body to take him into her mouth. He arched desperately toward her, and she took him with a deep, starving need that never seemed to fade no matter how she tried to slake it.

This was all she wanted. The taste of him. His rough lust. The guttural sound of her name in his mouth. His hands shaking against her hair. This was who she was. Who she wanted to be. His woman. His sin. His filthy, dirty secret.

How could this be more fulfilling than family, career, community? She was ashamed to even consider it. But the shame felt good too. She glided up his body and mounted him, and she let him fill her up with lovely, pulsing shame.

Afterward the bed smelled like them instead of him. Veronica hadn't felt this peaceful in days.

Micah turned toward her. He stroked strands of stray, damp hair from her forehead and watched her eyes for something she'd probably rather hide from him. "I love you, V."

Her heart froze. It stopped completely. Then it panicked and restarted itself with a jolt. He'd never said those words before. Not once.

"Micah . . ."

"I'm not good at this kind of thing. I'm not a family man. I wouldn't know how to be a husband. But I do know that I love you, for what that's worth."

A warning. A caution. But a gift all the same. Something she'd never expected even though her stupid heart had wished for it incessantly.

He loved her. And she'd loved him all this time despite her denials, hadn't she?

"I love you too," she said on a breathy rasp that barely reached her own ears. "I love you, Micah."

His hand framed her jaw. "Look at you," he murmured, and she wondered what he saw in her face. The stupid wonder of a child? The soft glow of unfettered need? Whatever it was, he whispered with his mouth against hers as if she might break under his touch.

"I love you," she said again, because now she could never stop.

CHAPTER 16

"I'm so sorry I'm late!"

Fitz and Trish barely glanced up from the sprawling board game they were playing with Sydney at the kitchen table.

"No problem," Fitz called. "Syd still needs a few more minutes to finish kicking her aunties' butts."

Sydney's giggle was only slightly maniacal in response. There were no video game systems at her aunts' house, so Sydney poured all her energy into games of elaborate strategy with weirdly colored tiles and names Veronica had never heard of.

"We haven't even had lunch yet," Trish said. "Do you have time to hang out?"

"Absolutely," Veronica drawled. She dropped onto the couch with a contented sigh. This was turning out to be the perfect day, which was quite an amazing coup, considering it had started with a police interview.

She kicked off her shoes and stretched into a sultry pose on the cushions. She'd showered at Micah's house, but he'd helped with the washing, which was why she was thirty minutes late despite her mad race down the freeway.

My God. He'd actually said it. He loved her.

It changed nothing, really. She still couldn't put Sydney through a divorce, and Micah still wasn't interested in being a husband and step-father. But it changed everything too.

If he loved her, he wasn't going anywhere. Not for a while, at least. She could relax and enjoy it again. Stop freaking out at every whisper of a perceived slight. She could just be his lover and stop worrying about all the rest. And that was all she wanted. She *swore* that was all she wanted.

Sighing, she let her head fall back into the cushions and smiled to herself.

"Hey."

Veronica felt a nudge and jerked awake, her wild eyes scanning the room around her before she registered that she was at her sister's. "What?"

"You fell asleep," Trish said as she held out a coffee cup. "Long week?"

"Shit, you have no idea."

Trish laughed and sank onto the other end of the couch. "Fatima and Sydney are making lunch."

"You're both so good to her. Thank you." She sipped from her coffee, then groaned with pleasure. "So good."

"Sydney's the best. So smart. And we can't seem to pull the trigger on having our own. It just feels like . . . I don't know. It feels like I already have a hundred and fifty kids to worry about."

"I know. You don't have to explain yourself to me."

"Mom, though . . . I swear to God, Veronica, I think she imagined that Fatima and I would have twice as many kids because we have two wombs."

"It's the clear benefit of having a lesbian daughter, Trish. Extra incubation space."

They giggled madly like they used to do when they were girls huddled in a tent on a backyard adventure. Trish put her arm around

Veronica's shoulders and she snuggled close, warmed by her sister's embrace and the burn of the coffee and the deep, dark hope that Micah had sparked inside her.

"Seriously, though," she said, "I don't know how you do it. All that energy you put into your students. Where do you find it? I can barely dredge up enough for one, and she's such an easy kid."

"They give it back in spades," Trish said.

Veronica shook her head. She'd never understand that. But that was why Trish was the teacher.

"Not that it isn't heartbreaking sometimes," her sister added softly.

"I know." Veronica tucked her hand into Trish's and squeezed. Last year Fitz had lost a student to leukemia, and it had broken both women's hearts. This year one of Trish's favorite kids had been deported. That had brought fury as well as pain.

Her sister was an idealist. Which was why Veronica could never, ever confide in her about her own problems. Trish wouldn't understand the affair. Oh, she would forgive it. She'd forgiven their father, after all. Her sister's idealism had kept her blind to all the hints that their dad had been cheating all their lives, but it also meant she wouldn't accept what Veronica was doing now. If she knew, she'd tell Veronica to end it or else, and that was the last thing she intended to do.

"How's Johnny?" Trish asked, as if she'd sensed a disturbance in the marital force.

"Good, I think. I'm hoping this morning will be his last interview. I was getting really freaked out by how the police were acting, but now that I know there was a crime committed, it all makes sense."

"What else have you heard?"

"Nothing, really. The same things you have. Apparently the kidnapper promised to release the boy near a busy trail, and Johnny was the lucky hero. Anyone could have found him that day."

"Wow."

"But it could have gone really wrong. Johnny said Tanner was scared and hiding in a ravine. I'm not sure if he would have found help without Old Man going crazy. But half the hikers in Denver have dogs. Another dog would have come by, right?"

"Don't think about that. He made it home safe and sound. The end."

Veronica shivered despite her cozy warmth. "Who would do that to a little boy? He's just a baby. Actually, it was worse than taking a baby, because he was old enough to be scared. Who would even think of doing that?"

"Someone desperate," Trish murmured. "Or out for revenge."

"Revenge. I didn't think of that. It was probably a disgruntled employee."

"Right. Someone who resents the Holcombs' money and power."

Veronica sighed. "I wonder if the police have any leads."

"With all the companies Hank Holcomb and his sons have started or taken over or partnered up with, my guess is the police have *too many* leads. Last year that little town near the ranch filed a water rights lawsuit against them, remember?"

"God. I just hope our part of this adventure is over. It must be, right?"

Trish kissed the top of her head. "I imagine they now have bigger things to worry about than the man who saved Tanner's life."

Determined to be positive on this glorious day, Veronica nodded and relaxed into her sister's side. "I think you're right. Our part is over and that little boy is okay, and that's all I need to know."

"And Fatima is making saffron rice."

"Oh my God, I thought it smelled delicious in here. This is genuinely the best day of my life."

Her sister laughed. "You must be starving."

"I am," she answered sheepishly, a blush heating her face. She'd forgotten that no one else knew about the best part of this perfect day and she should tone down her glow before someone noticed.

But she couldn't stifle it completely, and she didn't want to. Sydney raced into the room and jumped onto the last empty seat on the couch before snuggling her way in between her mom and aunt.

"Can we go see Grandpa today?" she asked.

Veronica's languid muscles cooled to solid rock, and Sydney noticed.

"Mom, come on. Pleeeeeease?"

Excuses traced across her mind like a breaking news story—all the justifications she normally used to get out of taking Sydney to her father's apartment—but those excuses were framed to stall a ten-year-old. They wouldn't stand up to her sister's adult credulity.

Damn it. "We'll see," she finally tried.

Sydney wasn't having it. "You say that all the time. I haven't seen Grandpa in a month. It's not fair, Mom."

It *wasn't* fair. Sydney was right and didn't deserve the irritation and anger gnawing at Veronica's tight neck. She couldn't put off this next visit forever, no matter how much she wanted to.

"I don't even know if he's in town . . . ," she stalled.

"He is! Aunt Fitz saw him last night!"

Trish cleared her throat. "She dropped off a novel she thought he'd like."

"Since when does Dad read fiction?" Veronica snapped.

"Since he got too much time alone, I guess." She shot Veronica a narrow look, saying with her eyes what she'd said with words plenty of times before. *He lost his marriage. He's paid for what he did. Mom is happy. You're just punishing Sydney now.*

"Mom," Sydney whined, "Grandpa is lonely."

"Fine," she finally bit out. "We'll stop by after lunch."

Sydney leapt to her feet. "Yay! I just need to get the card I made from home, okay? Can we stop and get it?" Done with her mother, she raced toward the kitchen with her arms raised in triumph. "We're going to see Grandpa!"

Veronica's perfect day was perfectly ruined.

No. No, that was pure melodrama. Nothing was ruined. Sydney was so happy, and seeing her dad would be fine, and Veronica still felt great.

And Micah loved her. She'd wear that knowledge like warm and fuzzy armor and nothing could hurt her. Not today. Not even seeing her father.

CHAPTER 17

It wasn't until she was watching her garage door rise that Veronica remembered the phone.

Sydney was singing along to some K-pop song, using made-up words, Veronica assumed, as she didn't speak Korean. Veronica waited impatiently for the clunky old garage door to stutter its way up. When its slow crawl revealed the blank space where Johnny's truck should be, she felt a surge of triumph she couldn't place for a moment. Relief that he wasn't home yet. Excitement that she could . . . what?

Then she remembered. The phone. The phone he couldn't possibly have taken to the police station this morning. He wouldn't have risked it. What if the police found the phone and got suspicious? He could tell them it was just for an affair, but would they believe it?

No, the phone must be in its hiding spot, unless he'd dropped by to pick it up later.

"I'll just run in," Sydney trilled as she opened the car door.

"Actually, I need to use the restroom."

"And then we'll go to Grandpa's?" She asked the question with suspicion, as if she thought Veronica might come up with an excuse to stay home once she went inside. Smart girl.

"Definitely. I just need to text and make sure he's there."

She'd been putting that off for as long as possible, willing her father to leave his place and be unavailable by the time Veronica reached out. But she couldn't avoid it any longer.

She pulled her phone from her purse as Sydney watched, then typed a quick message to her dad. Sydney wants to stop by. Are you home?

Sydney eyed the message and lingered a moment longer, watching for a sign that her grandfather was writing back.

"Go on! I'll let you know what he says."

She finally exited the car and Veronica followed her into the house. "I'll be back in a few," she offered as she aimed for her bedroom, but Sydney was already digging through a pile of construction paper on the kitchen counter.

Veronica's phone vibrated. She glanced at it to find that her dread had been justified. I'm home! her father texted. Can't wait.

Jesus, the man was finally present for his family. Great.

Dropping her phone back into her purse, Veronica stepped softly down the hallway as if Johnny's secret device might hear her coming and hide. She closed her bedroom door behind her as quietly as she could, then dropped cross-legged to the floor in front of the wardrobe and eased the left door open.

Her hand slipped unerringly inside the shoe as if she'd been sneaking peeks into his hidden stashes for years instead of days. She withdrew the phone and turned it on, her pulse pattering with quick excitement as it cycled through the opening screens. Finally the lock screen loaded. She typed in the password and then the message bubble dinged itself awake with a tiny number 1 that turned the stutter of Veronica's pulse into a driving rain on a metal roof.

She clicked on the icon and held her breath. This time she wasn't disappointed.

Don't let her see this phone. And don't ever mention my name. EVER.

The air whooshed from Veronica's lungs. She'd expected flirtation. Or jealousy. Or maybe even a sexy picture. But this wasn't some bimbo's cheeky text. This was fear of exposure.

"She's married too," she whispered to herself. And then she gasped. It was Neesa. It had to be. Neesa was married. And she would definitely not want her big ex-con husband to discover her affair.

Johnny was strong, but Neesa's husband K.C. was six four and built like a star linebacker, and rumor had it that he'd spent nearly three years in prison for stealing cars back in the day. Oh, he was an upstanding citizen now. In fact, he owned his own car repair place down the street from the gym. Then again, maybe that was a front.

No, Neesa wouldn't want to piss her husband off. But if Veronica didn't reveal that she knew, perhaps she and Johnny could maintain this dark, delicate balance for years, each of them toeing the dangerous edge and being careful not to topple them all down. They could all have what they needed. A little hit to get them through. Small escapes when they needed them.

She'd lost any desire to pull more information from this woman. She didn't want to be sure it was Neesa. If she knew for sure, she might give something away and be the one to tip the balance into disaster. She'd stay on her edge, steady and true, or as steady and true as one could be in an affair.

"Mom!"

She jumped so hard she hit the phone against the edge of the wardrobe door and flinched at the loud crack and the graze of pain against her fingers.

"I'll be right there!" she called through the door.

"Did he write back?"

"What?" she asked in shock. "Who?"

"Grandpa!"

Oh, right. "Yeah, he's home."

"Then hurry!"

"Sure," she muttered. But she didn't move. She sat there in her dim room on her cheap, worn carpet and she let a little peace seep into her bones.

She could do this. Just for a few more years. Johnny could have Neesa on the side. This would all work out.

Exiting the app, she started to shut down the phone, then realized she'd created a problem. The message bubble no longer indicated an unread message. If the woman texted again in the meantime, Johnny might not notice, but if he opened the app and found a previously read message . . .

Crap. She had no choice but to delete it. Better to raise suspicion that his off-brand phone had missed a message than a suspicion that someone else had been accessing it.

She deleted the text and shut down the phone, her heart lighter. Even the dread of seeing her father had lifted a little. Enough that the sight of her daughter waiting with a homemade card clutched tight in her hands brought a genuine smile to Veronica's face.

"Ready to see Grandpa?" she asked.

"Yesssss!" Sydney spun in a circle and held the card high. "I didn't use glitter because it's bad for the environment. Did you know that?"

"No. Why is it bad for the environment?"

"Microplastics," Sydney said solemnly.

"Oh, of course. That makes sense."

"We should take our bottles of glitter to the next Earth Day disposal thing."

"Sure." She draped her arm over her daughter's shoulders and walked out to meet her next challenge of the day. Today she could handle anything. Even revisiting her childhood.

~

Her father lived thirty minutes away, in a big development near the airport. It had been designed as a "walkable" neighborhood, and he'd latched on to a passion for discussing the walkability philosophy once he'd finally recovered from the shock of losing his marriage. It was a huge improvement over his first postdivorce apartment: a dingy one-bedroom a few blocks from the home he'd shared with his wife, a perch for him to await a forgiveness and grace that had never blossomed.

Now he lived within walking distance of a grocery store and a stadium-seat movie theater. The apartment had two bedrooms "so anyone could come visit," and the kitchen sported modern appliances. But there was still nothing on the walls, and the furniture all looked like soulless hotel chic. That was what he was used to. He probably felt more at home in a high-end hotel than he did in a house. He'd certainly always been ready to hit the road.

Veronica parked in a visitor lot and they walked a winding cement trail to her dad's ground-floor apartment. When they rounded a corner he was already outside, standing in front of his door with both fists on his hips.

"Hey, pumpkin!" he called to Syd, and Veronica's heart lurched with fierce nostalgia. He'd always called her "pumpkin," and she'd loved him more than anything in the world.

A good mother was easy to take for granted when a father was exciting and lively and often unavailable. He'd seemed like a movie star to Veronica. A classic star from the olden days, always tan and dapper. Always calling people "pal" or "chief." Or "pumpkin." He'd travel for a week or two at a time and then sweep back into town like a hurricane of charisma, swinging his daughters and even his wife into wide, spinning hugs, hiding gifts and candy in his luggage for the girls to discover.

When he was home, he'd been called up to be the disciplinarian, because his word was gold. Even the mildest scolding from him made Veronica blush with shame. She could ignore her mother for weeks, but she knew the insurrection would end as soon as her dad came home and told her to shape up.

But he'd countered his enforcement with pure indulgence. *Oh, come on, Janet, let them stay up a little longer. Come on, Janet, one scoop of ice cream won't ruin anyone's dinner. Come on, Janet, how often will they get to skip school to see the opening game of baseball season?*

Her mom had just been the rule maker, the gatekeeper, the cook, the helper. Dad had been the star.

Judging from the way Sydney raced to her grandfather and jumped into his open arms, he was a star to her too. He twirled her around in a circle that set her squealing.

"Did you see the pictures of me and Dad and Old Man?" she asked breathlessly as he set her down. "We were on the news."

"I sure did. Your dad is a bona fide hero, sweetheart."

"He is! My friends are all so jealous, Grandpa!"

"They should be."

"I brought you a card." She tried to hand it to him, but he pointed to his door.

"We'll open it inside. I've got a present for you too."

"But it's *your* birthday." A hollow protest, as she knew Grandpa always had a present for her, and she was already racing toward the open door.

"Hey, sweetie," her dad said as Veronica approached for a slightly more restrained hug.

"Hi, Daddy. How are you?"

"I'm good. Great. Just got back from Germany."

"Fun," she said with a forcibly bright smile.

"I do enjoy a good biergarten."

Out of respect for the lovely day, Veronica didn't ask whether he enjoyed the beer maids as well.

"How's your mother?" he asked, with only a shadow of the wistfulness he'd carried the year before.

"She seems good. She's been helping with Sydney this week."

"What a week!" he cried, throwing his arms wide. "Did you have any idea that boy had been kidnapped? Did he tell Johnny who took him?"

"No, we had no idea. He was scared and exhausted. He didn't say anything at all, I don't think. We were as surprised as everyone else."

Her father led the way into his place, and Veronica immediately noticed some bright touches that had been added since her visit two months earlier. His beige couch and chair were now accented with deep-blue pillows that picked up the blues in a soft area rug at her feet.

One of his casual partners had taken a more serious position, it seemed. "You get an interior decorator?" she asked dryly.

"A friend offered to help get this place more comfy."

"A friend, hm?"

He shrugged. "She's very nice."

"Finally ready to settle down after all these years?"

He grunted, his handsome face hardening a little at her jab. "Your mom *left* me. I'm not planning on spending the rest of my life alone."

"Oh, no one ever thought you would."

"Listen—"

Sydney came bounding out of the spare room, which was mostly decorated for her rare overnight visits. "Is this it, Grandpa?" She held up a rectangular box that had been wrapped in silver with an elaborate pink ribbon.

"That's it, pumpkin."

She bounced up and down a little, and Veronica took a moment to enjoy what could be one of her last glimpses of her little girl being a little girl. Hormones were already wreaking havoc on her life. She'd gotten her first pimple that summer. Some of her friends were already wearing dressier clothes and casting off their toys. Not Sydney. Not yet. But soon.

As she watched, her daughter took a deep breath and set her heels flat to the ground. "Okay, but you get your card first." She tucked the present close to her chest and handed him the glitter-free card.

It was made of yellow construction paper, but it looked nothing like a toddler's version of a card. She'd penned a beautiful sketch of a tree across the front, and when her grandfather opened the card, neatly written black script covered the right side. Veronica hadn't read it, and she wouldn't ask to read it now. Hopefully it wasn't another attempt to get her grandparents back together. It seemed as if Sydney had finally given up on that dream after last year's reconciliation-free holiday season.

"Oh, sweetheart. That was a lovely poem. What a perfect gift for an old man. Thank you, pumpkin." He pulled her high into another gravity-defying hug, and Sydney hugged him back with all her strength. After he set her down, she waited a respectable few seconds before holding up the wrapped gift.

"Can I?" She waited for his nod before tugging carefully at the ribbon. She'd always taken her time with gifts, which was a real boon for Christmas in a single-child household. If she'd been a ripper, the holiday would have been over in two minutes flat, even with too many presents from indulgent grandparents.

When she finally broke the tape and peeled back the shiny wrapping paper, she revealed a thin wooden box with a glass front. Veronica eased closer to look over Sydney's shoulder. Behind the glass were flat wooden cutouts of woodland creatures. When Sydney turned a little knob, they began to jump and move against a forest backdrop.

"Oh, Grandpa! It's so cute!"

"They make them by hand in a little village I went to. It can't compete with video games, I guess, but . . ."

"No, I love it. It's perfect." She gave him another hug and then took her arty little box over to the couch to turn the knob, first quickly and then slowly. She turned on the TV, but her eyes kept going back to the scene in her hands.

"That's really pretty, Dad."

"I thought she might like it. She likes to draw, and they carve them all by hand. But maybe it's too old-fashioned for a little girl these days."

"It's beautiful. Thank you for thinking of her."

"Thank you for bringing her by today."

She felt a little ashamed that he had to thank her. But seeing him broke open something inside her and left her exposed to all the pain and regret and guilt she could ignore in her everyday life. He'd been her hero, and she'd lied to herself and everyone else to maintain his heroic image for as long as possible. But that wasn't Sydney's fault. Hell, it wasn't even her father's fault. He hadn't asked her to cover for him.

But he'd known. When she was fifteen, he'd come home from a business trip without his wedding band, and she'd pointed it out quietly in the hallway. He'd taken out his wallet, slipped it from one of the plastic inserts, and put it back on. He'd winked and whispered "Thanks, pumpkin." A little secret between father and daughter. He hadn't known about the first secret she'd kept, but he'd known about that one.

That night her mother had asked him to enforce the curfew Veronica had been breaking. A typical request, because Veronica wouldn't argue with her dad. "Three nights in a row she came home after ten. She's only fifteen. This has to stop before she gets into real trouble."

Veronica had already turned beet red, afraid her father could actually see that she'd been making out with her new boyfriend on each of those nights. But instead of snapping at her to be more respectful of her mother, Dad had taken her side. "Let her have a little fun. She's a good girl. You're too hard on her." Veronica had felt triumphant at the tight twist of her mom's mouth. She'd also felt a little nauseated. From then on, it had been them against Mom, and he'd taken her side every time he was home. When he wasn't home, Veronica had thrown his support in her mother's face. Dad was reasonable. Dad understood her. Dad would never be so mean.

Had he known he was making that bargain? Had he known how ugly it was? Or had it just been a natural extension of his indulgent personality?

It shouldn't matter anymore. It had happened years ago. They were all adults now, and she had her own sins to justify. "I'm sure Sydney would love to spend the night . . ."

An olive branch. Today she could afford to be generous.

"Oh!" her father exclaimed, sounding genuinely happy. "That would be wonderful! But I'm afraid I have plans. A friend flew in and we're having dinner . . ."

Another friend. Of course. She nodded.

"In a few days?" he suggested. "Next week?"

"Sure. We'll see."

"I'll call you."

"Great. No problem." Her cheeks burned with embarrassment that she'd thought she was doing him a favor. "But hey, you should really let Sydney know that you're not lonely. She worries about you even though I've told her you're fine. More than fine, really. It seems like you're good as new."

"Were you hoping I'd suffer?"

"Oh, I don't know, Dad. I thought maybe you'd repent for a few years, at least."

He dropped his voice to a discreet murmur. "Listen, I was away from home a lot. It wasn't easy. After thirty-five years of marriage, I made a mistake. I've apologized to your mother."

Her laugh sounded like gravel. "After thirty-five years? Dad. Please."

He met her gaze without flinching. "I made a mistake."

"*A* mistake." The burn spread from her cheeks to her nose, the tips of her ears. It felt like embers beneath her skin. "One of them called the house once. I answered the phone."

"One of what?"

"One of your *mistakes*. I was fourteen. She thought I was Mom. She told me she loved you and you loved her and you were going to be together."

He still didn't flinch. He only frowned at her in innocent confusion. "What are you talking about? Who said that?"

"Were there so many you couldn't even guess which one it was?"

"This is ridiculous. I have no idea what you're talking about."

"I didn't tell Mom. I kept your secret. And the dozen secrets it was impossible not to notice afterward. It never even occurred to me that Mom might know too. I just assumed she was stupid and old-fashioned and clueless. *Weak.* I think I hated her for it. Like she wasn't smart enough to hold on to you. But of course she must have known. She put up with it for us. For me and Trish. I get it now. I really, truly get it."

Her father sighed. "Veronica . . ."

"I get why you did it too. Why not? You had the best of both worlds. A tidy family at home and fun on the road. You were a king."

"Hey. Come on. It was never like that. Yes, I made more than one mistake. Okay. I admit that. But it wasn't some conspiracy, all right? I was just . . . young and irresponsible."

"Jesus," she whispered. "Young? Are you kidding me? You were almost fifty when I found out."

His jaw had gone tight and he shifted from foot to foot. His burning cheeks matched her own now. "For God's sake, Veronica, I'm trying to enjoy a birthday visit from my granddaughter. This is outrageous. It's all over with, anyway. Why the hell are you rehashing crap from so long ago?"

"It's not rehashing," she countered. "This is the first time I've even mentioned it. How can that be rehashing?"

"Well, it's certainly old news with no bearing on anyone's life anymore. Your mother and I are divorced. That was what she wanted. The marriage is over, so how could this possibly matter now?"

How, indeed?

Veronica thought of what she'd done that morning. Of how much she'd loved it. If Micah had agreed that they needed to end it, if they'd gone their separate ways, would he have been her last lover or would she have moved on to another? And another? Just like her father. Anything so she wouldn't be her mother instead.

"Veronica." He sighed out her name like she was an unpleasant task he had to get over with. "Look, I grew up in a different time. I'm sorry things got so . . . messy. I'm sorry I hurt your mother. And if I hurt you, I'm sorry for that. All right?"

All right? No, it wasn't all right. Not even close. How could he just offer an apology like someone delivering a casserole because of an illness in the family? *I hope everything is all right . . .*

"It's done now," he said. "There's nothing I can do to change the past. I just hope your mother is happy and at peace. She deserves that."

Yes. Her mother was happy and at peace. But Veronica? Well, she was her father's child, apparently. Never satisfied. Never content. Maybe she should confide in him. Maybe they could laugh about it and exchange tips of the trade.

"Mom's great," she murmured. "Mom is just fine." She looked to Sydney, still alternating between watching TV and the toy. "I need to run a few errands. I'll pick her up in an hour if that works for you."

"Sure. Absolutely." His face shone with relief that this was over. They'd never speak of it again. Not if he had anything to do with it. "Love you, pumpkin."

He pulled her into his arms before she could brace herself, and his scent overwhelmed her. Crisp laundry, Irish Spring soap, subtle aftershave.

Veronica closed her eyes and let him envelop her. Her hero. She breathed him in and let the ache swell inside her. "I love you," she whispered into his chest, and it was true. She loved him in spite of his selfish, roving charm. Or she loved him because of it—how could she ever know?

She pulled back and turned away. "I'll text when I'm on my way back."

"Great. See you soon."

No. No. She didn't think she would be visiting again for a while. She had mirrors at home that she could use if she wanted to see more hard truths.

CHAPTER 18

"Neesa is throwing a party for me at King's!" Johnny called from the living room as soon as Veronica walked in.

Her head jerked back in shock to hear him shouting his lover's name at her. "What?"

"King's! Tonight!"

She frowned at Johnny, but he was looking at the TV screen as a cartoon car rounded a corner and crossed a finish line. "Nailed it!" he shouted.

"Dad!" Sydney called out as she finally walked in behind Veronica. "Look what Grandpa got me!"

"Bring it over here. Then I'll kick your butt at *Mario Kart*."

"It's on!" Sydney cried; then Old Man joined in with barking, racing back and forth between the living room and kitchen. Eventually they both jumped onto Johnny's lap.

Veronica just stood there, Walmart bags in hand, and shook her head again. "I'm tired," she said. "I'm not going to a party."

"What?" Johnny called.

"No party. I'm tired."

"Come on! Since it's the brewpub, even Sydney can go."

"Party, party, party!" Syd shouted, simultaneously logging in onscreen and picking a car to race. "Come on, Mom!"

Come on, Janet . . .

Jesus. More echoes of childhood? Hadn't there been enough today?

"Fine. Great. But we'll take separate cars. I'm not keeping Syd out late at a bar."

Both Johnny and their daughter made raspberry noises, but neither of them objected.

A night on the town with Johnny and his lover. She wasn't sure she was up to this. But she was a little curious to see whether it would be obvious when they were together. How long had it been going on? Would things look different now?

She dropped the bags of new hand towels and cleaning supplies and other household miscellanea on the counter. "I need to shower. What time?"

"Seven."

It was already six. But she'd be damned if she'd greet Neesa in her current rumpled state. She might not have six-pack abs, but she could at least be clean.

She raced through a shower and then put on skinny jeans and a flattering sweater and more makeup than she usually wore. Still competing. Always competing.

Before leaving the quiet safety of the bedroom, she checked her newsfeed for any updates on Tanner Holcomb. There was nothing from the family, but police revealed they had scent dogs searching the trailhead area where Tanner had been found to see if they could track his path.

Veronica slipped on heeled boots and left her bedroom with a wistful sigh. She'd been looking forward to a hot bath and a good book.

Johnny was waiting in the kitchen, head bowed and eyes glued to his phone.

"Ready?" she asked. He didn't respond. "Johnny?"

His head jerked up, brows snapping low. "What?" he barked.

"Calm down, I just asked if you were ready. Are you okay?"

"Of course I'm okay."

"Well, you seem really tense. Maybe we should stay home."

"Mom, no," Sydney whined from the hallway. She'd changed into her sparkly rainbow flip-flops, and she'd even dabbed clear gloss onto her lips. No way was she going to miss this evening.

"Okay, I was just kidding. Time to party, kid. Let's go."

"I want to ride with Dad," she said predictably.

Veronica glanced at her grumpy husband and shrugged. "Knock yourself out. I'll meet you there." Maybe he'd been counting on her bowing out so he could spend time with Neesa. Too bad.

She backed out quickly so Sydney could get into Johnny's truck more easily, then honked her horn and waved. Sydney waved back with the enthusiasm of an extrovert who was about to stay up late and listen in on adult conversations no one realized she could hear. Veronica turned up her music to try to get in the mood herself.

King's was one of a million Denver-area brewpubs, but it was near Johnny's gym, so it was a go-to hangout. She knew exactly where the party would be as soon as she pulled up. King's Backyard.

The Backyard wasn't a yard, of course; it was an outdoor seating area with a fire pit and lots of room to play cornhole and shuffleboard. Johnny loved it. Veronica spotted Neesa as soon as she walked through the doors. Steeling herself, she headed toward Neesa and the group of tables populated with a few people she recognized from the last party.

"Hey, Neesa," she said with as much warmth as she could muster.

"Hey, girl!" Neesa called as she popped up for a hug. It was too bad she was gorgeous and twenty-six and sleeping with Veronica's husband, or maybe Veronica could have liked her. She certainly had a great smile and a positive attitude.

"Grab a beer and a seat! Where's the man of the hour?"

"Heading in right now, I think."

"There he is!"

Veronica grabbed the beer and the seat and settled in for reconnaissance.

Neesa raced over to hug Johnny as soon as he stepped outside. When he let her go, she hugged Sydney with just as much enthusiasm. Veronica then heard her gasp and say the word *kidnapping* far too loudly. Neesa was fun and pretty and so excited. Her black hair was normally pulled into a sleek bun that accentuated her cheekbones, but tonight a perfect thick braid draped over her shoulder and she looked even prettier. Damn it.

Veronica glanced around to try to find Neesa's husband. He wasn't at the tables. Maybe he wasn't coming, and Veronica had been meant to stay home too. But then she spotted him leaning against the outdoor bar, looking intimidating and serious.

She actually shivered a little at the sight of him. He wasn't ugly. Far from it. K.C. was a big white guy whose arms were covered in tattoos. His brown hair was nearly shaved, and he kept his beard trimmed close too. He was muscular, but in a more workmanlike way than Johnny. Not chubby at all, but solid. And definitely mean-looking, with a piercing green gaze.

Did Neesa like Johnny just because he was so different from her husband, with his flat mouth and hard eyes? K.C. caught Veronica watching and raised a beer in her direction. His expression didn't soften even when she smiled back far too widely.

Johnny had used K.C.'s garage before, but Veronica preferred the friendly national chain down the street. They had coffee pods and Wi-Fi and no ex-cons as far as she knew.

Half a beer and a whole bowl of tortilla chips later, Veronica relaxed a little, tapping her foot to the rock music as Sydney danced near the shuffleboard tables. Neesa was hanging out with her husband now, and they made quite a striking couple. He was a good ten years older than she was and nearly a foot taller, even with her stacked heels. Her brown hand curled over the black and blue lines of the dragon on his forearm as Veronica watched.

Johnny was a little quieter than normal, sitting at the table next to Veronica instead of making the rounds. Maybe he didn't like seeing Neesa with her husband. Most of the rest of the party had broken up by gender, the men playing cornhole and the women laughing together nearby. Veronica watched them wistfully.

She needed to get back to that. She needed real friends. Maybe now that she'd accepted the state of her marriage, she could give up this twisted view of other women she'd had for too long. It was no accident that her only good friends were her lesbian sister and her sister's wife. Veronica didn't have to worry about them. She didn't have to be jealous.

But that needed to change. She needed to set a good example for Sydney. Hell, maybe she could even be friends with Neesa.

No, that was a bridge too far, Veronica decided when Neesa bounced toward their table. She wasn't at that moment of transcendence yet.

"So have you two talked?" Neesa asked cheerfully, and Veronica blinked in shock.

"What?"

Johnny shook his head. "Haven't had the chance yet."

"Johnny, come on!" Neesa said.

Veronica sat up straighter. "What's going on? Talk about what?" Were they going to do this here? Just get it out in the open? Work out some sort of strained open-marriage agreement?

Neesa cleared her throat. "You know Johnny and I started working together last year . . ."

Good Lord. Veronica glanced toward Sydney, who was only four feet away.

"Well . . ." Neesa looked at Johnny as if hoping he'd jump in. When he didn't, she took a deep breath that strained the buttons of her crisp shirt. "We're thinking of starting an interval training gym."

"A what?" She'd been doubtful Neesa would have proposed some kind of marriage swap right here in public, but she certainly hadn't expected this.

"The start-up costs wouldn't be huge, not compared to other kinds of gyms. We've been talking about it for a few months and—"

"A few *months*?" She turned to face Johnny fully, but he was looking at the table. "You haven't said a word about this to me."

"Johnny was a little nervous about bringing it up because of money, I think—"

Veronica cut a hand through the air. "I don't need you speaking for my husband."

"No, of course not. I get that. I'll let you guys talk it out. But I've got a lot of numbers nailed down and maybe we could all get together for dinner or something and talk through it." She actually reached out a hand to Johnny's shoulder as if to give him strength in the face of his mean wife.

Veronica glanced toward K.C., still holding up the bar, but he was looking over the crowd and paying no attention to them.

"I think you should go," Veronica snapped, and felt a hot surge of ugly triumph when Neesa's hand pulled back. "I need to talk to my husband."

So much for female bonding.

Neesa smiled nervously and gave a little wave before she left. Johnny slumped farther in his chair.

"A gym?" Veronica snapped. "You've been discussing this for months and you never mentioned it to me?"

"I knew what you'd say."

"Did you know what I'd say because we have no money and can't possibly afford to start a business?"

"Yes." He sighed.

"Mom," Sydney said. She'd moved closer while Veronica was distracted. "Don't fight, okay?"

"We're not fighting."

"Well, then, stop *frowning*."

Jesus. Veronica closed her eyes. She breathed deep. None of this mattered. There was no money for a gym. And she knew exactly what had happened. Johnny didn't like to tell people no. He certainly wouldn't want to tell his beautiful girlfriend no. So he'd let Neesa talk and plan until it had become too much for her to bear and she'd spilled the good news to Veronica. The good news about a gym Johnny could never possibly afford.

"We'll talk about it later," he said. "It's a good plan. I think it could actually work."

Veronica blew out a long breath, then glanced at Sydney's pleading eyes. "Sure, Johnny," she finally said. "Fine. We'll talk about it later."

He smiled. "Great."

Veronica took the rest of her beer and headed toward the small group of women who'd started playing shuffleboard. "Hey," she said to an older woman she'd never met before. "I'm Veronica."

They shook hands, and Veronica tried her best not to watch Johnny for the rest of the night, but she couldn't help noticing that when K.C. disappeared toward the bathrooms, Neesa made her way back to Johnny's table. She sat down and talked to him as he frowned at his phone. Her hand slid to his shoulder and, just like that, Johnny put away his phone and smiled again. He got up and they walked toward the cornhole area, laughing. Veronica turned her back on her husband and forced herself to forget about him and have fun.

CHAPTER 19

Sunday dawned gray and rainy, an unusual occurrence in Colorado. The mountains usually scraped any clouds wide open in torrents of flooding water and explosions of lightning that passed as quickly as they began. But this was a strange, gentle drizzle that made Veronica feel she was somewhere else, somewhere sluggish and dreamy.

She heard Johnny making breakfast and Sydney giggling over the clatter of forks, but when Johnny stepped back into the bedroom she faked sleep.

"New clients," he whispered. "I'll be gone a few hours."

She grunted and turned over with a sigh.

Once she heard the creak of the garage door and the rumble of his truck pulling away, she opened her phone to check her texts. Nothing. She got up to slip her hand into his shoe. No phone there. He'd taken it with him.

Whatever. He was out of the house and happy. What more could she ask for?

So much, a little voice whispered in her heart.

She shook her head. She had everything she needed right now. Wanting more had created most of these problems in the first place. Today she would be satisfied.

Though not as satisfied as yesterday afternoon at Micah's.

Smiling to herself, she padded to the kitchen to brew a pot of coffee and feed Old Man. Sydney wandered out and flopped onto the couch, so Veronica grabbed a blanket and joined her. Old Man curled up close too, and in that moment life felt perfect.

It was hardly a cozy scene of yesteryear, with Sydney on the tablet and Veronica reading the news on her phone, but was it so different? Would it mean they were closer if she were reading a newspaper and Sydney were drawing in her sketch pad? Impossible to imagine she could feel any more connected to her little girl than she did right now.

She kissed her daughter's head and cuddled her closer. The rain pattered like tiny fingers on the living room windows. They were safe here. Shrouded from the world. Old Man heaved a sigh and settled into sleep.

"Want to play Scrabble?" Veronica asked.

"Maybe later. I promised Jenn I'd meet her online at ten to play Wizard101."

"Got it. I should get some chores done then. No point in leaving the house today. Maybe you could play your ukulele for me later while I make some soup. Does that sound good?"

"Sure."

Sydney finally wandered away to hang out with someone her own age, and Veronica made herself stand up and stretch. Her lizard brain wanted to huddle close to warmth and leave chores for a safe, sunny day, but tomorrow she'd return to work and no chores would get done. Today she could clean the living room and put up Halloween decorations. Then she'd feel accomplished enough to spend the rest of the day reading.

In fact, she'd finish her new book without even mentioning it to Micah. He was busy. He'd explained that to her. She would do him the courtesy of understanding and respecting that and not reaching out for reassurance.

She'd had an extra day with him this week. Two, actually. And she'd see him again on Wednesday. She didn't need constant reassurance in the meantime. She *wanted* it, to be sure, but she didn't need it.

Cringing at her own ridiculousness, she put on some music and set in to decluttering their small living room. It accumulated layers of junk so slowly, it was almost unnoticeable. Small things put down over the days and never picked up again until one day you had half the space you'd started with. She did her best not to see it for weeks, but even she had been noticing lately.

She put on her Regina Spektor playlist and gathered pens and pencils to return to kitchen drawers and stacked old flyers and magazines to drop in the recycling bin.

By the time she got to dusting the blinds and lamps, Veronica had worked up a sweat. She stripped off her cardigan. She even cracked open a window to let the cool scent of wet leaves breathe over her. Maybe she'd clean the kitchen too. Reorganize the crowded cabinets and toss out the pots and pans that had rusted at the bottoms of the piles.

But first, the Halloween decorations. Then she'd vacuum up all the dust she'd disturbed.

She tried to be an enthusiastic, cheerful mom, but she'd gotten lazier about holidays with each successive year. At first, decorating for Sydney had been permission to unleash her own inner child and buy all the sparkling, flashing doodads she'd always wanted in her life.

Oh, her mother had decorated their home for every holiday, but the figurines and static lights had remained the same every year. The happy, fake jack-o'-lantern on the front railing on October first. The giant plastic candles at the end of the driveway installed every Thanksgiving and lit by one 60-watt bulb in each base. The thin plastic candy canes leading the way up to the front door at Christmas. There had been no upgrades over the years. There'd been no reason for it. Everything still worked perfectly, and burnt-out bulbs were easy to replace.

But for Sydney's first Christmas Veronica had spent money they didn't have on stuffed dogs that barked carols and lights that twinkled and flashed in time to music. For Halloween she'd bought door knockers that boomed like a monster banging on the door, and pumpkins that could be filled with liquid ice so that smoke drifted from their eyes. She'd bought fancy wooden turkeys for the dining room table and glowing Valentine's hearts for the front door.

So many decorations, and most of them stayed packed away these days. Last year she'd hung a "Happy Halloween" sign and twisted one string of orange lights around a bush, and that had been that. She'd just been too unhappy to do more.

This year she'd do better.

As she opened the basement door and turned on the light, she did her best not to think of Detective Reed following her down the stairs and peering into the shadowed corners of Veronica's life. That was over. Time to move on.

The shelves had been organized once upon a time, but since she'd started picking out individual decorations instead of unloading whole boxes, the stacks were a mess. Praying that she wouldn't find a nest of spiders—or even one lonely individual spider—she shifted a Christmas wreath off the top of the pile and opened the first cardboard box. Greeted by red and green ribbons, she moved that box to the side and opened another, only to find more Christmas crap.

If she were better at this sort of thing, she would have already marked the boxes. And if she weren't so lazy, she'd run upstairs for a marker to do it now. But instead she glanced idly toward the laundry area in hopes of spotting a stray Sharpie before shrugging and moving on. "Next time," she muttered, ignoring the fact that she'd definitely made that promise before.

The third box held a pastel explosion of Easter eggs and bunnies and baskets. She was already letting the flaps of the box close when her eye caught on a clear plastic bag filled with fake money.

Something from St. Patrick's Day, no doubt. She hadn't even known that was a holiday to be recognized until Sydney had come home from kindergarten with excited stories of leprechauns arriving during the night to wreak havoc in the classroom, dropping gold coins and chocolates as they searched for treasure.

But Veronica didn't remember buying fake dollars the next year, only some green beads and foil-wrapped chocolates to trail through the house on St. Patrick's Day morning. She'd phased that holiday out three years later on the grounds that even Valentine's Day seemed a bit much so soon after Christmas. And for God's sake, they weren't even Irish.

Puzzled, she lifted the flaps of the box again and freed the gallon-sized storage bag from a nest of fake grass. It was heavier than it should have been. The stacks of bills were thick. The ink intricate and realistic against creamy paper.

The bag hit the floor before she realized she'd let it go.

She stared at the stacks of fake twenties bundled together into bricks. Only they didn't look fake. And joke money always came in ones, didn't it? No. It came in hundreds. Twenties were an odd choice for a kid's practical joke, especially twenties that didn't look crisp and new.

The center of her vision grew brighter, sharper, even as the edges turned dark. She didn't need to pick up the bag to discover the truth. She didn't need to open it and touch the bills. The money was real.

Her heart hammered against the walls of her chest and the vibrations churned her stomach into sickness. Was this what Reed had been looking for in the basement? Or had she expected chains and a cot and dirty plates and cups?

She swallowed hard against the bitter touch of bile against the back of her tongue, working her throat to keep it down as she tried to calm her breathing. She realized she was rocking back and forth like someone enduring a trauma.

Had her husband kidnapped Tanner Holcomb? Had he stolen a child and exchanged him for money? What had they said? A million dollars in cash?

Her fingers tingled. The edges of her vision went from black to static, clearing or getting worse, she couldn't tell.

She'd touched the bag. Her fingerprints were on it. And not just her fingerprints but her DNA. They could pick up skin cells now, not just blood. And she was his only alibi. She was complicit.

But she really *was* his alibi. He'd been home. With her. That wasn't a lie or a cover-up. He'd had no time to snatch that little boy. That was the truth. She remembered it.

Didn't she?

Hadn't she complained plenty of times that her memory was shot? That pregnancy and the frazzled exhaustion of early motherhood had ruined her brain? She could have mixed up the days. Maybe she'd come home early on Thursday for some reason, not Friday.

She'd been so sure of everything, but now her world was jumbled, her vision static, her brain a wild, twisting storm.

How much money was it?

Stepping back from the bag, she raised the heavy, swimming weight of her head to look around the gray room. It swung sickly in her vision, careening back and forth, bringing her stomach higher into her throat. There would be a hell of a lot of her DNA on the bag if she vomited on it.

She stepped back and back again until her shoulders finally touched a cool wall. She closed her eyes. Pressed her body into the painted blocks of ice. She turned her head and felt the cold on her cheek. Her stomach gave up some of its fight and settled lower. The pressure at the base of her throat eased.

"Your daughter is upstairs," she whispered to herself. "Get your shit together. Don't be a coward. Figure this out."

But she *was* a coward and she *didn't want to* figure this out. She didn't want to even *know* it. But mothers couldn't be cowards. It wasn't allowed. No one told new moms that, but the realization flowed into their bones with the hormones. Calcium was leached from the skeleton to produce milk, and new knowledge flowed in to fill the gaps and give strength.

She couldn't ignore this. She couldn't walk away. She couldn't even turn it over to the police and wash her hands of it, not without hurting Sydney. She had no choice but to get her shit together and gather up her husband's shit too. The years of diaper changes were just practice for this moment.

Pushing off the wall, she moved her legs. They brought her to another plastic shelf, this one strewn with tools and tape and paint cans. A pair of dried-out gardening gloves sat on one of the cans. She made her arms rise and her hands grasp, and she tugged the stiff fabric on over numb fingers.

The plastic bag was waiting for her when she turned around. Afraid she might pass out if she stood still for too long, she dropped to the floor and sat cross-legged before it. For a moment her body refused to cooperate and reach out, instincts kicking in to protect her from danger.

"Do it," she ordered out loud. Then she took a deep breath and lifted the bag by the top two corners.

The plastic seal was difficult to separate with the clumsy stiffness of the gloves, but she picked and pulled until the seal gave way and the bag opened. Instead of reaching in and leaving yet more DNA behind, she tipped the bag up and carefully slid the cash onto the floor.

She could burn the bag, she thought. Put the cash back into the box loose, or even hide it somewhere new if she wanted to force Johnny to give her answers. Regardless, she didn't need the bag, and burning it would destroy her fingerprints once and for all.

Satisfied that she had an out, Veronica picked up the first untidy brick of money. A paper strap around the middle read "$2,000." She flipped a gloved thumb along the edge of the bills, and they fanned out in awkward clumps to expose a series of twenties, some new-looking, but most obviously worn and used. Two thousand dollars.

She counted the stacks. There were twenty-five. She was looking at fifty thousand dollars in cash. How was that possible?

She flipped through a few more of the bundles to confirm that none were filled with blank paper or, God forbid, the kinds of dye packs they used at banks. The bills all looked totally legitimate.

"What have you done?" she ground out between clenched teeth. "What the fuck have you done?"

Fifty thousand dollars. A fortune for them. A miracle. They could pay off their credit cards. Fix up the kitchen. It was a glorious jackpot. But . . .

She frowned at the money in front of her, her spinning brain trying to puzzle out the problem.

It was a fortune for them but not a fortune for Hank Holcomb. It wasn't even close to the going price for a man's own flesh and blood. For an innocent, invaluable child. It wasn't a million dollars.

She jumped to her feet and opened the next storage box on the shelf. Here were the Halloween decorations she'd been searching for. There was no bag of cash on top and nothing hidden underneath the fake spiders or orange string lights.

She opened the next box too. Nothing. No money. Just papier-mâché turkeys and a lot of fake fall leaves. When she dug through, she found only more decorations.

Veronica moved on to the next shelf and opened every box, however unlikely. She even grabbed a screwdriver and pried open the lids of the paint cans. Nothing. She opened the fuse box; she looked behind the washer; she checked every crevice; she popped the maintenance door on the furnace. The only treasure she found added up to about seventy-six cents in coins scattered near the clothes dryer.

But he could have hidden more money anywhere. Buried in the backyard. Stashed in the garage. Stuffed beneath the insulation in their claustrophobic attic space. It could be hidden in the glove box of his truck right now.

She was breathing too hard again, moving too fast. The tops of paint cans and boxes were strewn across the floor, though her eye was drawn to the pile of money whenever she looked around.

Panicked, she pulled her phone from her pocket, meaning to call for help. But help from whom? The police? That was who you called to report a crime or scream for rescue. That was who she should call.

But she couldn't. Because maybe there was another explanation. More important, maybe there wasn't and Johnny was a kidnapper and what did that even *mean*? That he should be taken away and punished, removed from his daughter's life forever?

Yes, obviously. Yes, that was what happened to kidnappers. But . . .

The boy was fine. He was safe at home with his family. Sydney wouldn't be fine if her father was sent to prison for a spectacular, notorious crime. She wouldn't be anything close to okay ever again.

Veronica's face burned with shame, but she didn't call the police. She at least had to get the truth from Johnny first. She couldn't bring hell down on him if she wasn't even sure.

There had to be another explanation. Something to do with Neesa and her idea for a gym. Because, even aside from Veronica knowing he was home, he just wouldn't do that. He was a little hapless and a little immature, but he'd never been a bad guy. Not truly.

She shook her head and then she couldn't stop shaking it and that scared her. "Stop," she whispered. "Stop." She breathed until she could control her body again.

Instead of dialing 911, she opened her contact list and stared at Micah's name. She needed him, and he loved her. He could tell her what to do. Or he could tell her she was being silly and list the reasons why.

Her finger hovered over his name, quivering as she trembled with fear and need. But she didn't touch the screen. If there was even the smallest chance this had something to do with Tanner Holcomb, telling Micah would pull him into a crime. A felony. Christ, he could probably be prosecuted for not alerting the police. That would be considered abetting, wouldn't it? Wasn't that what she was doing right now?

That thought stopped her cold. She'd thought of Micah as her confidant, but he would be a witness as well. Right now both of Syd's parents might be complicit in a crime, but no one could prove Veronica knew, not unless she told.

So no. She couldn't run to Micah. She couldn't put him in danger, and she couldn't put herself in danger either.

And that meant she couldn't call anyone, because telling her mom or sister or sister-in-law would bring the same risks. She had to do this alone.

The realization sank into her the way a cold front soaked through thin walls. A surface cold at first, but it permeated slowly and deeply. No one could give her advice on what to do.

She moved slowly, joints stiff, as she picked up each bundle of bills and dropped it into the plastic bag. She sealed the bag, scrubbed the corners with her gloves to smear any fingerprints, and then tucked it back into the box of Easter baskets and bright-green plastic grass.

When she closed the cardboard flaps and tugged off her gloves, she felt strangely calm. It was shock, probably, because there was no reason for calm. She'd figured nothing out. She had no plan.

And she may have just become a ruthless criminal, bargaining one child's justice away for the sake of another. Nothing would ever be the same again.

CHAPTER 20

Johnny came home in a good mood. A great mood. He shouted a greeting to her from the back door and headed straight for the fridge to start a smoothie. "I had two new clients this morning!" he called as she stepped from the hallway. "And they both seemed pretty serious. I'm gonna be damn busy for the next few months, Roni. Shit, maybe for the next few years. This is exactly what we've been hoping for."

She could only nod. *Sure, Johnny. That's great, Johnny.*

"Everything is really working out perfectly."

What the hell did that mean? Her eyelids fluttered. She couldn't think straight. *Working out perfectly.* Was that a normal thing to say? Maybe it was.

"Hey, the place looks great."

She nodded again as her scrambled brain tried to catch up.

She watched as he prepped the blender. He looked so relaxed. So typical. He grabbed frozen fruit from the freezer. Then baby spinach from the fridge.

This was the time. The burner phone weighed down her pocket like a brick. He'd left it behind this morning, perhaps worried that the police would pull him in for another interview. She could say she'd been cleaning the bedroom and she'd discovered it. She could see how he explained the phone first. Once she was satisfied—or furious—with his explanation for that, she could move on to the money.

Veronica opened her mouth. She shut it. Opened it again. She had a strange moment of déjà vu. Had she done this before? Had she stood here and struggled? Maybe. Maybe on one of the days she'd been seconds from suggesting divorce.

"Hey, I'm meeting up with Trey tonight," he said lightly, deliberately calm and casual as he scooped protein powder into the smoothie.

"Trey?" she asked hoarsely.

"Yeah. No big deal." A preemptive reassurance so she wouldn't ask any questions. And that was when it hit her. That thing that had been lurking at the edges of her vision, too quick to get a good look at. Trey.

Johnny fired up the expensive blender he'd spent far too much money on, and her whole body filled with a rumbling roar of machinery and shock.

Maybe that was it. The answer to the question she'd asked herself hours before. Why only fifty thousand dollars? The ransom had been a million. Why did he have only fifty thousand?

Because perhaps it wasn't a ransom. Perhaps it was drug money. Johnny and Trey were dealing again. Fifty thousand was a hell of a lot for dealing, but maybe Johnny was supposed to pick up a big supply or something. What if the drama of the kidnapping had blinded her to the far more obvious truth? Johnny needed money to start a gym with his girlfriend, and Trey knew how to make some quick cash.

Dealing steroids was stupid. It was criminal. But it was not unforgivable and not irrevocable. If that was all it was, they could come back from this. They'd done it before. It would barely be an irritation in the face of the horror that had been pulling her under.

Relief sucked all the strength from her body and she slumped into the kitchen cabinets.

The kitchen exploded with silence when he hit the Off button. "Hey, you okay?" Johnny asked.

She felt as pale as the dingy white linoleum at her feet. "Sure. I'm good."

"You look tired."

She nodded absently again but pushed up to stand a little straighter. "I'm good. Thanks." She needed to figure this out. Trick Johnny into giving up some truth. The déjà vu returned, but this time it wasn't the least bit mysterious. "So you've been hanging out with Trey a lot."

He shrugged and turned his back to her to pour out his purplish-green meal.

"Johnny? What's up?"

"Nothing's up. We're hanging out."

The tide of relief receded. Anger was at the ready, waiting to take up its natural place inside her rocky chest. Anger that he was putting her through this and risking so much. *Again.* "Does it seem like a good idea to be hanging around a drug dealer when the police are watching you?"

"The police aren't watching me!" he snapped.

"Are you sure?"

"Yes, I'm sure! They're out there trying to catch an actual kidnapper. What the hell would they want with me?"

"You're the only lead they have. Whether they want you or not, they've got you. So maybe hanging around a goddamn criminal isn't your best move right now."

He rolled his eyes. "Give me a break, Veronica. He's not a criminal."

"Give you a *break*? Are you kidding? I know exactly what Trey is, Johnny. Don't you try to play it down. Why the hell are you so close to him again all of a sudden, huh?"

"We've been hanging out at the gym! That's all!"

That's all. Another stupid reassurance he thought she couldn't see through. "And who else have you been hanging out with?"

Another roll of his eyes. She wanted to slap them right out of his head.

"Are you just selling," she asked, "or are you using?"

He laughed at her. He laughed right in her face. "Jesus Christ. You've lost your fucking mind."

"Oh, is that right?" She shoved her hand into her pocket. Curled her fingers around the phone, ready to yank it out and throw it at his stupid, thick head right between those stupid, rolling eyes.

But why? To what end?

She hesitated, the muscles in her arm trembling with the need to lash out.

If Johnny and Trey were selling steroids at the gym again, it was par for the course. It had felt like an unbearable threat five years earlier, but Johnny had graduated to a kidnapping investigation, and now it felt like nothing. Just another hobby to keep her husband busy and out of her hair. No different from the woman on the other end of this phone. He was screwing around and dealing drugs and all of it kept his eyes off of Veronica.

Why throw a bomb into the situation? Micah had asked. Why indeed?

Her fingers eased their grip. Her lips curled back down to cover teeth she hadn't realized she'd been showing. Johnny shook his head and shoved a straw into his smoothie.

She hoped he choked on it.

Her eyes slid down his body. Were his arms a little bulkier? His shoulders a little wider? She hadn't truly looked at him in so long that she couldn't say. But maybe.

When the front door flew open, Veronica jumped, her heart and body both leaping with fear. But it wasn't a police raid. It was only Sydney and Old Man bounding into the living room, leash jangling, music from an ancient iPod blaring.

"Dad!" she cried out. "You missed Frisbee!"

"Sorry, honey. I had work again."

"Movie night?" Sydney asked, and Johnny winced.

"I'll be out for a while tonight." When her face fell, he hurried to reassure her. "Let's catch up on *The 100* while I drink my smoothie. Okay?"

Sydney literally leapt for joy before racing to the couch. Old Man jumped around a little too, excited by the palpable happiness. Now Veronica was the only sour one in the house. It definitely wasn't the first time.

She closed her eyes and let the counter take the weight of her body again. Sydney's happiness was why she was here. This was her whole reason for staying. And it was good and right, even if she wasn't.

A strange bell chimed softly. Frowning in confusion, Veronica glanced around the kitchen for some new appliance that might have appeared on a counter unnoticed. From the corner of her eye she caught Johnny's movement. He reached for the front of his body, his hand sliding down his hip, then back up again.

As she turned toward him, his other hand repeated the same movement on the left side. His eyes were round as quarters, his forehead stamped with furrows of shock.

Oh my God.

Her own hand moved before she could stop it. Her fingers touched the hard rectangle of the phone through the denim of her jeans. Johnny's gaze fell. His jaw dropped, parting his lips into a little hole of fear.

No. She'd decided not to do this. She'd decided to let him be. But now he was stepping toward her, one hand out as if to grab her wrist, as if stopping her from reaching for the phone would somehow reverse her knowledge of it.

She tried to step back, but she was already against the counter.

"Roni," he said. Just that. Just her nickname like some kind of dire warning. His hand hovered so close to her arm that she could feel the heat of it. She pressed her fingers harder to the layer of denim against glass. The corner of the phone dug into the hollow of her hip.

"Roni, what are you doing?"

"Nothing."

He dipped his head, his body curving to crowd hers. "What the fuck are you doing?" The hushed words scraped roughly against her ear, his mouth twisting them into a snarl. "Give it to me."

"No." She hated the way his growl shivered through her nerves.

"Give me the goddamn phone."

She glanced past his arm toward Sydney, but their daughter seemed lost in something on the tablet, and the TV was already blaring. "Get away from me," Veronica whispered. She'd held this man much closer than this, but suddenly his body had transformed from familiar to an unknowable threat.

Instead of retreating, he wrapped his hand around her wrist. There was no affection or comfort in his touch, only strength. When he crossed his other arm over to try to dig in her pocket, she jerked her body quickly to the side.

"No!" She tried to say it quietly, but she caught the movement of Sydney's head looking up.

"Come on, Dad. Let's start!"

Veronica clenched her teeth and spoke as quietly as she could, though her fear made everything seem too loud. "Let. Me. Go."

"Give me the phone," he growled back. Without loosening his hold on her, he cleared his throat and pasted on a smile to call out to his daughter. "Just give me another minute, sweetie!"

"Okay." Veronica could tell by the sound of Sydney's voice that she'd already lowered her head again.

"Whatever you're thinking," he murmured, "it's not that."

Veronica couldn't believe she managed to laugh, but she did. "Oh, really? What am I thinking?"

His grip tightened until she winced. "We can't talk about this here."

"No, we can't. Take your hands off me and we can talk quietly in the bedroom."

"That's not what I meant," he hissed.

"Take your hands off me right now or I will call the police, and I doubt you want to discuss your secret phone with them. Do you, Johnny?"

She'd meant it to be snide, but his face actually paled with fear. He let go of her, nearly tossing her arm away from him as he stepped back.

His reaction scared her, but it thrilled her too. Because he'd frightened her with his strength and he deserved to feel small and helpless now. She stood straighter, and this time it was her body stepping into his as she sneered at his alarm.

"Should I tell them about your phone, Johnny?"

"Be quiet," he ordered.

"No? You wouldn't like that? I bet you really wouldn't like it if I showed them the fifty thousand dollars I found."

Veronica wasn't sure what happened then. All she knew was that she was suddenly out of the kitchen and flying down the hallway, her arm locked in a vise, her feet tripping to keep up with Johnny's speed.

He yanked her into the bedroom and closed the door. His wild eyes rolled, checking the corners and the window and the door before he grabbed her by the shoulders and his gaze locked on hers. She stared back in utter shock.

"Keep your fucking mouth closed," he said.

"Are you *insane*?"

"Stop talking, Veronica." He shook her. Her head snapped back. "Not another word. Just stop talking."

"Get off me!" she gasped, twisting hard to break out of his grip. She staggered to the side in panic before realizing she was moving farther away from the door.

"We'll talk about it later."

"What the hell?" she yelled, backing away. "Have you lost your mind? I find a bag of cash in the basement and you think we'll just talk about it later?"

"Stop!"

"*You* stop! Stop *lying*! There's fifty thousand dollars in—"

She heard the crack before she felt the pain. Terror didn't rush in when it should have. Instead she felt only confusion at how the room had shifted, and then there was the surprising flash of her hot skin as she raised a hand to touch her cheek.

It wasn't until she pushed up from her landing place on the mattress that she registered Johnny looming over her, his breath coming hard and fast, his face a blotchy mess of red and pale white.

"I'm sorry!" His voice had lost the rage and soared high into panic. "I'm sorry. Just please stop talking!"

Finally her fear revealed itself and slipped into her skin. All of her skin, all at once. Goose bumps rose, but she shrank into something smaller as she tried to squeeze more deeply into the mattress.

"Roni, I'm sorry. Please. I'm sorry. I didn't . . ."

She wanted to turn away from him, but she had to look. Had to watch his hands and his wide shoulders—they were wider, weren't they?—so she could know if he was moving toward her. If he was going to hit her again. This man. Her own husband.

So she watched him. Watched his hands clench into themselves. Watched tears well in his eyes. Watched him hunch closer until she flinched away.

"You hit me," she whispered past a throat clogged with tears.

"I'm sorry."

"Get away from me. I hate you."

"Don't say that. *Please.*"

"Don't ever, ever touch me again."

"Veronica, please. You have to understand . . ." He went to his knees and started to reach for her, but he drew his hand back when she growled. At least she was looking down on him now.

"You're using again."

"No. No, but we can't talk here." His hands opened, begging with his palms. "I'm afraid."

"Afraid." She shook her head, the skin beneath her fingers burning hotter. "Fuck you."

"Roni, please. I'm afraid they're *listening*."

"Who?"

He grasped his skull in his hands. Squeezed his hair tight between fisted fingers. He raised his tear-filled eyes and held her gaze for a moment before he mouthed two words. *The police.*

The fear writhed and shifted inside her, sliding out from under her skin to curl into a knot in her gut. "What did you do?"

He shook his head and kept shaking it until he let his face drop to the twisted comforter. The shaking moved to his shoulders then. He sobbed like a child.

Veronica held the burning cinders of her face and watched her husband cry. "What did you do?" she whispered again, but he didn't even raise his head.

CHAPTER 21

The world didn't stop turning, no matter what happened. Even during the darkest tragedies life went on, unaware and cruel, completely unconcerned with whether you could manage to catch up.

Veronica sat on her bed and stared at a dark wall as the sounds of a distant battle played out on the living room television. Johnny had kept his promise to Sydney and fired up their favorite TV show. Cars passed on the street in front of the house. The man next door yelled at his dog to get inside, *get inside*, just as he did every afternoon around this time.

Veronica stared at the wall and waited. For what, she had no idea.

Sydney had knocked on the door, and Johnny had scrubbed his face with his hands and whispered, "We have to act normal. We'll go for a drive later. We'll talk then. I promise."

We, we, we, as if she were any part of this. As if they were a *team.*

Veronica just sat there dumbly, waiting for someone to tell her what the hell to do. Her hands lay open in her lap, her lips stayed parted in shock, but her mind was a tightly closed shell. She couldn't access any part of her brain that might give her ideas.

At least her cheek had stopped burning. Still, when she blinked, the corner of her left eye felt angry and injured. Each blink was a reminder that she was no longer a woman who had never been struck by her partner. He'd slapped her and she'd cowered there like every woman in every made-for-TV movie about abuse that she'd watched as a girl.

One tear welled there and spilled over. Even with all her privilege, even being the one who paid the bills, the one who could walk out, she felt the suffocating weight of that shame. The immediate urge to hide it from everyone.

But I can leave now, something inside her said, though it was just a memory of her previous self. She could leave now, but it would hardly be a triumph. Sydney would still be devastated. The only difference was that it wouldn't be Veronica's fault. Was that all it took to make it right in her head?

Thirty minutes passed, or maybe sixty. The shadows shifted slowly around her body until finally something stirred inside her and she remembered she still had the phone.

Tipsy with shock, she moved slowly and deliberately to tug it from her pocket. When she pushed the button, the message icon gleamed. Two messages. With none of the usual thrill of anticipation, she opened the app.

Is everything cool at home?

The first message shocked her so much that a sob exploded from her throat and immediately twisted into a laugh. No, everything was not cool at home. Everything was very far from cool, goddamn it all to hell.

Then the second message: Don't start second-guessing.

That was more puzzling. Second-guessing what? An affair? Selling drugs? Or a kidnapping plot?

She stared at the phone through a haze. Should she reach out? But how? Maybe she could say *Remind me of everything that's going on?*

She laughed again, that awful sound of pain, and clapped a hand over her mouth to stop it.

Johnny knew that she knew about the phone now. This might be her last chance to reach out. But she couldn't think. She couldn't think at all, and what she wanted to type was *HE HIT ME.*

She touched the *H* and then the *E.* Another *H.*

Then she let her hand fall back to her lap. No. She couldn't make it real like that.

She delcted the letters.

Just as she lifted her finger, the bedroom door swung open and Johnny was standing there in the gray space of the hallway. He'd shaped his face into regret, but that faded as soon as his gaze fell to the phone in her hand. Whatever peace offering he'd come to make was left in the hallway when he leapt forward to snatch it from her.

Veronica flinched away. Disgust roiled her stomach, a burning, horrified hatred of him and herself.

He checked the messages and then tucked the phone into his pocket. The loud music of a commercial drifted down the hall from the living room.

"I told Sydney you and I needed to run an errand in a little while. We can talk in the car."

"Where are we going?"

"Nowhere. Just out of the house."

"I don't feel safe with you," she murmured.

"Jesus, Roni! You know that's ridiculous. We just need a safe place to talk."

"Safe for who?"

He swallowed hard and dropped his eyes. Now that he had the phone, he was contrite again. "I panicked. I'm so sorry. I never . . . It won't ever happen again."

"No, it won't," she said as if she were brave.

"I promise. I wouldn't hurt you, Veronica. I'd never . . . I just freaked out and lost my mind for a second."

"That's all it takes, isn't it?"

He winced and nodded, then shook his head and winced again.

"Are you ready?" she asked.

"Ten more minutes in the show." He walked out of their bedroom like everything was normal. Like it was an average Sunday evening with time to kill with his daughter. After all, he had his phone now. What did he care?

Veronica wondered if she'd just lost her last best chance at getting to the real truth. But she wondered it from a distance, still too numb to be invested in the future.

But even through her numbness, she knew she had to watch out for Sydney, so she texted her mom. I'm going out with Johnny.

The dots of a return message began immediately. Do you need me to take Syd? I was going to go out to the bookstore, but . . .

No, we'll only be gone a few minutes. Things are a little tense & we need to talk some things out. I just want you to know in case you call the house. Sydney won't answer the phone if we're not here.

Are you ok?

No. Tears welled in her eyes at her mom's concern. No, she wasn't okay. But she knew she'd hide it until she was forced not to. I'm fine, she typed. Things have just been so crazy. I love you.

I love you too. Call if you need anything.

She stood unsteadily, waiting for the room to stop its swinging before she went to the bathroom. A flick of the light switch and her face was revealed. Veronica stared in horror at the truth.

She looked fine. A tiny hint of red at her cheekbone and the edge of her eye, but no swelling or bruising or scalding fingermarks against her skin. No proof of how profoundly she'd been injured. Her body had absorbed the hurt.

She looked fine.

"I hate you," she said to her reflection. Her reflection looked unmoved by the admission.

She brushed her tousled hair and pulled it into a ponytail. She washed her hands, though there was no reason to think they were dirty. Instead of drying them, she patted her wet fingers against her eyelids, then wiped off any remaining salt.

She was ready for the truth. Or she wasn't. It hardly mattered now.

When Johnny came for her, he whispered that they should take her car, and that gave her a little comfort as she followed him down the hallway. They'd be in her space, not his.

"Do you want to go to the duck pond?" he asked as she got behind the wheel.

"Sure," she said, sounding so normal, as if they were taking their little girl along just like they used to, loaded down with a picnic basket and a bag of stale bread to feed to the ducks and catfish. She'd still thought they might have the dream then. Nice cars, nice house, an annual trip to Disney World. A little debt on occasion, sure, but who didn't have that? She'd thought Johnny would grow up soon and get a real job, but she hadn't even asked him to. She'd wanted him to work through it on his own so he wouldn't resent her. But then, of course, she'd resented him. Somebody eventually had to do it.

Another bubble of laughter as she eased her car down the alley. Johnny shot her a look of concern, but she ignored it. "Well?" she demanded. "Talk."

"Not yet."

"The cops haven't bugged my car, Johnny."

"Probably not."

"Jesus. What the hell have you done?"

He didn't answer that. She hadn't expected he would, but she wanted it out there just the same. Whatever was happening here was entirely his fault, and she wanted him to feel the ache of that in every cell of his body. And she was very, very afraid that she knew what he was going to say.

The next five minutes were silent aside from the tapping of Johnny's foot against the floorboards. His knee bobbed in a jagged, nervous dance, and his frantic tension made her drive more slowly, putting off the horror of what he would reveal.

When they reached the parking lot of the pond, Veronica blew out a sigh and sat behind the wheel for a long moment even as Johnny got out of the car. There were two families along the edge of the water. Johnny gestured toward the far side of the pond, and Veronica finally opened the door.

"Tell me," she demanded as soon as she got out.

Instead of answering, he glanced toward the people throwing crackers into the water, and then began walking toward a bench halfway around the pond. Veronica rolled her eyes and followed.

Johnny found a bench he liked and dropped hard onto the curved metal. He slumped down to hold his head in his hands. Veronica sat a full foot away from him and waited. It took only a few seconds for her impatience to get the better of her.

"Well?"

"All I did was find the kid," he said to the ground.

Veronica's heart stopped. She'd known this must have something to do with the kidnapping, but it was so unthinkable, so horrifying, that it hadn't really been possible until he'd said it aloud.

"Johnny . . . ," she breathed.

He nodded as if she'd said something more and sat up to stare out at the water. "I didn't hurt anyone."

"No," she said. "This can't be true. Tell me you didn't do this."

"All I had to do was go hiking at a certain place on a certain day. That was it. I helped out a child. That was all."

She shot to her feet and stood on shaking legs. Her stomach trembled too, threatening to tip her into nausea. She walked away, not toward the parking lot, not toward home, but just *away*, over yellowing grass and around pine trees as quickly as she could. *No, no, no,* she muttered as she moved. The grass ahead brightened into an impossible green, and when she reached the chain-link fence, she realized it was the golf course. Men in pale clothing shifted around on the grass as if nothing bad were happening a hundred feet away.

Veronica grabbed the metal rail of the fence and squeezed as hard as she could. Her knuckles turned white, and then her vision too as she tipped her head back and stared at the bright clouds above her.

He'd ruined them. All of them. He'd ruined their lives and their futures and even their pasts, because this was all he'd ever be now. This monster. *Why?*

"They won't find out," he said from behind her.

She swung around to find him standing ten feet away, tears sliding down his face and dripping from his jaw.

"There's no evidence," he insisted. "I didn't do anything *wrong*."

"Are you kidding me? You . . . you helped in a kidnapping!"

"I only helped in the rescue."

"Do you think anyone will care about stupid details? Why would you *do* this?" She was nearly screaming now, her tight throat barely keeping the words low enough for discretion.

"I needed money. Veronica. I . . . I wanted . . ."

When his words stalled, she sneered. "You *wanted*. It's her, isn't it? You did this for her and your precious gym! She talked you into it."

"Who?"

"Neesa! You did it for her!"

"No! I mean, I wanted the money to invest in the business, yeah, but for *our* future."

"Oh, come on! Who planned it? Her? Her husband?"

He shook his head. "I can't talk about that. Ever. I made a promise."

"To Neesa?"

He shook his head. "I can't."

"Or it's Trey, right? Trey and his stupid friends! They helped you come up with this plan?"

He shook his head again and kept shaking it, his tan cheeks pale and splotched with a guilty flush.

"Tell me who it is!" She raised her fists, shaking them, wanting to shake him.

"I can't, Roni. I can't. It's better if you don't know. Can't you see that? I can't ever tell you."

"God, you're all idiots. Do you really think you won't get caught? Only one person needs to screw up, and then the police will link you to them, you giant fucking moron."

"I'm sorry," he whispered. "I'm sorry." He didn't even flinch when she marched across the grass and pushed him as hard as she could. He didn't flinch and he barely moved, which only made her angrier. "You helped torture a child! Do you know how afraid he must have been?"

"I didn't. No. He was fine. He wasn't . . . I mean . . ."

"How could you do that? How could you put him in danger? How could you put *us* in danger? Sydney will . . . My God, this would kill her, Johnny! You're her hero! And now . . . Now you're a monster."

His face crumpled into a sob. "Please don't say that."

She watched him crying like a scared little boy and her fingers stretched themselves wide. Her palms tingled. She could slap him. She *should* slap him. He'd hit her and he deserved it and she *wanted* to.

"There's no evidence," he panted.

"After all the time you've spent watching ridiculous TV shows, do you really think there's no evidence? Phone calls. DNA. Tracks. They've got dogs out there, Johnny! And you can't even use that money, you know. The serial numbers have been recorded! As soon as anyone uses any of those bills, it's over. They'll show up at our house one day, and . . . Jesus, Johnny, you've ruined us!"

"No. No. It's going to be fine. I promise. We've talked it all out. There are ways around all of this. They're nonsequential bills. We won't—"

"That phone?" she spat at him. "Is that how you communicate with them? This whole time I thought it was just for your girlfriend, but I guess you wouldn't have slapped me over that."

He shook his head, raising his hands in a helpless plea.

"If they find anyone else's phone, whoever you've been talking to, they'll be able to trace this one. What the hell is it doing in our house? You have to get rid of it."

The moment the words left her mouth, she realized what she was doing. She was helping. She was conspiring to cover up a crime. A real crime this time. Not just an assumption of one.

She shook her head at her own terrible wrongdoing, but Johnny was nodding now. "Yeah. You're right. I need to get rid of it. I will."

"No," she whispered, but then she stopped talking, because yes, he needed to destroy that phone and leave the remnants far away. He should burn it somewhere. Obliterate their fingerprints and DNA.

No, a little voice inside her insisted. She ignored it.

"The dogs won't find anything," Johnny said. "I don't know where exactly, but he wasn't kept anywhere near where I found him. I know that."

She shook her head again. She didn't want to know this.

And was there any chance at all that Trey and his friends could pull something like this off without leaving bread crumbs of evidence across the forest floor? Were they in any way competent enough to get away with an elaborate heist? She didn't think so. But then again, maybe she was just being a judgmental bitch. None of them had ever gotten caught dealing as far as she knew.

But if it was Neesa and her husband—

"Veronica?" Johnny whispered. His hands were still palms up, his neck bowed. His lower lip looked swollen with childish regret, and she still wished it were swollen from her blows.

She finally cracked, because apparently he needed her to play an interactive audience. "What?"

"Are you going to tell the police?"

Fury glowed inside her, heating until it spread to every nook of her body. "I can't, can I? I can't turn you in or I'll destroy our daughter. You fucking asshole. Don't think for one second that I care about protecting you. You deserve whatever happens. But she deserves none of it."

"I'm sorry," he breathed.

"We need to hide the money. Somewhere not in our goddamn house."

He nodded.

"And the phone. Take out the SIM card. Smash it to bits. Then take it all somewhere isolated and burn it. Pour acid over it. Something."

"Okay."

She looked out at the golfers and marveled that they'd just watched her transform willingly into a criminal and they couldn't even testify that they'd seen anything change. She looked the same. Just an average mom on an average day. But now she was a part of the horror too.

CHAPTER 22

She stared at her husband in the faint slices of moonlight that cut across the bed. How could he just lie there and sleep? How could he leave her here with all the questions she hadn't known she would have at one in the morning?

She'd been too in shock to organize her thoughts into more questions at the duck pond, and since he refused to discuss anything inside their home, he was safe from her here.

Were there devices that could help them discover any bugs? Were the police even suspicious enough to surveil them?

That was her biggest question right now. If there was no evidence, why did Johnny think they were being watched? But she knew the probable answer. If they really had no evidence about the kidnapping, Johnny was their only shot.

After she'd pointed out how stupid his plan was, he'd agreed not to hang out with Trey tonight, at least. Just the fact that she'd had to steer him away from it gave her little hope that he would get away with this crime.

He'd left for a while to dispose of the phone; then he'd returned home and raked the yard, as if finally taking care of that task might appease her. He'd thrown some steaks on the grill. Then movie night. A lovely family evening. Sydney had been so happy.

Veronica had spent half of the night in the bathroom with an upset stomach.

And now her husband slept like nothing was wrong, like he hadn't put a child's life in danger, like he was still a normal person. He'd set her whole world on fire, and now he was *sleeping*.

She stared harder at his face. The heavy light-brown eyebrows, the fan of short eyelashes against tan skin, the large nose and strong jaw.

When Sydney had been a baby and Veronica had spent far too many hours looking down into her sweet little face, there had been a few weeks of disorientation. Sometimes when Johnny was talking to her, she hadn't been able to hear him because she'd only been able to think *Why is his face so freakishly huge?* The thought had consumed her. Was his face a normal size? Had it grown? Could a human have a nose that big? How had she ever thought him handsome?

The obsession had passed within weeks, and she hadn't thought of it since, but it returned now as she watched him sleeping. His face was huge and ugly. The face of a caveman, all brute force and no intelligence.

Back then she could have reached out for advice. A question for other new mothers. *Does your husband's face look too big after staring at your baby?* But now what could she ask? *If your husband committed a terrible crime, do you think his face would look huge and ugly to you?*

Maybe she could find a Reddit board.

She laughed softly, but her mood didn't change. Finally she poked him. Hard. "Did you really get rid of it?" she whispered.

He squeezed his eyes more tightly shut and shook his head.

"Johnny! You really took care of the phone?" When he'd come home from the errand, he'd only nodded, and when she'd pointed at her own cell phone, he'd nodded again. But now she couldn't stop imagining he'd gotten distracted by a shiny Under Armour shop on the way and forgotten about the whole plan. "Johnny!"

"What?" he croaked, finally opening his eyes to slits.

"The phone!" she demanded.

"Yes. Be quiet. It's gone."

"You destroyed it?"

"Yes."

"Where?"

"I'm not saying that. Jesus. Go back to sleep."

"I wasn't sleeping," she hissed. He rolled over, and now she didn't have to stare at his face anymore, at least.

In the morning she'd confront him on paper and end this little fantasy that he didn't have to answer her questions. She'd write them down and he could print out his confessions, and then she'd burn the pages. And the pages beneath the pages. She'd read enough mysteries and thrillers to know that pens left behind indentations.

Johnny's breathing evened out. She turned to her back and stared up at the vague darkness of the ceiling.

How had they done it? Had they lurked in the trees at the edge of the sprawling Holcomb estate? It wouldn't have been difficult. There were two main houses plus a guesthouse by the pool, then acres and acres of trees and paths and man-made hills and curves for BMX biking. She'd seen it all on the news. A whole army could have hidden unseen on that land. The police had even discovered a cave somewhere close by, but it had been shallow and the dirt near the entrance undisturbed according to a press release they'd written.

The Holcomb grandchildren had treated the estate like a fantasy camp. They'd run wild, by all accounts. They'd spread out through the woods at every given opportunity and returned only for meals.

Tanner had been too young for that, hadn't he? People had whispered about it on the first day of the disappearance. By the second day they hadn't bothered whispering. The boy was too young to play unsupervised. Colorado outdoorsiness was all good and fine, but the Holcombs had taken free-range parenting to a whole other level. When adults were that irresponsible, children went missing. Of course they did.

And sometimes when adults were that irresponsible, children were taken by bad men. Bad men like Johnny.

Veronica groaned in distress and finally sat up. She'd been avoiding coverage of the kidnapping since Saturday, determined to stop worrying and put it behind them. But now that she knew the truth, she needed as much information as she could get. She got up, grabbed her phone, and headed out to the living room for a cup of tea.

Once she'd microwaved water and dropped some bourbon in with the tea bag, she curled onto the couch with a blanket and her internet access.

The police had released more information this morning, and her starving mind grabbed at the skittery bits of story. At only three years old, Tanner couldn't remember much about the kidnappers, or at least couldn't convey reliable details to the police. Veronica couldn't imagine Sydney trying to describe anything at that age. She'd once said President Obama had "small hair" and she'd called the bespectacled old woman who worked at the pool concession stand "owl parts," whatever the hell that meant.

Little Tanner couldn't describe a voice or height or guess where he'd traveled, but he did remember playing hide-and-seek on the estate before a person picked him up. So someone had definitely snatched him from the Holcomb property on purpose.

Then Tanner said it had gotten really dark, so the police suspected he was either put in a car trunk or bundled inside a blanket. They were currently looking for tire tracks, but with all the search parties in the area after his disappearance, there wasn't much hope that anything would come of it. They'd had no luck with search dogs at the time of the disappearance either. Tanner had been running those trails all afternoon and all summer. His scent was everywhere.

After being taken, Tanner remembered a room with a "dirty" floor and what police said must have been a cot. There were blankets and crackers and juice. And the last detail they revealed made Veronica wonder exactly how the police had looked as they had conveyed this fact: Tanner said that Chewbacca had taken care of him the whole time.

The theory, of course, was that a man wearing a Chewbacca mask had fed the boy and kept him comfortable. But she wondered whether Tanner believed the actual Chewbacca had been his companion. If so, would *Star Wars* bring bad dreams from now on? That poor baby.

Tanner did not appear to have any injuries. He hadn't been sexually assaulted, thank God. But they had found evidence of sedatives in his system.

Veronica touched her throat when she read that. She pressed her palm to her neck and swallowed hard.

How much of the planning had Johnny helped with? What had he known? He claimed his only role had been retrieval, but why would he confess the whole truth to her at this point? He needed her sympathy, after all. He needed her help.

But these idiots—or maybe just one idiot; maybe just Trey or Neesa's husband—had drugged a small child. They weren't doctors or any sort of medical professionals. What did a three-year-old weigh? Thirty pounds? They could have easily killed him.

Had Johnny known about the sedatives? If the worst had happened and Tanner had disappeared forever, would Johnny have told anyone?

No.

She didn't have to sit with the question to know the answer. No, of course he wouldn't have told anyone, because then he would have been involved with the murder of a child, and what would be the point in confessing? Every realization now led her to a worse thought. Every worry brought another horror.

But even with all of their problems, Veronica could not reconcile this criminal, callous Johnny with the man she knew. He was a great father, a good friend. When he volunteered at Sydney's school, some of the kids literally cheered when he walked in. Veronica had seen it with her own eyes.

How could that man have so thoughtlessly put a tiny child in danger? He wasn't evil. She knew he wasn't evil. But . . . he was immature and gullible. He always had been. Someone had talked him into this scheme, and—instead of being strong and standing up to his friends—he'd gone along with it.

Despicable.

When her conscience raised its weak voice and reminded her that she was going along too, Veronica slapped it down hard and shook her head. The deed was already done. Given the chance, she would have stopped it. But she hadn't been given that chance. Now it was too late to take it all back.

She set her jaw and crouched back over her phone to do more research.

Johnny might have been right about one thing: the police didn't seem to have any leads. They were asking the public for help finding a small cabin, possibly with a dirt floor, but they couldn't offer any details on a search radius or even what kind of car might have been parked outside it. The boy could have been driven hours from the Holcomb estate. He didn't remember, and he'd been drugged either before or after arriving.

She wanted to wake Johnny right now and ask about the cabin, but she understood that she was better off not knowing. Hopefully Johnny really didn't know either.

Unless he'd been there at some point.

Frowning, she tried again to re-create the days after the kidnapping. Had there been any unusual gaps? She didn't think so, but there had been the *usual* gaps, hadn't there? He'd gone to work, she'd slipped away for a jog, he'd driven to the store. He'd run other errands, surely, but maybe all those trips had been a pretense? How would she ever know? He'd changed everything for their family forever.

It didn't matter how much information she found online. No set number of facts would satisfy her. She'd never feel secure again.

Veronica curled lower in the couch and opened her messaging app to review the few messages saved from Micah. She ached with the need to reach out to him. Her skin felt tight and cool from the lack of his touch. Johnny had taken this from her too, finally. She couldn't lean on Micah any longer or she'd have to reveal something he could never know. Loss burned like a cold stone in her belly.

She wouldn't be able to see him Wednesday. Maybe she'd never be able to see him again. She'd felt free with him. Beautiful. New. But the beauty was smashed to bits now. She'd have to hide the glaring, howling horror that was her whole world from now on, and how could she set that aside for even a moment?

I miss you, she typed out, hitting SEND as her vision blurred with desperate grief. Without even hoping for a response, she pulled the blanket higher and shoved a pillow beneath her head. It was too late to stagger back to the bed she shared with Johnny. She closed her eyes and dreamed of shadows running through a forest. Most of them looked like her.

CHAPTER 23

"Mom?"

Veronica sat up with a gasp that turned into a grunt of shock when an empty mug rolled off her thigh and thumped onto the carpet. "Hey," she croaked. "Hey, sweetie. What's up?"

"Why are you sleeping on the couch?"

"Uh. I fell asleep watching TV, I guess."

Sydney turned narrowed eyes toward the blank screen.

"Oh," Veronica croaked. "I meant . . . I must have fallen asleep after watching TV."

Her daughter shrugged, but her gaze swept down her mother's body before she turned to head toward the kitchen. Veronica looked down to see a pale-brown tea stain on the front of her baggy shirt. "Crap," she whispered. The couch was black leather, at least, and wouldn't be stained, but bourbon fumes drifted up from her body when she shifted.

Great. One more sparkling memory between mother and daughter. She'd had only one spiked mug of tea, but now it looked like she'd passed out sloppy drunk. Not that she hadn't earned the right, but if Sydney was going to remember it that way, Veronica would've preferred to have actually indulged in a drunken night.

Johnny strutted into the living room, eyebrows flying high at the sight of her. "Hey, babe. There you are!" His voice shone bright with relief, as if he'd worried she'd snuck out in the night.

Ignoring Johnny and still bundled in the bourbon-scented blanket, she pushed up from the couch and brushed past him on the way to the bedroom. She didn't have to be at work for two hours, but she could tell that the last wisps of sleep were past her. Still, she climbed back into her bed, determined to enjoy the space now that it was blissfully husband-free.

She listened to the sounds of breakfast, then the sounds of packing up; then their voices faded as Sydney and Johnny left the house. The engine of Johnny's truck rumbled, which meant he was dropping Sydney off instead of walking her to school. No doubt he wanted to head straight to work to avoid Veronica's glares and questions. Fine. She'd have plenty of both waiting for him when he got home.

Once the house was quiet again, she rose and headed straight for the basement door.

She barely noticed the grit and dust against her bare feet as she descended the old wooden stairs. For once she didn't cringe at the feel of a cobweb brushing her elbow. She lived in a house with a giant slithering snake of a husband. Everything else felt easy now. She could certainly handle a tiny arachnid touching her arm.

When she lifted the flaps of the box, Veronica was almost surprised to see the money still there. After all, what did she really know about Johnny? How could she have been certain he wouldn't just take the money and run? She certainly hadn't expected him to be involved with kidnappers, so anything was possible at this point.

In fact, maybe she should have been concerned that he might skip town with Sydney. Take the money and his daughter and start a new life somewhere. For a moment Veronica dared to wonder whether Sydney would go along with it. She was a daddy's girl, after all. Would she really even care if Veronica was out the picture?

The thought made her dizzy, because the answer was very possibly no.

Nonsense. That was just her feeling pitifully sorry for herself. Her daughter wouldn't just blithely write her off and move on. That was the whole reason Veronica had stayed in this marriage. Because Sydney idealized family to an unhealthy degree.

It was meaningless dramatics, anyway. The money was still nestled in its box, safe from Johnny and any plans to escape. But it wasn't safe from her, was it? She lifted the bag and felt the remarkable heft of it again.

If she took the money and ran, would that make her an accomplice or just a double-crosser? If it were five hundred thousand it might be worth finding out. But fifty thousand . . . Johnny didn't pay the bills. He probably thought this was a genuine fortune. But if they used it to pay off their debt, they'd be left with about thirty thousand, and they would easily blow through that in three years of normal household expenses. Her husband was a cheap grifter on top of everything else.

They had to get it out of here, just in case the police came poking around again. She supposed that at this point they could refuse a request to search the house just on principle. Johnny was a hero, so why did they keep bothering him? But a refusal would only make the police look harder, and they certainly couldn't risk that. The money had to go.

She briefly considered that she could hide it in her mother's house. Bury it beneath a pile of old board games in her mom's closet, tell Johnny she'd taken care of it, and it would be emergency money if they needed it. But she considered that option for only a few seconds. It wasn't fair to put her mother in danger for Johnny's sake.

So where? Maybe bury it on public forest land, and they could dig it up later? She pictured Johnny running from tree to tree sometime in the future, certain the treasure was at the foot of this pine tree or maybe the identical one next to it, or maybe they'd taken the wrong fork in the logging road a mile back.

Snorting, she tucked the bag back into the box and closed the flaps again. There was no point moving the money until they had a plan. She might just make the situation worse.

Then again . . .

She shoved her hand between the cardboard flaps and drew the bag back out; then she opened it, withdrew two of the bundles of bills, and sealed the bag again. Whatever plan she concocted with Johnny didn't mean she couldn't have a plan for herself. If everything went sideways for him, she'd still have a daughter to support.

Two thousand dollars fisted in each hand, Veronica stomped up the stairs and into the kitchen. She wrapped the stack of bills in foil first, then in a kitchen towel; then she stuffed the whole bundle into a new plastic bag and sealed it tight.

She couldn't pull her family into this, and unfortunately they didn't have any inherited land nestled in the foothills somewhere. She'd have to make do with what she had.

After shoving her feet into an old pair of tennis shoes, she headed out the back door to the garage to grab gloves and a shovel. Old Man followed her and flopped onto a sun-warmed square of grass. "No, not there," she murmured to him.

Not the backyard. That was too obvious. Paused on the cement patio lodged between the back door and the detached garage, she turned in a slow circle. There was a narrow side yard, but it was mostly a stone walkway and a privacy fence. The fence ran all the way behind the garage to their property line at the alley.

It wasn't their fence, of course. The neighbors had asked them to contribute, but the old chain-link fence had worked fine for Veronica and Johnny, as it had been more in keeping with their fence budget for the year: zero dollars. Their neighbors had huffily paid for the fence themselves, and Veronica had left them to it, but she'd taken advantage of the clearing done by the fence company. Once the brambles along the back of their garage had been ripped out to leave working room for the installers, she'd planted a few shade-loving vines and never set foot there again.

She eyed the two-foot space between the fence and the wall, wrinkling her nose at the thought of how many spiders must live back there. Hundreds, certainly. Thousands? There were probably black widows lurking in their strong, wiry webs, waiting for her to brush against them.

"Oh God," she whispered, shaking her head in admonishment for even thinking of sliding into that space. But she knew it was mostly dirt there. She'd run into only a thin layer of gravel and a few rocks when she'd dug in before.

"I fucking hate you, Johnny," she said. He wasn't forcing her to hide some of the money for an emergency, of course, but she certainly wouldn't be in this position without his help. He wouldn't be facing prison. He wouldn't be facing bond and attorney fees and unemployment. How would she support Sydney through all of that?

Content with blaming him even for her betrayal, she blew a long breath through pursed lips and nodded. "Get it over with," she urged herself, tightening her hold on the shovel. She'd get in, get out, and race into the shower to scrub off the creepy-crawlies.

The first foot wasn't so bad. It was fairly clear of cobwebs. She forced herself to push into the second foot of space, waving the shovel ahead of her, scraping it over the garage wall and then along the ivy leaves, hoping to scare away any danger.

Something scuttled through the dead leaves on the ground ahead of her, and she froze with a little whine of terror. *Far enough!* her brain shouted at her, and she agreed and dug the shovel into the ground. It clanked against a rock but then sank an inch into soil. She dug out a chunk and then another.

Something tickled her cheek, and she failed to bite back a scream. When she jerked away to swipe at her face, her elbow scraped along the garage, but she barely noticed the sting of pain as she swatted her cheek in panic. A wisp of her own hair flew in front of her eyes, scaring her even more deeply. It was only as she drew her chin in that she realized it had likely been her hair tickling her all along.

She held her breath and waited to see whether she felt anything else moving on her skin. After a few moments she convinced herself she was fine, but she couldn't slump against the wall to regain her strength. That was just an invitation for more spiders to explore her body.

"Get it over with," she reminded herself, then dug frantically into the dirt. Once she had a decent-sized hole, she kicked the package into it and scooped the dirt back into place. No matter how hard she stomped on it, she couldn't make the mound perfectly flat, so she leveled it out as well as she could, then scraped some old leaves on top of it.

"Not bad," she muttered as she eased back to look. "Not bad at all."

"What are you doing?" a voice asked from behind her.

Veronica shrieked and tried to spin toward the threat, but she flung out the shovel at the same time and it bounced against the garage wall with a bone-jarring clang. Plaster flew up and chittered against the leaves behind her.

"Hey! I'm sorry! It's just me."

When she finally craned her head enough to get the person in view, she realized it was Neesa, fresh and beautiful and standing in the backyard like she belonged there.

"Oh God!" Veronica yelled. "You scared the crap out of me."

"I guess so." She cringed and then chirped out another "Sorry!"

Veronica felt like she was on the verge of a heart attack. "What are you doing here?"

"I wanted to talk and no one answered the door. I thought I heard someone back here."

"So you let yourself into the backyard?"

"I'm sorry. I thought maybe I could catch you guys before you left for work."

She pushed her way past the last vines to get out of the claustrophobic space. "Johnny's not here. It's just me."

"You're the one I wanted to talk to, actually."

Her heart was already beating so hard, it felt like her whole chest was shaking. She'd been caught doing something very, very wrong. Something utterly incriminating. And now her husband's lover or partner in crime or whatever she was wanted to have a *talk*?

Desperately trying to hide her panic, Veronica said, "Oh, sure," and tugged off her gloves. She left the shovel where it had fallen and stepped into the open. "I caught a mouse," she explained. "Sydney doesn't like it when we throw them in the trash."

"So you bury them? That's sweet."

"Thanks."

Neesa paused as if she were waiting for something.

"Did you want to come in?" Veronica asked finally. "I can pour you a cup of coffee, but I really need to jump in the shower soon."

"No, that's okay. I need to get to work too. I just wanted to stop by and let you know that I've put together some good numbers on the gym. It's not just off-the-cuff. I really believe we can make this work. K.C. and I have so much experience running the garage, and it's doing really well, so . . . Johnny has the spreadsheets already, but can I email them to you?"

Veronica cleared her throat, attempting to look serious as she tried not to scream that she didn't give one damn about their stupid gym right now. "That's good. Sure. I'll look at what you have, I guess. Johnny and I haven't really had a chance to discuss it yet, but money is pretty tight, so . . ."

"Of course. But I know Johnny has been saving up, and I just hope you'll hear him out, Veronica. He's really good at what he does."

Irritation bloomed in her veins to join all the other emotions rioting inside her. "I know he's good at training, Neesa. I've known him a long time. In fact, we're married."

"Right. Of course."

She kept talking, but Veronica's irritation had already fizzled out and she was thinking about what Neesa had said. That Johnny had been saving money. Johnny hadn't been saving money. There hadn't been any extra money to save. Not until Tanner Holcomb had come along.

"Where did you get your half?" she asked.

Neesa had been speaking, but she paused to let her mouth hang open and her eyes stare in shock at Veronica's question. "Excuse me?" she finally asked.

"You said Johnny has been saving money. You two have obviously been discussing this for quite a while. It's a big investment. How much money would it take? Fifty thousand? A hundred?"

"I . . . I have the numbers drawn up. Like I said, you can—"

"Where did you get your half of the money, Neesa?"

Neesa pulled her chin in. For a moment she looked as if she wouldn't answer, but then she relaxed her tight hands and nodded. "Well . . . Like I said, we have the garage . . ."

"The garage," Veronica repeated doubtfully before waving a dismissive hand. "Whatever. I need to get ready for work." She couldn't think about this now. Not in front of Neesa. It could be Trey, but it could also be Neesa and her husband. He could very well be running stolen vehicles through that garage, honing his criminal skills, making connections, making plans.

"Okay, but—"

"Thanks," Veronica shot out for no reason, and darted toward the back door. "I'm late."

"Sorry!" Neesa called after her, sounding sweet and helpful again. But was she? Or had she actually planned this with Johnny to finance her dreams?

Veronica slammed the door behind her and pressed her back to the wall, ears straining for any suspicious sound.

But she was being ridiculous, right? Neesa was just a harmless little fitness buff. And Veronica was losing what was left of her mind. But if Neesa was involved, if there was any possibility at all, she'd just watched Veronica bury part of the ransom behind the garage.

"Fuck," she breathed, then froze at the crunch of footsteps along the side of the house. A few dozen heartbeats later she heard the thump of a car door closing, and then the purr of an engine that soon faded.

What the hell was she doing? Why was she digging herself deeper? Her entire focus should be on making sure she didn't make things worse.

Silently repeating a few choice curse words on a loop in her head, she checked the front window to be sure Neesa was actually gone; then she rushed back outside, tugged on the gloves, and plunged into the narrow space behind the garage without thinking once about spiders.

A few minutes later she had the wrapped stacks of bills in hand. Making sure to keep the gloves on, she tossed the plastic bag in the trash and even managed to work the foil off before returning the cash to Johnny's hiding place in the basement. For good measure, she dumped the bills out of the plastic bag she'd touched when she'd discovered it, then raced upstairs to hold a match to it over the trash can. The plastic quickly curled and melted, taking her fingerprints into the ether.

Finally she took off the gardening gloves, dropped them in the trash too, and washed her hands.

She wasn't turning Johnny in. That was wrong, but she wasn't sinking any deeper than that. She couldn't.

No, that wasn't quite it. She could. She'd just done it, in fact. But she *wouldn't*. Not anymore.

Her shaking legs finally gave out and she dropped down to the cold linoleum. She put her hands, cool and raw from being scrubbed in icy water, over her face. She wanted to cry, but she couldn't. Something was stuck inside her, shut down. So instead of crying she just wailed into her own skin. The low, helpless whine of an exhausted animal.

She should have left him. She should have left and put Sydney in therapy and been a stronger, better woman. After all, hadn't she learned from her own childhood that shoving things down only made everything worse? She'd watched her parents as they'd perfected this dance of loving pretense over the years and she'd learned. How to lie and tough it out and put off happiness and ignore problems. She should have shown Sydney honesty instead.

Now Veronica desperately needed help, comfort, and love, and she couldn't ask anyone for it. She didn't even deserve it.

"Oh God, oh God, oh God," she chanted into her hands. How would she get through today, much less years of living with this? It was too much guilt. Too much uncertainty.

A strange buzz vibrated through her. It took her a long minute to realize it wasn't fear or anxiety shaking loose from her bones. It was her phone.

She scrubbed her dry face and took a deep breath before tugging her phone from her pocket. "Please don't be awful," she prayed.

And it wasn't. It was Micah. I can't wait for Wednesday, V.

Still no tears, but she did feel that stuck place inside her melt a little. But only a little, because there wouldn't be a Wednesday with Micah this week. There might never be again.

She hit the little call button and cradled the phone against her ear.

"Hey, V," he murmured, his voice low.

"Hi. I won't be able to make it this week. I'm sorry."

He went silent for a long moment. "Is everything okay?"

Her eyelids fluttered until she had to close them to stop the strobing light. "No," she whispered.

"Are *you* okay?"

"No."

"What's wrong, V?"

"Everything."

"Hey, you're kind of scaring me here. Is something really wrong?"

"Micah . . ." There were so many things she couldn't say. So many truths she could no longer speak to him. So she latched on to the one thing she could tug free from her pain. "He hit me."

"What? Who hit you?"

"Johnny."

"What the fuck, Veronica? He *hit* you? Are you okay? Are you safe?"

"Yes. I'm safe. It was yesterday."

"*Yesterday*? You didn't call me? I could've . . . I . . ." His voice cracked, and her throat closed up in response.

"I'll kill him," Micah growled, and God, she loved him for it, and she felt so stupid for the bubbly gratitude that fluttered through her chest. Gratitude that he cared enough to want to protect her. Pitiful but it was true.

"I'm fine. It was . . . He panicked and lost his temper, but I'm fine."

"What happened?"

Now what? She couldn't explain what had caused Johnny's panicked rage. "He . . . he caught me looking at that phone. We argued and he freaked out and slapped me."

"Oh, Veronica. I'm so sorry. That stupid asshole. Do you need to get away? Can you stay with your sister?"

She knew she couldn't stay with Micah. It wasn't even remotely feasible under the circumstances, but still . . .

Still.

He didn't ask.

Veronica nodded. "No, it's fine. He's contrite. I'm not going to leave right now. Not yet. I'll work it out."

"Do you need me to come over?"

Yes. She wanted him to come over. She wanted him to never leave. But this wasn't a fantasy. Hell, it wasn't even real life anymore. It was some weird nonsensical nightmare where she was digging holes behind the garage to bury bundles of cash.

"No," she rasped. "I'm going to work. I'll be okay. I'm not hurt. I'm just in shock, I guess."

"Do you want me to talk to him?"

She frowned and rubbed a hand over her eyes. "What would you say?"

"I guess I'd try to get him to tell me it happened, so I could tell him it had better never happen again."

"God, Micah. No. You don't need to be dragged into this. But I love you for offering."

"I love you too. And I'll call him, regardless. He'll listen to me."

He *would* listen to Micah. He looked up to his former roommate because Micah had made something of himself. He'd paid his way through college by working landscaping jobs, and then he'd gotten into landscape design and he'd started his own company. Now he made beautiful worlds for wealthy people, and Johnny often said Micah was one of the smartest men he knew.

"Did you tell your family?" he asked.

She shook her head hard. "No. I'm too embarrassed."

"You don't need to be embarrassed. And it's good to talk about things. You should talk to your mom. Tell her what happened."

"Maybe later. If I leave him, I'll tell my family about it so I don't have to listen to twenty iterations of 'Are you sure? He's such a good guy, Veronica. You should try to make it work.'"

"I have to admit, I thought he was a good guy too. I never thought Johnny would stoop that low."

"Thank you for talking to me," she whispered. "You made me feel better."

"Can I stop by tonight? Make sure everything's okay?"

"You'd better not," she said slowly, forcing the words out of her mouth.

"Okay, but . . . stay safe, V. I love you."

"I love you too, Micah."

Her throat tightened as she hung up and stripped off her clothes. Naked, she tossed her clothing down the stairs to the basement floor before heading straight for the shower to scrub her whole body down.

It was only a matter of time, she assured herself. At some point she'd leave him. She'd be free. A few more years, that was all.

Maybe Micah would wait for her. Probably not, but after that phone call she could almost convince herself that things would eventually work out.

Almost.

CHAPTER 24

Despite her busy schedule, she had to tamp down ruthless anxieties all day, like stomping out scattering roaches. Every time she started to lose herself in her work or her patients, her guard would relax and a stray thought would skitter into the light to distract her.

Did that car door closing just outside the rehab center belong to a police detective? Was her phone buzzing because Johnny had been arrested? Was Trey being hauled in at this very moment, Johnny's name at the ready on his lips? Or was it actually Neesa or her husband? She needed to make Johnny tell her the truth so she could know which person she should watch out for.

Then again, she had no control over any of it, so there was no point worrying. Better not to know more. Better to be able to claim ignorance. But no matter how often she told herself, she couldn't make her own advice stick. She needed to know.

By the end of the day she was exhausted and managed to issue instructions to her patients only by rote.

Throughout the day people peppered her with questions about Johnny's heroics. She'd hoped interest would die down soon—people moved on quickly these days—but everyone seemed reminded of the story as soon as they glimpsed her face. Each exclamation of Johnny admiration screeched like nails on a chalkboard for Veronica, but she had to grin and nod and proclaim her breathless gratitude for the wonderful man in her life.

The queasiness carried over into the drive home, and instead of stopping for groceries she drove straight through. Johnny could damn well fend for himself, and Sydney would be happy with the chance to gobble down a couple of microwaved hot dogs. As for Veronica, all she needed was wine, and lots of it. And tonight he would tell her who was involved even if he had to write their names out on the Etch A Sketch.

How had she fallen so far, so quickly? She'd started shedding threads of herself somewhere along the way and now she was willingly unraveling, tossing off tendrils and strings until they tangled around her like some warped aurora.

Her whole life she'd assumed she was a decent person, maybe even a good person. She didn't steal or do drugs. She contributed to society. She protected her child. She drove safely and always wore her seat belt. Heck, her entire career was built on helping people who most needed help.

But this year, at every crossroads, she'd willingly taken the crooked path. She'd *wanted* that. She'd felt entitled to rewards for all the good decisions she'd made. She'd put in her time. She'd *earned* her right to do wrong.

And she was doing it again. But what other choice did she have? She had to protect Sydney. There wasn't a better option, was there?

As she pulled into her neighborhood, she puzzled over the question. Maybe there was a better option and she was too close to see it. For instance, maybe Johnny could leverage what he knew into a bid for leniency. He could turn in his friends and claim he knew nothing of their plans. What if they hadn't told him about the kidnapping until *after* it was done? What if he'd seen their request to retrieve the child as a way to help and not hurt? After all, the boy was already in danger, and Johnny had known that the child would be safe with him. So yes, he'd taken the money, but his primary motivation had been getting little Tanner Holcomb out of those woods.

It could work.

She'd been operating on pure panic for the last twenty-four hours, but what she needed was calm and a little distance. If they could think rationally, maybe . . . just maybe . . . they could get out of this mess for good.

She wished there were someone else she could talk to. No, not *someone* else, of course. She wished she could talk to Micah. He was smarter than Johnny and more logical than Veronica. He could help.

But it wasn't fair to ask. It just wasn't. She wasn't worth that kind of danger.

And there it was. Her greatest fear. That she wasn't worth it. That Micah would realize that one day. That he likely already had. And somehow the fear made holding on to him seem so much more important. The fear made her hold tighter and try harder, just as it had with Johnny years ago.

Because she knew she wasn't really worth all this trouble. She knew she had to dress it up and make it all more pleasant, or he'd walk away. Was that the truth or just one of those insecurities she was supposed to fight against? Should she trust in her own worth and tell Micah that she needed help?

Hell, that wasn't even the right question. The question was why was she measuring her own self-worth based on what a man wanted? Again. Girl power: doing it wrong since age fourteen, at least.

So the question wasn't about Micah. The correct question was . . . what would she tell her daughter to do in this situation?

The thought hit her hard in the gut. She almost grunted from the force of it. What would she tell Sydney to do if her husband had helped kidnap a child?

First of all, she'd say, "Jesus Christ, girl, you are a mess." And wasn't that the God's honest truth? But what else would she say?

Veronica reached her street and drove straight instead of heading toward the alley so she'd have a few more moments to herself. And as she drove by her house, she got the shock of her life. Micah's car was parked on the curb. Her heart leapt as she rolled by, and she forgot all her girl power and switched immediately to yearning to see him. Another swift fall among many.

He was here. He'd come to protect her. And she felt happy.

She was covering up a crime, stealing cash, lying to her husband, her lover, her family. And still, right now all she cared about was knowing Micah loved her. Pitiful.

She pulled into the garage and turned off her car's engine; then she sat there for a long time assuring herself there was nothing to plan at this moment. She wasn't going to tell Micah anything tonight. Right now she just needed to walk in, say hello, meet his eyes, and feel his presence without throwing herself into his arms. She needed to hug her daughter, pet her dog, and do her best not to start hitting and kicking her husband for screwing everything up.

She could do all those things. She was almost sure of it. She forced herself to get out of the car slowly and walk toward the house with a little dignity.

Johnny opened the door before she reached it. "Hey. Micah's here. He was waiting when Syd and I got home." He ran the words together as quickly as possible, as if staving off an argument about having guests over when their world was in chaos. But Johnny looked like he'd already had an argument. His brow was tightly folded into a frown and his hair was a rumpled mess. In fact, his eyes looked shot through with red, as if he'd been crying or on the verge of it.

Micah really had sat him down for a talk, it seemed. Gratefulness swelled hot and soft in her chest.

She nodded and walked forward until he had to move aside and let her in. "Hi, Micah," she said, the words too husky by far, but she no longer cared. He stood up from the couch and watched her, his gaze warm and bruised with emotion.

"How are you doing?" he asked.

She only nodded in response.

"I hope it's okay if I stay for dinner," he said, the words a rumble of relief in her ear.

"As long as you're okay with Chinese food or whatever else we can pick up."

"That sounds great."

She didn't ask Johnny. She didn't even look at him.

"Mom!" Sydney called. She raced down the hallway with Old Man at her heels. "Mom, can I go to Grandpa's? Please? Pleeeeeease?"

"What?" She finally granted Johnny a look, and he shrugged.

"I told him it would be okay."

"Oh, great."

"Mom, pleeeeeease?" Sydney repeated.

"Honey, I don't even know what's going on here."

"Grandpa says I can spend the night. He said we could go to the indoor water park and—"

"It's a school night," Veronica interrupted.

"I already did my math sheets and he said he'd drive me to school in the morning. Please? You've let me stay at Grandma's on a school night! Pleeeeeease?"

She wanted to say no out of sheer irritation. None of this was cool. Her dad should have run this by her. By going to Sydney and Johnny first, he was manipulating the situation. Of course he was. That was his specialty. Easier to ask forgiveness than permission.

"Please, Mom? I already told him I have to be in bed by nine. And you know how much I've missed Grandpa." Sydney's eyes suddenly shimmered with tears, and Veronica's heart twisted into a guilty pretzel. Damn it. She knew it was bad precedent to give in to this kind of emotion, but in all honesty she could use a break too. And after Micah was gone, she and Johnny could go for a walk and he could tell her exactly what had happened.

"Nine o'clock bedtime," she said firmly, and Sydney burst into an excited scream and threw her arms around Veronica's waist.

"Thank you, Mommy. He'll be here at six."

"So it was already arranged?" she asked over Sydney's head. Johnny shrugged.

Whatever. Veronica was too tired to care, and she didn't want to be a nagging harridan in front of Micah anyway. "Let's get you packed," she murmured.

"I already started."

She caught Micah's smile as she left and smiled right back, not bothering to hide the joy she felt from seeing him right there where she needed him.

Did they even have to hide their involvement at this point? The marriage was over. Even Johnny must know that. He'd committed an unforgivable crime. And he'd hit her. They were done. So done she didn't even need to pretend.

But Micah wouldn't want to hurt Johnny, she supposed. And he probably didn't want anyone to see him as the guy who'd sleep with his buddy's wife. She'd have to take her cues from him.

Sighing, she grabbed Sydney's toothbrush and comb from the bathroom, then added a beach towel to her overnight bag. "You got your swimsuit?"

"Yes!"

"Be sure to listen to Grandpa and the lifeguards, okay?"

"I know, Mom."

"And don't let him feed you too much junk."

Her daughter didn't even bother answering that ridiculous request. Her grandfather was great at spoiling kids. Great at swooping in like a magnificent, unreliable fairy godfather to upstage all the hard work of the women doing the actual child-rearing. He'd done it to his own wife for years. Now it was Veronica's turn.

Sydney would no doubt come home with a tummyache and fifty dollars' worth of useless gifts from the gift shop. She'd rave about him being the best grandpa in the whole world, eclipsing the everyday love her mother and grandmother put into keeping her life steady. But that was part of childhood. Or it had been a big part of Veronica's childhood, anyway. And she was doing fine, wasn't she?

Sydney looked up at her mom's laugh, but Veronica just shook her head. "Underwear?" she prompted.

"It's in there."

"I'll give you the iPad so you can text or FaceTime us if you want to."

Sydney offered another hug and then hauled her backpack onto one shoulder and her overnight bag on the other. "I'm ready!"

"All right. Call me if you change your mind and want to come home."

"Mom, come on!"

"Worth a shot."

After Sydney hugged her dad and Veronica locked eyes with Micah for another secret smile, she and Sydney walked out to sit on the front step and wait for Grandpa.

Her daughter chattered about the last time she'd spent the night at his place and how he'd taken her to the Cheesecake Factory at the mall and then shopping afterward. Above Sydney's delighted voice, Veronica could hear the deep murmur of male conversation on the other side of the door. It wasn't the normal give-and-take of them bullshitting each other. It was low and solemn.

Her ears burned to think of Micah defending her and admonishing Johnny. Then her cheeks went warm. Then her whole face flushed hot, a strange combination of self-consciousness and gratitude and maybe a little shame. She strained her ears, hoping to pick up a word or two, but nothing jumped out from the dark stream of murmured voices.

At 6:05 her dad pulled up, and Veronica walked Sydney to his car and opened a rear door. "She still needs to sit in the back, Dad."

Sydney groaned at her mom's insistence that she stay out of the front seat until she reached the recommended height, but she climbed in anyway.

"Please watch her carefully in the water, okay?"

"I will. We'll have a great time, won't we, pumpkin?"

"And next time call me instead of Johnny," she added.

Her dad rolled his eyes. "*Johnny* called *me*."

"Oh." She frowned, but the reason was damn obvious. He didn't want Sydney overhearing any talk of physical abuse. "Bedtime is nine," Veronica said.

"Yep. No problem."

She kissed Sydney goodbye and shut the door carefully, relieved the interaction was over. She was still waving at the retreating car when Micah emerged from the house.

"Are you leaving?" she asked.

"Just to pick up dinner."

She stood there with her arms crossed and imagined walking back inside alone. "I'll come with you."

He glanced over his shoulder toward the front door. "Think that's a good idea?"

"I think I don't give a damn anymore."

He flashed a wide smile. "All right, sexy. Let's go."

She smiled and hopped into his car, relieved for this brief moment of escape.

Even as he pulled away from the curb, he threw little glances toward her. "What are you smiling about?" he asked.

"I've never been in a car with you."

"What?" He laughed. "Is that true?"

"Yes. We've never been on a date, you know. It's all been secret, steamy hookups in the dark."

"Steamy, huh?"

She felt her smile tip into something wistful as she reached over to touch his thigh.

"Well, I guess you're right. But I did take you up to the rooftop deck a few months ago. Remember? That was kind of a date, wasn't it?"

"Of course I remember." She sighed, thinking of that unseasonably warm night in June. He'd held a finger to her lips to shush her, and then he'd pulled her right back to the elevator she'd just exited. Instead of going down, they'd risen all the way to the top of the building.

They'd emerged onto a beautiful rooftop deck, the limestone tiles scattered with wooden lounge chairs and small potted trees. A few gas grills awaited visitors, but they were alone. "Look at that view," she'd exclaimed, her hand tucked deliciously into his. The sun had been setting behind clouds that tipped the mountains of the Front Range, the rays blazing orange and pink on the horizon.

"It's even better over here," he'd purred, tugging her toward a low stone wall.

When they reached it, she balked. It wasn't the edge of the building, but it was an unfinished portion of the roof, about a foot lower than where she stood.

"It's perfectly safe," he assured her, ignoring her yelp of terror when he hopped over the wall and landed on the pebbly surface below. "I hang out here all the time."

She blinked away some of her fright and finally saw the patio cushions piled at his feet. Then she saw the bottle of wine and the two glasses.

He winked. "Come on in. The water's fine."

Unwilling to play the coward in front of Micah, she stepped carefully up onto the ledge, took his hand, and let herself slide down into his arms. Unwilling or not, she let out a little scream, but he smothered it with a kiss.

"Now," he murmured, "look at this."

He turned her, and they were closer to the edge of the roof now, with no other buildings between them and the mountains, and she sighed with wonder at the sight.

"Micah. It's so beautiful."

"I knew you'd like it."

He poured them wine and made a little propped bed of the cushions. They'd lain there, hidden from the world, and laughed and sipped wine until they were tipsy. Then they'd made love with nothing but sky and clouds above them as a lightning storm began dozens of miles away beyond Longs Peak.

It had felt like a dream. A fantasy. But it had been real and, in the days after, she'd teared up every time she'd thought of it. Of lying there exposed, his body above hers, inside hers. And he'd watched her face so closely, mapping out each moment of pleasure.

Afterward, watching the bright electric flashes against a darkening sky, Micah had worked a stone loose from the wall behind them and withdrawn a pipe and a small bag of weed. She'd demurred but stretched out naked on the cushions, her legs over his thighs, and watched his face soften as he smoked.

"You're so gorgeous," she purred to him, delighting in his lazy smile of delight at her words.

"Not half as gorgeous as you are."

"You're just saying that because I'm naked." A joke that invited his attention, and he'd given it, stroking his hand up her thigh to her sex to cup her there.

She wanted that again. She wanted it forever.

Watching him as he drove, she squeezed his thigh. "You talked to Johnny?" she finally asked.

"Yes."

"He admitted it?"

"Yes. And I let him know if it ever happened again, I'd personally beat his ass with a pool cue."

"Good."

"He is sorry, though. He seemed . . . I don't know. Almost distraught. Something is going on with him. I'll dig a little deeper."

Yes, something was definitely going on with him. This was her chance. She could just blurt it out. Ask for Micah's help and support.

But she wanted that night on the roof again someday, even if it was years from now. She wanted a real date. Wanted to get dressed up and go out and spend a romantic evening on the town before they went back to his bed. And then she wanted to sleep there. The whole night. Wanted to slide into dreams as he whispered *I love you* in her ear.

Or else she really, really wanted an escape fantasy from her real life.

Whichever it was, the truth would send him running. She'd run from it herself if she could. And even if she couldn't be with him, she still needed him as a friend. So she shook her head and shrugged. "Who knows. He's been really busy with work. And that girlfriend, I guess."

"Yeah. He's definitely stressed about something."

They pulled up to the restaurant, and Veronica waited in the car while he ran in to pay for the food. She breathed in the scent of his soap warmed by the leather of the seats. The car was neat, all the surfaces shiny and dust-free. She poked at a compartment over her head and it opened to reveal a pair of expensive-looking sunglasses.

With a glance at the restaurant door, she opened the glove compartment as well. She reached for a pair of black driving gloves and the leather yielded to her touch with hardly any pressure. She wondered how much they'd cost. Wondered if they'd been a gift and from whom.

When the restaurant door swung open, she withdrew her hands with a squeak and slammed the compartment closed.

She'd poked around in his apartment once while he was sleeping. Everything had been clean and neat and in its place. The opposite of her own home.

Maybe she wasn't in love with Micah. Maybe she was only interested in his high-end lifestyle.

He caught her grinning when he slid back into the driver's seat. "What?" he asked as he handed her the big white bag of food.

"Nothing. You're just cute."

He gave her a quick kiss like they were a real couple. She resisted asking him to drive around town for a while so they could hold hands and listen to music. But just barely.

Her smile faded as they drove the familiar streets back to her house. "I can't leave yet," she finally said.

"What do you mean?"

"I can't leave Johnny yet. But I will one day."

Micah shook his head and blew out a long breath. "I told you not to confront him."

The words stabbed her in her softest place. The little spot where she nurtured her secret hopes. The place she held her love for him. She heard a growl leave her throat. "You . . . Are you trying to talk me into staying with him? Long-term? After what he did?"

"I didn't say that."

"No. No, you didn't say *that*. But you just reminded me I shouldn't rock the boat. You want things to stay the same, even if I have to stay with a man who hit me. You want me once a week. Maybe twice if you sneak into my bathroom when my husband is drunk and distracted. That's enough for you, right? Anything else would be too much?" She ran her hands over her face with a disgusted sigh.

"Come on, V. Calm down. I don't want this all to end badly for you guys. You have your daughter to think of. That's all I'm concerned about."

"I don't need to be reminded about my daughter, thanks."

"I didn't mean you should stay with him forever. I just meant let's handle this carefully. He's not going to do it again. He's genuinely ashamed."

Her lips parted, but what else could she say? She'd just admitted she couldn't leave Johnny now anyway. But she'd wanted Micah to fight, damn it. To fight for her or them or something.

Veronica stared out the windshield as the houses slid past. She watched the world shift as Micah turned onto her street. Watched her house grow slowly larger and then her husband stand up from the porch step she'd been sitting on herself not twenty minutes before.

Micah was delivering her back to Johnny. He'd eat dinner with them, and have a few drinks with his good buddy, and at the end of the evening he'd say goodbye and leave her there.

"You said you loved me," she whispered, lips numb and tongue dry as bone.

"I *do* love you, V. I just want everyone to be happy. I don't want to destroy anyone's life." *Most of all mine.* He didn't say it, but she heard it clear as day.

And she saw it then. The truth. That she was clinging to Micah just as she'd clung to her father—just as she had to Johnny. One more hard-to-hold man whose attention she needed like oxygen. She was the same desperate little girl she'd always been. Only the name of the man had changed.

Micah pulled next to the curb and she scrambled out of the car to get away from him. In a parody of choosing her husband, she made a beeline for Johnny, rushing toward the door at his back.

"Hey, babe. You went with Micah?"

"Yes, Johnny. I went with Micah." She held up the paper bag as evidence as she walked past him and into the house.

After dropping the bag on the counter, she dug out the pork lo mein and the entire bag of crab Rangoon; then she added a fork and a beer to her haul and headed for the bedroom. She didn't want to pretend with either of them anymore. She didn't even want to look at them.

"I should've grabbed another beer," she muttered as she kicked the door shut behind her and set the food carefully on the mattress.

"Babe?" Johnny called faintly from the kitchen.

"I'm watching something on Netflix!" she yelled back.

That seemed to satisfy him. She heard their voices again, woven together, both conspiring to enjoy their evening without her. She popped open the beer, turned on the small TV atop the dresser, and called up the trashiest reality show she could find. She ate every last crab Rangoon before they could come looking for them. She knew they were Micah's favorite, and that made them fantastically, maniacally delicious as she washed them down with Johnny's beer.

She'd done everything wrong. She'd tried to improve her unhappy life with one man by turning to another. So stupid. She needed to work on herself and take control of her own crap. Stop chasing men, begging for their attention. She was so far from control now that it felt almost impossible to grab it again. She had to do better.

The show blared on the TV, but Veronica's mind easily tuned it out, refusing to be distracted from her worries. She searched for news stories on her phone about the kidnapping but found no updates.

No news was good news. Or no news meant the police were quietly surrounding the house with long guns loaded, ready to break down the door and drag them to jail. She couldn't know. She could never know. It might be today. It might be next year. It might be ten years from now when someone finally cracked.

Thank God she'd put the money back. They couldn't convict her of anything.

Or maybe they could.

She'd eaten only a few bites of lo mein when her stomach turned and she had to set down the container. Wives couldn't be compelled to testify against their spouses, but were they required to turn them in for crimes?

Aware that she was likely leaving an easily traceable trail, she searched *criminal liability spouse* on her phone. Most of the results that popped up were explanations of spousal abuse. She snorted a humorless laugh and tried again.

Can a spouse be an accomplice? God, she was really painting a picture for the police here. She typed in *I didn't do anything criminal but my stupid husband did*, just for a laugh. Her phone suddenly froze and then powered down.

She tossed it aside with a curse and reached for the charger at the side of her bed. Her fingers found only air. The cord was still in her purse and her purse was in the living room, and she refused to set foot in there. She'd been so happy with Micah for a few sweet minutes and then he'd ruined it all.

"Fuck." She checked Johnny's side of the bed, but of course he hadn't conveniently left a cord. Why make things easier for her?

She snatched up her half-empty beer and quietly opened the door. The men were still talking, their voices more normal and relaxed, now that the uncomfortable question of Veronica had been brushed aside. They were back to being friends, the kidnapping wife slapper and the cuckolding buddy. Even now, when Micah's laugh echoed down the hallway, Veronica's stupid heart lurched.

She told herself none of it mattered. Her feelings were hurt. She ached deep down inside. But he'd never promised her anything. Hell, all she'd even bothered asking for was a little niceness, and how pitiful was that? He'd signed up for an affair, and he'd never hinted at spinning something more from those threads.

But he loves you, a pitiful voice whispered inside her.

Sure. Sure, he did. He also loved crab Rangoon, and maybe she was just another consumable item.

"Bastard," she whispered before tiptoeing to Sydney's room and closing the door.

Once she'd settled at Sydney's desk, she wiggled the mouse to wake the computer. The CPU whirred and the sound of the fan reminded her it was past time to vacuum the dust out of it. The thing seemed overheated as soon it was touched.

She swigged her beer and waited impatiently for the screen to wake up. The fan roared with effort. She took another sip. Nothing happened. She wiggled the mouse again, then tapped a key on the keyboard. "Come on."

When there was still no response from the monitor, she set down her bottle with a groan and dipped her head to find the power button. A nose full of dust later, she pressed the monitor's hidden On button. Still nothing. She tried again. No response. No error. Not even a light.

With no other choice but to crawl under the tiny desk, she shoved the chair back and got on her hands and knees to trace the cord down to the power strip. It lay useless and unplugged on the floor.

"Victory," she murmured, plugging it back in. When she finally got her head above the desk, the monitor was glowing white, most of the screen a blank expanse of unwritten document. But there was one lone word. Johnny.

Frowning now, she stroked the wheel on the mouse and shifted the document down. The largely blank page disappeared and revealed that the first page was a letter addressed "To The World." And it started with "I'm sorry."

Johnny was confessing.

She reeled back in the chair, hand flying to her mouth to cover her horror or surprise or relief, she didn't even know. Had he decided to turn himself in? Did she even want him to?

If he went to jail, Sydney would know everything. Her friends and schoolmates would know everything. Her daughter would be devastated. Her poor little baby.

But Veronica shouldn't try to stop him if he was doing the right thing. But what the hell was the right thing, anyway?

"Okay, okay, okay," she whispered to herself. *Read the letter. Then think. Then decide.*

> I'm sorry. I never wanted it to be this way, but everything got so out of control. I just wanted a better life.
>
> I haven't been able to provide for my family. Not really. I wanted to give my little girl the best and I couldn't. I needed money.

Her eyes welled up from reading Johnny's pain. She didn't begrudge him his hurt. She knew he'd always had dreams; he just hadn't been able to make them come alive. "I'm sorry," she whispered, briefly blinded by her tears.

They hadn't had the right time together. If she hadn't gotten pregnant, maybe she'd have had more freedom to nurture him. Maybe he would have matured and they'd have built something grand. More likely they'd have dated for another year or two and grown apart. Either way, he might have been more focused and successful. Instead he'd just gotten lost, overwhelmed by new responsibilities. They'd both gotten lost.

She wiped her eyes on her T-shirt and tipped her gaze toward the ceiling until the urge to cry faded. Once Micah left, she and Johnny could figure this out. He might serve hardly any time at all if he struck a deal to testify against Trey and company. Bro loyalty or not, he had Sydney to protect. Surely he would do it.

One more swipe of her eyes and she had it together enough to focus on the screen again.

I needed money. I wanted to start a real business.

I thought if I could just make this plan work, everything would be better. No one would get hurt. I could pay my bills, buy a better house, maybe my wife would even stop cheating on me.

Veronica's heart froze.

"Oh God," she moaned. He knew. She'd told herself she didn't care if he knew, but it wasn't true. She hadn't wanted to hurt him; she'd just wanted to stop her own constant, aching pain. "Jesus, Johnny. I'm sorry."

The Holcombs seemed like an easy target. I didn't think they would even miss the cash. I didn't hurt the boy. I swear. I never hurt him.

She frowned. That didn't make any sense. Why was he taking all the blame?

The cops are getting closer. They won't stop asking questions and they'll find the phone records eventually. I can't go to jail. My daughter . . . My daughter will be better off without us. Sydney, I'm so sorry. Grandma will take good care of you.

The chill started at the top of her head. It coiled behind her ears and then slid down her neck and chest until her nipples drew tight with prickling terror.

What the hell did he mean by *us*?

"No," she whispered. Then she said it more loudly. *"No."*

This was why Johnny had arranged for Sydney to be out of the house. Not because he was getting a lecture from Micah but because later he was he planning to . . .

She sprang up from the chair with such force that it rolled until it hit Sydney's bed. Her body rocked back and forth. She just stood there, unable to make another move. She didn't have any idea what to do. Her phone was dead in the next room. Her husband was down the hall between her and both exits from the house.

But Micah was there too. Micah was here. Thank God. Imperfect, inconstant Micah. He was still *here* and he'd come here to protect her.

She stepped carefully to the door and put her ear to it. Nothing. But Johnny could be on the other side, waiting. What if Micah had left and she hadn't heard the front door close? What if Johnny was lurking there, ready to put his plan into action?

Her breath came faster and faster until she was panting. The door loomed like a threat, as if the wood itself were the danger. She backed away from it, stared at the knob.

He wasn't standing there. She knew that. He wasn't there.

She closed her eyes and strained her ears, and even over her hammering heart she could hear a low rumble of conversation from the front room. Still, her hand shook as she reached out. Once you realized your husband was planning to kill you, reality felt a little less concrete. Any minute now an ax head could burst through the wood and he'd be standing there Jack Nicholson–style, and she'd be trapped.

Fighting every instinct her body had to retreat and hide, she gripped the knob and forced herself to turn it. Slowly, slowly. Once the latch was fully free, she eased the door open a quarter of an inch and put her eye carefully to the gap.

The hallway was empty. Of course it was. What she'd thought was conversation was actually a basketball game, but she could hear Micah's voice too, thank God. He hadn't left her.

Slightly calmer, she opened the door all the way and stepped into the hall, craning her neck to see as far around the corners as she could. Johnny could be in the kitchen. He could be getting a beer. But she didn't hear any creak or shift of floorboards, and the fridge hummed on steadily without the loud hum of the fan that signaled someone had opened it.

Veronica tiptoed across the old wood. When a board snapped under her toes, she cringed and froze as if stillness could take back the sound. Her breath a rock in her throat, she waited, but the game jangled on in the living room. They couldn't hear anything over that noise, surely.

She reached the hated basement door and eased past it. Two more feet and she was at the end of the hall. But she wasn't strong enough to brave a look. She pressed her back to the wall and whispered a soundless prayer for courage.

Just a few more inches. Johnny would be sitting in his favorite chair, his back to the hallway. He always sat there unless he was snuggling with his family. Why would anything be different just because he planned to murder her?

Holding her breath, she eased her face past the corner, then jerked it back again. Yes. Johnny's back was to her, and Micah was on the couch.

She stepped out from the wall and exposed herself, one finger already to her lips to signal Micah to silence. His eyes stayed locked on the television for an eternally long moment as her heart tried to pound its way out of her chest. When she saw his eyes shift and his head swing up, Veronica was already shaking her head in warning, finger pressed so hard to her lip that she tasted the copper tang of blood.

No, no, don't react! Please don't react!

His eyes widened. He jerked his head back to the TV.

When he glanced over again, he barely turned toward her. Finger still locked to her lips, she gestured for him to follow and then she moved as quickly as she could back to Sydney's room. Through the open door she could just make out Micah's offer to get Johnny another beer.

"Sure, thanks," her husband called out.

"Here you go, man. I've got to take a piss."

Veronica clenched her hands tight to her throat and waited. Micah walked past the doorway, then stuttered to a stop and backed up. She frantically waved him in, then shut the door behind him as quietly as she could.

"He's going to kill me," she whispered as she grabbed his arm with both hands.

"Why?"

"No, I mean he's really going to kill me. *Johnny.* I found a note. He plans to kill me and himself."

Micah laughed. He actually laughed and shook his head. "Come on, Veronica. It's Johnny. He's not going to kill you."

"I found a *note*!" she repeated, tightening her hold on his biceps, shaking him, trying to make him believe. "And keep your voice down. Please."

His smile froze to a grimace before finally fading. "What do you mean? Like a suicide note?"

"Yes. Yes!"

His amusement had disappeared, but he still shook his head again. "I don't believe it."

Veronica growled and let him go to gesture toward the monitor. "Read it! It's right there. He even knows about you and me! I need help. I need to . . ."

He moved to the desk and she just stood there, arms still raised, fingers still curled to try to grab on to anything that might help her. "I need to get out of here," she whispered.

"What the fuck . . . ?" Micah was murmuring. "What the hell is he talking about? Is this about the steroids?"

"No. It's bigger than that. Micah, I need to leave now. Sydney is with her grandfather, so she's safe, but I'm . . . He must have bought a gun, I don't know. He used to shoot for fun, but I wouldn't let him have a gun in the house with Sydney."

Micah stood and turned to her, his mouth a straight, hard line. "What do you need from me?"

"I don't know. If you can distract him . . . I need to get to my car. I need my keys. I can just . . . I don't know! If we call the cops, anything could happen. He could start a firefight. I don't know what to do!"

He reached for her, ran his hands up her arms, squeezed her shoulders. "Shh. It's okay. I'm here."

"Oh God, Micah. I don't want you in danger either. If he thinks you're helping . . ."

"Listen. Can you climb out one of these windows?"

"I . . . Yes. I think so. Sure."

"You get outside. He'll have no idea that you're even gone. I'll stroll back into the living room and tell him I got a call from a client I need to return. I'll say my goodbyes; then I'll pull around to the mouth of the alley and pick you up. We'll get somewhere safe and figure this out."

She nodded and nodded, relieved to have a plan. "Yes. Yes, this will work. Just be careful. He knows we're having an affair, apparently. He might be out to hurt you too."

"Don't you worry about me, V. Just get out and stay safe until I pick you up. He's had four or five beers. He's not going to notice anything." He kissed her then. Kissed her quick and hard, then wiped the pad of his thumb gently over a tear on her cheek. "You know what to do? Out the window, then get to the end of the alley."

"Yes."

"I'll see you in a few minutes."

Micah swung open the bedroom door as if he weren't afraid of anything. Instead of walking toward the living room, he turned left into the bathroom and flushed the toilet.

Veronica stayed frozen for a moment before realizing she should use the rushing of the old plumbing as cover for opening the window. She closed the bedroom door, then raced toward the window, popped the locks, and pushed up as hard as she could. The old metal groaned, but the toilet was still running loudly. Thank God for the ancient ten-quart tank. She forced herself to keep shoving until the pane slid fully open. Then she pressed the springs on the screen and pushed it out, letting it fall to the rocky dirt below.

She was too old for graceful window scaling. First she tried to put one leg through. Then she tried the other. Then she gave up, pulled Sydney's desk chair close, and climbed onto it. Once she was standing with both feet on the sill, she lowered herself to a sitting position, let her legs dangle, then ducked her head outside as well, until the only part of her inside was her butt.

It was only a four-foot drop, but she still held her breath as she pushed off, praying that she wouldn't break an ankle or scrape her entire back against the wall.

She landed before she could even finish the prayer. And she was fine. She spun on one foot and took off running for the alley and the safety of Micah's car.

CHAPTER 25

Micah wasn't there. He wasn't there and that was okay, because he hadn't promised to spring out of the house and race his car around the corner with tires squealing, but . . . he still wasn't there.

Veronica paced down the sidewalk for a moment, then back. Had he meant the other end of the alley? He couldn't have. Their house was only a third of a block from this corner. The other end of the alley was twice as far away.

Still, she spun and stared down the long cement line, suddenly aware of just how many bushes and garage overhangs had been put there to block her view.

"Damn it."

She heard a distant car door close and held her breath. Was it him? It had come from that direction. But maybe it was Johnny. Maybe he'd already shot Micah and he was coming to hunt her down. She assumed she would've heard a gunshot, but people were killed all the time and not found until days later. So maybe—

His car turned the corner and headed up the narrow street toward the mouth of the alley, and Veronica sobbed with relief. She bounced on her toes and covered her mouth to keep from crying out.

As he was pulling up, she raced to open the door before he'd even come to a complete stop. "Thank you!" she cried as she slammed the door shut. He didn't wait for her to order him to drive. He hit the gas hard and they were racing out of the neighborhood before she even had her seat belt in her hand.

"Oh God, Micah. This is insane."

"What should we do?"

"Call the police."

"If he has a gun, he could end up dead," he cautioned.

"I'm not sure I care at this point."

"Okay, I'll call." He reached for the phone he'd tossed on his dashboard.

"Wait. Should we check to be sure Sydney is safe first? Johnny could go after her."

"He sent her away so she'd be safe. He wouldn't hurt her."

Veronica covered her face. "I know, but I didn't think he'd hurt me either. Jesus, I don't know what to do! If we call the police . . . That's what we should do, right? But if he has a gun they might *kill* him. He needs help. And I . . ." She couldn't think. "Micah, this is such a mess. I don't know what to do. I'm sorry to even get you involved."

"I'm not sorry. If I hadn't been there tonight, who knows what would have happened? I talked to him a little, but then he said we'd talk more after Sydney was out of the house. I never thought . . ."

She nodded. "I know."

Micah turned right on a main thoroughfare, then stole a glance at her face.

"What?" she asked.

"You said this wasn't about dealing drugs?"

"Oh God." She sighed. "No. It's something much bigger. And I screwed up and got myself involved too."

"With what?"

"You don't want to know."

"Veronica." He set the phone back on the dashboard. "I want to know. I want to fucking fix this. Say the word and I'll call the cops right now. Or we can drive and you can tell me what the hell is going on. I'll do whatever you want, whatever you need. I'm here. Okay?"

He was here. He'd just rescued her from being murdered by her own husband. And if she was going to call the cops, Micah would find himself smack in the middle of this investigation whether he wanted to be or not.

"The letter said something about the Holcombs . . ."

She stared at the mountains ahead for a moment. The Holcomb estate was up there somewhere, with a view of the whole city beneath them. On a hilltop, safe above it all, they'd felt invincible and let their guard down.

"He was involved in the kidnapping," she finally blurted out.

"No. No fucking way."

"He was. I found fifty thousand dollars in the basement. And there was the phone. It wasn't for his affair."

"You're saying he kidnapped that kid?"

"I think it was Trey. Or maybe it was Neesa or her husband. Johnny said he just agreed to 'rescue' Tanner. You know? He said he wasn't there for the kidnapping, and I know that's the truth. He was with me that day. He has an alibi. But in the letter he confessed to everything. It makes no sense."

"Are you sure he couldn't have done it?"

"He was only out of the house for an hour that afternoon. He went for a run."

"But you're the only one who can confirm that?"

"Yeah." She shook her head. "It must be Neesa. He's trying to protect her." Veronica laughed and threw her hands in the air. "My God, he's in love with her and he was trying to protect her by killing me! Apparently I don't know anything about him! I didn't even know he could write a decent letter. Half of his texts are abbreviations."

Micah patted her hand. "So I don't get it. How are you involved? Were you in on it? You knew?"

"No! Of course not. I didn't suspect anything until I found that phone. And I didn't *know* anything until I found the money. Even then I thought it might be drugs. Jesus."

"So you found the money and he confessed?"

"Yeah." The mountains loomed larger. Veronica slid a little lower in her seat and tried to relax enough to think. "Then I took some of the cash. I thought Syd and I would need it if Johnny was arrested. It was a mistake. I put it back, but I'm still worried. What if they find my DNA on the money?"

"Jesus, V."

"I know."

Micah's phone rang, the buzz so startling that Veronica yelped with fear. Johnny's name appeared on the screen and her yelp turned into a groan. Micah touched the phone and silenced it.

"Okay, listen. Don't worry about him. Let's go somewhere safe for the night. If he can't find you, he can't . . . do anything. We'll figure out a strategy for approaching the police. Maybe contact a lawyer. We'll do this the right way, without rushing into anything. We need to frame our involvement as something innocent."

"Yeah. That's a good idea. You're so smart. We should get Sydney, though. I don't want to scare her, but what if he decides to . . . Jesus. He'd never hurt her, would he?"

"He won't hurt Sydney. If he wanted to hurt you, it was because of . . . well . . . me, I guess."

"Did you tell him?"

"No, of course not!"

"He never mentioned it to you?" she pressed. "Hinted that he knew?"

"I had absolutely no idea. He never let on. I never wanted him to know."

She nodded, fully aware Micah had meant to keep everything on the down-low. "Let me think about Sydney. They're out in public right now anyway. She's safe with my dad for a couple of hours."

Micah turned right and they curled through Golden, rising higher, the mountains now blocked by the foothills. "Do you think we should find a hotel?" she asked, aware of how excited she would have been by the idea just an hour ago.

"Yeah. We can't go to my place, obviously. He'll look there."

"If he thinks we're together."

"Your car is still home, and apparently he knows why you'd leave with me."

"Right." She let her mind drift for a while, still turning over the pros and cons of getting Sydney. How would she explain that her daughter needed to leave her grandfather and come with her mom to a hotel without scaring her? But maybe she *should* be scared. Sydney's father had orchestrated a kidnapping and was planning to kill her mom.

"Johnny was going to kill me." The words fell from her mouth, pushed by the sudden horror of it welling up in her. The initial shock had worn off. The stark fear had faded. Now she felt the dark cavern of this knowledge she would carry with her the rest of her life. She'd loved this man, married him, borne his child, built a life, and he'd meant to cut her down and take away his daughter's mom and dad in one cruel act.

She curled up in the seat and wept. Past her sobbing, she distantly felt Micah stroking her hair. "Even"—she drew a shuddering breath and sobbed again—"even if he hated me . . . how could he do that to Sydney?"

"He's not thinking straight."

"Clearly!" She tried to wipe her face, but the tears kept coming as they rounded a curve. She ducked her head and let herself cry until she couldn't anymore.

"I'm sorry," she choked out as she wiped her face on her shirt. She sat up a little and blinked hard. "Where are we?" Even past her tears she could see that the road was narrowing and the houses were farther apart and higher up.

"Near Black Hawk. Plenty of hotel rooms, and he won't find us there. We can get a room. Have dinner and drinks."

"Dinner?" She couldn't imagine eating right now, but that didn't mean Micah wanted to starve with her.

She wiped her face on her shirt again, but she really needed something more substantial. Her nose was clogged up and she didn't want to imagine what had already leaked out.

She popped open the glove compartment. "Do you have Kleenex?"

"Hey," he said as she moved aside the black gloves. Beneath the gloves lay a black canvas case that felt heavy when she shifted it. Micah's hand darted past hers to slide it from the glove compartment and out of her way.

"Napkins." She sighed with relief and pulled out the small stack, thinking she'd need all of them.

"Hey," he repeated as he grabbed a phone that had been hidden at the bottom of the compartment.

A phone. She frowned and glanced at the phone on Micah's dashboard, then back to the one in his hand. "What's that?" The question sounded like an echo in her hollowed-out mind.

"Oh." His eyebrows jumped and he cleared his throat. "That."

"Yes." She snatched it from his fingers and touched a button. The screen lit up with a lock screen she recognized. "Micah? What is this?"

"Yeah. Well . . . Johnny asked me to hold it for him."

"This phone? He asked you to keep it?"

"Yes."

They rose higher, climbing the road toward the little gambling town perched in the mountains. The sky was turning a darker blue, edging toward sunset. "He told me he destroyed it."

"I had no idea it had anything to do with a kidnapping, or I wouldn't have taken it. He's going to get me into trouble."

"He is." Trouble. Trouble that was starting to turn to a strange static in her mind. She cleared her throat. "You should just take me back. Drop me at a police station."

He shook his head and kept driving.

Veronica sat up straighter and inhaled, filling her lungs with oxygen, fighting off the static of fear and the fog of stress that had been pushing her down. It cleared a little, revealing a sharper emotion. The shivering edge of panic. "This is too far. Let's go back. I think I need to get Sydney."

"I need to keep you safe."

"We can go to any hotel, Micah. He won't be able to find me as long as I don't use one of our credit cards. Let's go back to Denver."

"Sure," Micah said, and some of that sharp fear receded. "Let me get to a turnaround."

She waited for the next turn, but they'd already driven past all the neighborhoods and were surrounded by nothing but trees. Acid burned in her throat, and her stomach tightened. Too many twists in the road. Bile rose up. So did the hairs on her neck.

Why had Johnny given Micah the phone instead of getting rid of it? Even if he hadn't wanted to destroy it, surely he would have given it to an accomplice. Not Micah.

Not Micah.

Her mind flashed to an image of Johnny hunched over the computer keyboard, hunting and pecking out that suicide note. How long had it taken him? He'd taken time with it, obviously, laboring to be sure there were no typos or misspellings.

Micah was waiting when Syd and I got home.

Chills chased down her arms like sparks. She tried to repress a shiver, but she couldn't quite tamp it down.

"Cold?" Micah asked softly. He reached to turn on her seat warmer, then rested a hand on her knee.

She stared down at his tanned fingers, so familiar and beautiful to her.

Johnny had never said it was Trey. Or Neesa. He'd never confirmed or denied it. He'd refused to say a word.

Micah's fingers squeezed her knee, then patted her reassuringly before returning to the steering wheel.

Why were they even driving into the mountains? They didn't need to get out of town to evade Johnny. There was no way for him to track her down even if she was only a mile from home.

Veronica's mouth dried until her tongue felt stuck to her palate. Another chill flashed through her. Her lungs worked too quickly, pushing out air before she'd snatched the oxygen from it. This couldn't be happening. She was jumping to ridiculous conclusions.

Not Micah. No.

"Micah?" she croaked. "Why is his phone on? Why would . . . why would he give it to you?" She turned to look at him, and he frowned as if he were concerned and confused by the question. But as she watched, his face lost its tension and fell back into smooth lines.

He shrugged one shoulder and made a little clicking sound with his mouth. "Don't freak out. We'll be there soon."

Every hair on her body stood up. *Don't freak out* was secret code for *You'd better freak out.* She reached for the door handle, but Micah sped up and eased a little closer to the rocky shoulder of the mountain road.

"Calm down," he murmured, as soothing as if he were speaking to a frightened child. "If you jump out here you'll lose half your skin and probably most of your skull."

Her eyelids fluttered with shock at his words as she tried to shut out the horror. "What are you doing?" she whispered.

"Taking you somewhere to talk."

She shook her head no. No no no. More lies. Too many of them. "About what?" she managed to ask.

Micah had been waiting for Johnny. He'd been at the house before Johnny got home, and he knew they kept a spare key under a big rock near the garage. He knew because he'd once come to feed Old Man when they were on a weekend trip. So he could have been in the house. He could have had access to the computer, and he could have written that note quickly and with no typos. He never misspelled anything in his texts. That was one of the many things about him that had turned her on. One of the things she'd *loved.*

And now . . .

She glanced toward the rough canvas square on his lap. He'd opened a flap, and she saw the butt of a handgun beneath it. Everything inside her lurched. Her lungs seized up. "Micah," she croaked, his name a terrible, twisted whine in her parched throat.

"I just want to talk," he said.

She shook her head again, denying everything. He didn't need to drive her into the mountains to talk. He didn't need a gun to talk. And she'd already done everything wrong that she could have done. She'd left her phone at the house. She'd told no one where she was going. She'd let him move her to another location.

"Micah." Saying his name again set off a quiet explosion inside her chest. She'd let this man into her body. She'd loved him and craved him and lied so she could have more of him. And he was a kidnapper. And probably worse than that.

"There's more money," he said, so friendly and calm. "Another fifty thousand for Johnny once the storm has passed. All you have to do is keep your mouth shut."

She started to shake her head one more time but then realized her mistake and nodded. He wasn't her lover anymore. He wasn't someone to argue with. Of course she'd keep her mouth shut. Of course. She nodded over and over, but she couldn't even feel it. Her entire head felt numb even as her chest burned.

"We can come to a separate agreement, you and I. You know I'd never hurt you, V."

But he'd written that note. It was so clear now. He had the gun. He'd written the note. He'd somehow talked Johnny into getting rid of Sydney for the night. He'd invited himself to stay for dinner so that he could get Johnny drunk and stage a murder-suicide. Maybe he'd meant to slip her something too so he could arrange them at will for the final shots.

She heard a soft noise come from her own mouth. The mouth this man had kissed. The mouth that had made love to him. A sound of grief and horror.

"The phone," he said softly, almost to himself. "The phone has been to the Holcomb property. It's been to the cabin. I gave it to Johnny the day before the rescue so I could send him the pickup location via text. He happily accepted it and has kept it in your home ever since except when he took it to his work. It places him at every important spot since the day before little Tanner was kidnapped. You know what that means?"

She should. She knew she should, but her brain was a Tilt-A-Whirl, spinning and sliding. Veronica shook her head. She felt a tear slide off her cheek and hit her hand.

"What?" she pushed out.

"His possession of the phone implicates Johnny and maybe you. After all, he says he was home that day, but how could he have been? His phone was in the mountains."

"But he *was* home that day."

"Really? Who says he was?"

Oh. Oh God. She was the only witness. Well, Sydney, yes, but people would discount her story. She was ten. The police hadn't even bothered interviewing her.

Veronica was his only alibi. And Micah had just passed the exit for Black Hawk and kept driving.

It had been him on the phone the whole time. Not Neesa. Not Trey. She'd told him she'd found the phone, so he'd sent messages that would reinforce her fears and keep her quiet.

Micah slowed to take the next turn onto a narrow road, and before she could think about it, before she could let herself change her mind, Veronica yanked on the door handle and threw herself free.

Or she tried to.

The door swung open and she was reaching for the seat belt when her head jerked back and exploded with a thousand shards of pain. When he slammed on the brakes her body pitched forward, but her head stayed tight in his cruel grip. The door clapped shut from the force of the movement before he eased the car to the shoulder. Micah's fist twisted in her hair and she heard several strands pop free of her scalp even though she didn't feel it.

She reached desperately for his wrist, digging her nails into his skin in a parody of passion. "Please," she begged. "Please, Micah. I love you. Don't. Please."

"I said I didn't want to hurt you. What the hell are you doing? I just want to talk."

"Yes. I'm sorry. I'm just scared. I panicked. Please."

"Lock the door."

She slapped her hand against the door and hit the lock. "Okay. I'm sorry. I want to talk too. I'm just confused, Micah. I'm just . . . I thought you were my friend. I thought . . ." The words broke off on a sob she couldn't contain as his grip loosened and the agony in her scalp eased.

"We *are* friends, V. Just like Johnny and I are friends. You didn't seem to think that should stop me from fucking his wife."

"I'm sorry. I know. You're right." She'd say anything. Anything he wanted. He was a stranger. A killer. He wasn't Micah anymore. She didn't know who he was.

"Jesus Christ," he sighed, sounding for all the world like an exasperated parent being put out by an unruly toddler. "Just calm down, okay? Everything's fine."

"Yes." She nodded, turning toward him, finally catching a glimpse of the open case and the gun in his hand. Her bladder threatened to let loose at the sight. She clenched her thighs tight and pressed her shaking hands to her knees.

"If I'd wanted to kill you, I would have done it at the house. I just want to go somewhere to talk."

"Yes." No. Whatever he'd planned at the house had likely not involved them both awake and sober. This was plan B. "I'm calm," she assured him as he stared at her. She tried a smile but it twisted into a grimace.

"Don't try anything again."

"I won't."

He took his foot off the brake and they were back on the road, weaving through towering pine trees and sheer rock walls that made her feel like they were the only people in the world. There was no help for her here. No one to save her. No one to take her back to Sydney.

"Fuck," he suddenly huffed, chuckling a little. "You really are brave, V. I didn't think you'd actually try to jump from a moving car. But I should have guessed. I've always loved how bold you are."

The compliment cut like a blade, freeing memories like blood. The time she'd lured him into a bathroom at a pub, the time she'd texted Johnny from Micah's bed even as Micah went down on her, and just last week when they'd had sex on her own bathroom sink.

She'd craved compliments like that. She'd wanted him to know how wild she was. Not just a wife and a mom and a career woman but a hungry *force*. Now he tossed his dirty, tattered compliment at her as if he thought she'd still be happy she pleased him. She burned with awful shame. Regret swelled the wound inside her. She deserved this. She'd been dumb and desperate and awful, wanting more when she'd already had everything.

She'd thrown her life away for this monster.

As he took another turn, this time onto a dirt road, Veronica realized the most horrible truth of all. He was showing her exactly where the cabin was. He hadn't even asked her to close her eyes, much less ordered her to blindfold herself. Even the dumbest criminal wouldn't give her this power over him, and Micah was so damn smart.

There was no question he meant to kill her. And whether Veronica deserved to pay for her sins or not, Sydney didn't deserve to be left alone. She had to find a way out of this. She had to get back to her daughter.

"Micah?" she whispered.

"Hm?"

She cleared her throat to try to get her voice back from its hiding place. "Why? Why did you involve Johnny? Wouldn't it have been less risky on your own?"

"He needed the money."

"Oh, you were being selfless?"

He actually flashed a smile at her sarcasm. "Okay. He needed the money and I needed insurance. I didn't plan on sacrificing Johnny. But if things got too heated . . ."

"He's your fall guy."

"Yes. But he needn't be. All right? It's in your best interest to stay quiet, V. On every single level. Keep your mouth shut, keep your head down, and in a few months Johnny gets the rest of his money, and I'll give you a bonus too."

"How much?" she asked, as if she really believed this ridiculous lie.

He had the nerve to wink at her. "Depends how convincing you are."

"Are you saying I have to keep sleeping with you?"

"Have to?" Another smile, this one warm and welcoming as he glanced at her. The smile of a con artist. "I'm not a rapist. It's always good between us."

She looked away, bile surging in her gut at the affection in his voice. How could he do this? And how could he sound so sweet while he did? Who the hell was this man? She pressed a hand to her mouth at the thought of everything she'd willingly given him.

He sighed. "No, that's not what I meant. Come on. I'd miss you if you cut this off, but I guess I understand. Things have changed now. But I really do care about you, whether you believe that or not."

Did *he* believe that? Could he justify all this to himself, or was he some of kind of sociopath who needed no justification at all? He'd had a rough start in life. She knew that. His dad had left before he was born. He'd never once met him. His mom had remarried several times, and Micah spoke of his stepfathers with dark bitterness. His mom he didn't speak of at all. Had his childhood warped him into a monster?

God, she'd never sensed that from him. He'd been driven, yes. Ambitious. And he'd loved the finer things in life. She'd seen that as a grasp at the security he'd never had in childhood. She'd admired that he wanted something better for himself. She'd wanted that too.

The road narrowed until the trees blocked out the last lingering light of the evening. They dipped into a rut and back out. They had to be close to the end. The end of the road. The end of her life. No one would even find her body up here. The Holcomb estate was south of Golden and they were north. No one would search here. She'd just be one more woman who'd disappeared. Sydney would never know. She'd spend her whole life motherless and suffering.

No.

"Micah, we've had our talk. We can go home. I won't say anything to anyone. I wasn't ever going to say anything! Why would I? I'd lose everything."

But she'd spoken too late. Micah took a slow left turn onto a trail so unused and narrow, she wouldn't have spotted it if they'd driven by. Pine needles and branches scraped the windows and the top of the car. They were being eaten, swallowed, devoured, by a green-black night.

"Micah, please."

"I just want to talk." He said it so sadly, like a goodbye. He wasn't even pretending she'd get out of this now. Unless the sorrow was a lie too. It had to be.

"Please don't do this to Sydney," she said as a sob rose up and tore from her throat. She gave up the pretense that she believed him and grasped his arm in a death grip. "Please. Sydney is just a little girl. I have to get back to her. She needs me. She needs her mom."

The car suddenly popped free of the forest's hold and they were in a narrow, shadowed clearing. She whipped her head around in a panic, hoping beyond hope that there were people already there or neighbors or something that would promise safety. But all she saw was a little wooden cabin listing slightly to the right, the windows shuttered and the roof covered in moss and pine needles. Her coffin.

Micah was ready for her attempt to escape this time, and his gun pressed into her temple when her fingers touched the door handle. "Don't move." Goose bumps spread over her arms and down her body, pulling her skin so tight it hurt.

She heard the click of his seat belt. He opened his door.

Veronica had the courage to wrap a hand around her own handle. She even tugged it toward her. But she didn't push the door open. Her arms were cowards that refused the order. And then Micah was there, pulling the door open for her, the gun waiting patiently at eye level.

"Unbuckle," he said gruffly. Her gaze locked on the tiny black hole that promised a bullet.

She knew he didn't really want to talk. He was proceeding with this charade of a discussion because he didn't want evidence in his car.

Evidence like her blood and brain matter. Veronica shook her head and braced her feet against the floorboard.

"Unbuckle the seat belt and come inside. We'll spend the night here, then go back tomorrow."

"No." She wouldn't make this easy for him. She had to fight for Sydney.

"Veronica, get out of the car."

The second "No" was only forming on her tongue when he grabbed her hair and yanked her halfway out of the car, playing tug-of-war with the seat belt that pulled at her neck and waist. Her head flamed with pain. She grabbed his fist, trying to hang on, trying to ease the tension. And then something heavy fell and dropped her into numb darkness.

CHAPTER 26

Her head throbbed and spun. Her shoulder ached. Something was very wrong with her. There'd been a wreck of some kind. Johnny had rolled the truck. Or she'd crashed her car? Was that what had happened?

The skin of her neck and hip burned, and she thought she could map the injury in the shape of a seat belt. But those pains were a vague annoyance compared to the throbbing beat that had once been the left side of her skull. Every pulse of her blood swelled the pain to an unbearable level before it briefly subsided again.

She tried to raise a hand but, instead of touching her head, she hit herself in the face. That one small defeat felt too difficult to overcome, so she gave up with a groan and let her hands fall to her stomach. She wanted to dip back beneath the surface again. She wanted to sleep until the pain was over. If someone had given her morphine, it had worn off.

"Help," she whispered. "Help." The word stirred alarm inside her rib cage. Her heart fluttered and stammered out a faster beat, and she felt a tear leak from her eye at the quicker pace of the pounding in her head.

Had Veronica been alone? Was Sydney okay?

The eyes she'd kept tightly shut popped open at that thought. Veronica braced herself for the bright lights of a hospital room, but she was met by only a gentle glow somewhere behind her. The rest of the space was a shadowed gradient of brown to black. The soft light behind her revealed only a circle of her world. The bright-blue nylon fabric that covered her chest. A few drops of blood on her sleeve. The vague shapes of her hands. She raised them again, and both her hands came together, bound by a zip tie.

Help.

Not a car accident. Not an accident at all. She remembered the drive and the mountains and she remembered Micah.

Air choked out of her, as if she were retching it from her body.

Micah had shot her. Micah had killed her.

But no. He hadn't done a very thorough job of it. Not only was she not dead, she could still move all her limbs. Careful now that she knew her hands were bound together, she slowly raised them and stretched to touch her scalp as softly as she could. The flesh felt swollen but not destroyed. When she drew back, her fingertips were smeared with only a tiny amount of blood.

Drawing encouragement from that, she touched again, probing a little more firmly. It hurt like hell, but she didn't feel any skull or brain. Apparently he'd only pistol-whipped her.

Did that mean he wasn't going to kill her after all? Even more unlikely, maybe he hadn't even hit her. Maybe she'd just tumbled from the car and slammed her head on the ground.

"Micah?" she croaked. When he didn't answer, she felt a surge of hope that he had simply left her there. She couldn't fathom why he would, but she could hardly think at all. Perhaps he'd changed his mind. Perhaps he'd found his soul.

Her eyes had managed to focus a bit more in the dark. Now she could see a wooden wall across from her and a closed door. She shifted and the bed she was on shifted a little too, making her grab awkwardly at the edge to hold herself still. Her hands found a metal bar. Not a mattress. She was on a cot. The same cot Tanner had slept on, no doubt.

As soon as the thought hit her, she realized she could smell urine, and she pictured poor little Tanner huddled here for four nights, terrified and alone. A man she'd thought she loved had done that to him.

Horror rolled through her, turning her stomach. She swallowed against it. Tried to breathe. Panted instead.

She'd told herself that Johnny had been just as guilty as anyone he'd conspired with, but it wasn't true. Johnny hadn't grabbed that boy and covered his mouth. He hadn't heard that child crying. He hadn't stuffed him with drugs to keep him docile. Micah had done all of that, and—lying here in this dark, dirty cabin—she could feel the terror of it. The heartlessness.

If Micah had left her alone here, she had to escape. If he hadn't, she'd do whatever she needed to do to get back to Sydney.

Veronica twisted to her side and dropped her legs over the edge of the cot. Her shoes scuffed against grit and dirt as she pressed her hands against the stiff edge of the cot and pushed up as hard as she could. Her head screamed in protest and her stomach lurched. She felt her throat pushing up, bile rising, and dropped to her hands and knees on the floor just in time to vomit.

"Oh God," she panted as soon as the waves of nausea subsided. "Oh God."

Everything felt steadier, though, as if her body had made its objection clear and was willing to calm down. She spit and closed her eyes for a moment, waiting for her head to stop spinning. The cold air soothed her and cleared her mind. She could do this.

Sliding her hands back onto the cot, she braced her weight in the middle of the canvas and pushed up, wincing as the frame rocked under the force. But the muscles of her legs eventually decided to contribute and she managed to unfold herself into a standing position.

A brief flare of triumph blazed in her chest, but it faded to nothing when she remembered that standing wasn't the ultimate goal and wouldn't be close to the hardest part of this. She wanted to collapse and cry, but she straightened her shoulders instead, readying herself to walk across the room. She just had a bump on the head. She was fine.

She turned carefully, arms outstretched for balance as she shuffled across the floor, terrified of tripping over some unseen obstacle. When she made it to the door, she leaned against the rough, swollen wood in relief.

There was no knob, only a kitchen cabinet–style handle. She pulled gently at it but felt no give. Holding her breath in fear, she pulled harder. The metal handle dug into her fingers. The door didn't budge.

Hoping it had only swollen into the frame over the decades, she gave up on subtlety and yanked hard, then yanked even harder. Her fingers slipped off the metal, singing with pain. The door wasn't stuck; it was locked or bolted or nailed from the other side.

Pressing her hands to it, she held her breath again and strained to hear any noise through the wood. Was this the front door of the cabin, or was there another room? She'd had only the briefest glimpse when they drove up, but she thought she remembered shuttered windows. There were no windows in this wall. There was another room on the other side, then, and Micah could be right there.

When she turned to survey the rest of the room, there wasn't much to see. An electric lantern hung from a hook in a ceiling beam, and it revealed the cot, a bucket, and a cooler sitting on a bare dirt floor.

The dry sourness of her mouth suddenly overwhelmed her, and she stumbled to the cooler to open it. Fetid air greeted her with no hint of cold. The cooler contained no ice, only an old stick of string cheese and a juice box. She snatched the juice box up and managed to work the straw loose; then she held the box between her knees and pierced it with the straw.

Her stomach rolled when she drank it, but she kept sucking until it was dry. She could almost feel the sugar hit her bloodstream as she walked the perimeter of the room. There was a window just past the cot, or there had been. It had been boarded over with thick planks of wood screwed into the window frame. She gave one of the planks a hopeless tug, but it proved as immovable as the door.

That was it. There was nothing else. Escape was off the table. She'd never get back to Sydney. Never see her as a teenager or adult. Never tell her that her father had done something wrong, but he hadn't hurt that boy. He wasn't a monster; he was only a fool.

She felt her face crumple with tears and groaned. No, she wouldn't break down. She wouldn't give up.

Returning to the door, she leaned close, drawing up every ounce of courage in her cowardly soul. "Micah?" she rasped. He didn't answer. She pressed her ear to the wood and listened for movement. "Micah, are you there? Can we talk now?"

Nothing.

Head pounding, she lowered herself carefully to the floor and slumped against the door to wait for the dizziness to pass. Then she'd try the door again. The window. She'd dig at the dirt of the floor. She'd find a way out.

Sleep must have pulled her under, because she jerked awake at a faint crunching sound, her neck protesting the sudden movement with a jolt of pain. Utterly disoriented, she looked blankly around the room for a moment. A car door closed somewhere, and she was still trying to piece her memory together when she heard a voice.

"What the hell's going on, man?" the muffled voice shouted.

Johnny. She'd run from him earlier, but now her heart leapt with desperate hope. "Johnny!" she croaked out.

"We need to talk," Micah replied, the words soft through the walls.

"Johnny!" she tried again, her voice barely scraping past her parched throat. Her eyes filled with tears as she was buffeted by twin gales of hope and despair. He was here. Here to save her, maybe. Here to talk, even. Maybe Micah would let them go.

But she knew Johnny was really here because Micah wanted them in the same spot. She pushed up to her knees and banged her fists on the door.

"Is this the place, man? What the fuck? I thought I wasn't supposed to know where it was!" He sounded near tears, as if he'd just realized the danger himself.

"Johnny!" This time she had a real voice but she still wasn't loud enough. With a cry of desperation, she got one shaking leg beneath her and forced herself to stand.

Micah murmured something too soft for her to hear past the wood walls of the cabin. Then he said, "I told her everything. She's on board."

"No!" she screamed. "Run! Johnny!"

A moment of silence, and then he shouted, "Babe?"

"Come on," Micah called cheerfully. "We'll have a beer and you can drive her home."

"Thanks," Johnny answered, his voice closer now. *Thanks*, as if he owed Micah his gratitude for this.

"Johnny, run!" she yelled, trying to warn him. "Run! *Run*!"

A lock slid on the other side. She backed up. "Wait. No! Johnny don't—"

The door opened. Her husband surged through the opening. She held up her bound hands, reaching for him, warning him, as he grasped her shoulders. *"No!"* she screamed.

"Babe, what the hell—?" And then he was gone. Not all of him, but important parts of him. His right temple. Part of his eye. A big piece of his head flew off. Her face felt hot and wet as she blinked at him falling away from the gun that had pressed to the right side of his head.

Johnny disappeared and it was only Micah standing there, his lips a tight, white seam. No husband between them anymore. No one at all.

Johnny was dead.

"I didn't want this." His words were far away and muted by the ringing in her ears. She took a step back, shaking her head, her whole body a terrified mess of fight or flight, the muscles screaming for help.

Micah lifted a hand, palm up, as if asking her to understand him. "He was supposed to pick up the kid and be a hero. That was all. He was excited about it. And that was going to be the end. It would have been good for you. For your family. But he couldn't keep his mouth shut. He couldn't even hide a goddamn phone correctly. This is his fault for being an idiot, V. You see that, right?"

She moved away from him, away from the light, as if the darkest corner of the room could protect her, could save her so she could get back to her daughter. Sydney's father was gone, but her mother was still alive. Veronica couldn't give up.

But there was no way out. He'd brought them here to stage a murder-suicide. The only reason he hadn't killed her hours ago was because they both needed to die at the same time, their blood mixing on the floor together.

She could see it all. Johnny's heartfelt suicide note. The blow to her head to keep her quiet. The phone tracing Johnny's path up the mountains. The cabin as a perfect tie wrapping up this gift to detectives. *This is where I kept the kid, and this is where I killed my wife and myself when the investigation closed in on me.*

The end.

Veronica blinked hard, trying to stop the strange movie playing in her head. "No," she whispered.

Micah threw his hands in the air. Hands that had once caressed her and would kill her at any moment now. "Why the hell did he tell you?" he barked. "All he had to say was he was sleeping around. That was it. I gave him the fucking story. You were already jealous of Neesa. I told him exactly what to say."

"Please," she sobbed. "Sydney. She's my baby. She can't be an orphan, Micah, please. She can't be all alone."

"I'm sorry, V. Come on." He reached out his hand as if she'd take it. He wanted her close to Johnny, and he thought she'd just walk over there with him and make it easy. She backed all the way to the wall and slid down into the corner to make herself small.

All she wanted was to return to her daughter. To her life. The perfect life that she'd held in her hands with no appreciation for what she had. That boring, safe, no-frills life she'd being trying so hard to escape. She wanted it back now. She'd had everything. She'd had Sydney. A safe and happy home.

"Micah," she tried. "You love me. You love me; you said you did. Please don't do this. I'll tell the police I lied about his alibi, okay? I'll tell them he came here to commit suicide. I'll write a new note on the computer explaining everything. Just don't leave my baby all alone. Don't kill me. I'll do anything. She *needs* me."

He moved closer, blocking the light, reduced to nothing but a silhouette looming over her as she shifted, pressing her back to the wall, steadying her body. Micah was huge above her. A giant shadow of death, his familiar shoulders distorted by the low light into a darkness that filled her world.

"I'm sorry," he muttered. "I swear I'm sorry. But it's over. I talked Johnny into getting your kid out of the house for the night. I did that. I'm not a monster, Veronica. I wouldn't hurt her. I didn't want to hurt her."

She felt mad, wild, unable to fathom his stupid words. *"How?"* she screamed. "How are you not hurting her? I'm her mother. She *needs* me."

"Johnny did this," he insisted. "Not me. This is his fault."

"This is you," she tried, desperate to change his mind. "*You're* doing this. You don't have to, Micah. You don't have to. Just stop this. It's not too late. I don't care about any of this. I'll lie. I don't care!"

He ducked down and she screamed when he put a hand to her cheek. This man who'd touched her a thousand times. She screamed at the horror of it.

He murmured a soothing "Shhhh," as if that would make her accept her own death.

Her thighs burned from holding her weight. She shifted forward to her toes. "Help me?" she whispered, the words rising with the sickness in her throat. "Help me up and hold me for a minute, please? I'm so scared, Micah. I don't want . . . I don't want to die like this."

"Hey." His hand moved gently to her shoulder.

"I love you," she sobbed, the words a fiery lie in her throat.

"Come here." His left arm slid toward her elbow; his voice hovered just above her. She could see the shadow of the gun in his right hand, pointed toward the wall. "Come on." His breath just above her as if he were whispering all the endearments she'd wanted to hear from him once upon a time.

Wincing in anticipation of the explosion of pain, Veronica ducked her head and surged up, springing tall with all the strength she could summon in her legs. And they were good legs. Runner's legs. She hit him hard, the crack of his nose breaking loud in her ears like the crack of a stick against her head and then his scream filled the room.

She swung her arms high, doing her best to knock his right arm away from her. The gun went off. A flash of light and horrible sound, but she felt no pain, not even a dull punch. Maybe he'd missed her. Maybe she had a chance.

Using the momentum of her own stumbling body, she pressed him farther back, toward the light, toward the—

He fell away from her, tumbled over. The backs of his knees caught against the cot, and the weight of his torso carried him past its corner and down to the floor. A black shape flew toward the doorway, and it had to be the gun or she was dead. If he still had it in his hand, he could easily shoot her whether he was on the floor or not. She jumped toward the doorway and the gun—yes, the gun—had caught up on the rough floor and stopped just outside the threshold.

"Veronica!" he roared, his voice so close behind her. His hand closed over the heel of her shoe, but she jerked her foot free of him and grabbed the gun in both shaking hands. Turning, she fired blindly into the dim room, her bones exploding with each round, arms and head battered by the force. She fired and fired, and then it clicked and clicked and clicked in her grasp.

She was panting. Keening. Each breath a little scream of terror. Her ears sang like twin bells, and if he was coming for her, she couldn't hear him, and she couldn't shoot him. He'd win.

But he didn't move forward. He didn't move at all. He was twisted over Johnny's legs, body slumped against the ground, and part of Micah was missing now too. Part of his jaw. His eyes were on her, though, watching, unblinking.

She stared back, the gun a blur in her shivering hands. "Don't," she croaked one last time, still trying to calm him. He was angry. He must be angry. And she needed to calm him down. "Just don't."

But he was calm, she realized then. He wasn't glaring at her. He wasn't furious. He was a blank. Micah was dead.

Her arms fell. The gun was searing heat against her thigh. She looked from Micah to her husband. Micah's arm was over Johnny's face, hiding the ruin there.

"I have to go," she whispered to Johnny. "I have to leave you here, I'm sorry."

But she sat there still. Her thigh burned. She felt limp as a rag doll and nearly as lifeless. She could sit there forever, she thought. Just give up. It wouldn't take her long to die. She'd already lost blood. She was concussed and in shock.

"I have to *go*," she said again, reminding herself. "I have to go to Sydney."

She dropped the gun to the side and scooted back on her ass. Once she felt safely out of range of Micah's clawed, reaching hand, she twisted to her hands and knees and pushed up to leave both men behind.

CHAPTER 27

The Holcombs had wanted her charged with aiding and abetting. They'd demanded it. But every news story had flashed pictures of Veronica red-eyed and weeping, stitched scalp black and scabbed against the freshly shaved patch on her head.

She'd looked stunned and helpless in that first bright day after the cabin, one of her temples purple with bruising, and she'd denied every accusation. She'd known nothing. She'd planned nothing. The DA had found no proof to contradict her and their case was solved. Both suspects were dead. The kidnapping crisis was over.

Over but still dragging on. And on and on. Six months had passed in a flash, and the news trucks had long since driven away, but they would be back. She'd heard a TV movie was being made. Of course it was, because this story had everything. A rich family. A child in danger. Greed and lust. A dirty, filthy love triangle.

She couldn't even pretend she wouldn't have watched it herself, given half a remove from the horror of it. But they were moving on. Moving away.

She watched Sydney sort which stuffed animals were going to charity and which were going with her. Her bowed head was a common sight these days. She'd never held her head that way before.

"Your new room isn't huge, but we can hang a net near the ceiling to hold them all if you want."

Sydney shrugged. She was eleven now. She probably wouldn't get her animals out of the moving box once they got to their new place. She was growing up, and she'd never be her old self again. She'd never be a child.

She'd lost her father but, more than that, she'd lost her identity. She was no longer a confident daddy's girl with a school full of friends and every ounce of love she could possibly gather in her little arms.

Her father had been murdered. He'd died a criminal. Her mother was an infamous slut who'd shot her own lover. That was a scandal with eternal legs, and it would never leave her. Veronica had been afraid to put her daughter through a divorce, and now her entire world had burned down around them.

Sydney was broken. But she wasn't destroyed. Veronica told herself that over and over. She would recover.

Sydney would have a chance to have friends again once they were settled. Maybe Veronica should have kept her in school, but pulling her out had felt like the only solution. The other kids had taunted her. Those who hadn't had reluctantly told her they weren't allowed to hang out with her anymore.

Veronica couldn't even blame them. She couldn't rage. She wouldn't have let her precious child hang out in a den of crime either. So Veronica had been homeschooling her for the past few months. Her mom had been doing a lot of the heavy lifting, but Veronica had done her best to stick with it every day. This was *her* mess. *Her* chaos. She couldn't ever get tired of putting it right.

But Sydney couldn't be homeschooled forever. It wasn't her nature to be alone, isolated, even if it was all that Veronica craved anymore.

"Okay, pumpkin," Veronica said cheerfully when her mom stepped into the room. "Grandma will help you finish packing. I'm going to pick up a few things and I'll bring lunch back, okay?"

"Okay. Hi, Grandma!" Sydney sounded like her old self for one sweet, brief moment, but when Veronica kissed her, she ducked her head again.

"Don't forget to label the box with all your swim stuff. We'll only be two blocks from the beach, so we'll need to get it out right away."

"I know," Sydney muttered.

"And Grandma will be down to visit in just a few weeks."

"As soon as you're settled!" Veronica's mom said cheerfully.

"I know."

Sydney hated Veronica a little. Or more than a little. Veronica knew that because her daughter had said it often enough. But she also knew that they'd get past it. They were both alive and they would grow and live and love. She wouldn't allow any other option. Sydney went to therapy twice a week to help deal with her grief and anger, and they'd already found a new therapist for her near Galveston.

Galveston. They'd gone there once with Johnny. A road trip to the beach because they couldn't afford any other kind. Sydney had been seven, and for the next three years she'd talked about going back. She'd loved that place, and Veronica wanted to give her a reason to love again.

Veronica had suggested it two months earlier, expecting Sydney to object and say she'd miss her Grandma and Grandpa too much. But, to Veronica's surprise, she'd asked to think about it. A day later she'd said yes. "Let's move. I don't like it here anymore."

Here in Colorado or here in this house, she wasn't sure, but she'd taken her daughter's approval and run with it.

"Get something for your father too!" her mom yelled as Veronica grabbed her keys. "He's coming to help load the trailer."

"Got it."

She wasn't avoiding her dad anymore. He was no longer the greatest villain in her life. He didn't even make the top three. Those slots were reserved for Micah and Johnny and . . . the last slot was for herself. She prayed to God none of them would ever be dislodged. She'd happily wear that crown forever if it meant nothing bad ever happened to Sydney again.

Her father had made mistakes, but she was the one who'd put him on his pedestal. And now she could see who her real hero was. Her mother. Who'd always been there. Who'd never budged. Who'd hung the same Christmas decorations in the same spots year after year while her shiny, sparkly husband floated in and out of their lives like stardust.

Her mother, who was the only one who'd never asked what Veronica had done. She'd only held her so tightly it had hurt and murmured "You'll be okay. You'll be okay for Sydney" over and over, and maybe she'd even made it true.

Veronica stepped into the garage, startled by walls so recently cleared of their clutter. Once the police had returned Johnny's truck to her, she'd sold her own car and there'd been so much space then, even before she'd thrown out most of the accumulated crap.

She'd been waiting for months. Just waiting. And now they were free.

Her phone buzzed. It's really done? Fitz texted. Like DONE done?

Yes. I got a heads-up last week, and official notification this morning. No charges.

Wonderful!!! Trish says congrats. And so do I.

Thank you both! Trish had drawn away after the deaths. Not at first. At first she'd offered nothing but relief that Veronica and Sydney were alive and well. At first she'd been almost proud of her sister's survival.

But slowly, slowly it had sunk in that Veronica had been lying to everyone, that she'd had a whole life she'd been building outside her marriage. And then parents at Trish's school had begun to complain. She hadn't lost her job, but the school district had asked if she'd be willing to take a brief leave of absence until her notorious family of kidnappers wasn't on the news every day.

So Trish had pulled back, and Veronica had let her go. But Fitz kept them connected, determined that this rift would heal. And it would. It had to. Because Veronica had lost so much already.

Stone-faced despite the smiling emoji she sent to Fitz, Veronica got behind the wheel and backed Johnny's truck out of the garage. Johnny's truck. Not hers. A stupid way to keep him in their memory maybe, but there it was. She wouldn't put him away and erase him. He deserved better. He hadn't been innocent, but he hadn't deserved to die.

She'd loved him once. She'd loved him recklessly, stupidly, and she'd forgotten all that in the years of disappointments and betrayals and weariness. But she remembered now, too late. That sweet college romance with a lovely, shining boy.

Veronica set her jaw and drove. Today wasn't a day to think about the past.

They needed more cleaning supplies, more drinks, more snacks for the road. She'd purchased a smartphone for Sydney as a surprise for the road trip, and she wanted to get her a gift card too, so her daughter could buy all the apps she wanted. But instead of stopping for supplies, she drove past every store and continued on until she reached the ugly brick building she hated so much.

When she asked for Detective Reed, she was directed toward a far-too-familiar office packed full of desks. By the time she got there, Reed was already standing next to her chair, clearly alerted by the officer in reception.

"Mrs. Bradley. I wasn't expecting you."

"We're leaving today. I promised I'd give you an address."

"Thanks. I appreciate that."

Veronica handed over the address, written in pink marker on a notecard. Detritus from packing up their junk drawer. "No offense, but I hope you'll never get in touch. I hope it's all over."

"Perhaps it is. Unless there's anything else you'd like to contribute?"

Veronica laughed. She'd given up everything. Her blood, sweat, and tears. Her love and horror. She'd handed over every detail she could remember from every interaction with Micah. Everything she'd heard him even whisper to her or Johnny. She'd confessed to every moment she'd spent with him. Every moment but one. She'd kept that one evening for herself.

So she smiled and shook her head. "You know all my secrets, Reed. It's time for me to take my daughter and start over. You know about the name change?"

The detective stared at her. She stared hard, arms folded, lips a disapproving line. But she finally relented and tipped her chin in a nod. "So you didn't find anything else while you were packing up?"

"No. Nothing."

"Micah never gave you anything?"

She sighed but kept her face relaxed and friendly. "He was determined to kill me after I found out about the kidnapping. Why would he have paid me off?"

Reed shrugged. "Doesn't hurt to ask. They're still looking for that last four hundred K they never recovered."

"Maybe Micah bought a fucking yacht or something. I have no idea. I haven't worked in six months and I'm selling the house my daughter grew up in so we can afford a two-bedroom apartment in Texas. Feel free to drop by on your next vacation if you want to make sure we're still poor."

The detective held up her hands. "All right. I get it."

"Let the internet sleuths enjoy their treasure hunt," Veronica added bitterly. The missing money kept everything fresh and new online. Veronica had shut down every social media account long ago, and she no longer even had an email address. The stalking and accusations had become too frightening. She'd even caught a man in her backyard with a metal detector. A metal detector. As if he were looking for gold bullion instead of cash.

"If we move again, I'll let you know," she offered. "I don't want you to think I'm running. It just isn't safe here. Sydney . . ."

Reed's face finally softened. Veronica knew now that she had two daughters of her own. "I know. She's a sweet girl. I get it. You two stay safe."

They exchanged stiff goodbyes, and Veronica left that place behind, hopefully forever. She hit the freeway, checking her rearview mirror the whole way just in case. She was sure they must have tailed her at some point, but even if they were still suspicious, there weren't unlimited resources and there were new crimes committed every day.

Still, she took an early exit and circled downtown Denver twice before she found a nonmetered parking spot and slipped on her sunglasses. She took off her ball cap and tugged off the brown wig she'd been wearing, exposing her short new dirty-blond style. Even Sydney hadn't seen it yet. Another surprise for the road. Blond enough to change her appearance, not so blond it would draw attention. Frankly, the color wasn't even flattering on her. All the better to blend into the crowd. She put her hat back on and grabbed her slouchy purse and the brand-name shopping bag she'd brought along.

Three blocks of practicing her most confident stride and she was ready. She pulled her cell phone from her pocket, swung the crisp bag that proved she'd been out shopping, and strode through the glass doors of Micah's old building.

Her ruse wasn't foolproof, but it proved far more than she needed. The woman behind the welcome desk barely looked up from her own phone as Veronica jotted down a random apartment number and signed a few loops for a name. Veronica gave her a wave and made a beeline for the elevators. As soon as she'd passed out of sight, she ducked her head and hit the Up button.

The elevator flew up. She watched Micah's floor pass with only the tiniest lurch of her gut. And then she was past the penthouse and at the top, and the elevator doors opened to the rooftop hallway. Heart thundering as she prayed no new security had been installed, she reached for the door and turned the knob. It wasn't locked.

One more obstacle passed.

And here she stumbled. She'd hoped that the middle of a workday afternoon would mean privacy, but two women were on the rooftop patio, drinking wine at one of the small tables and typing away at their laptops. She felt a brief moment of jealousy for whatever jobs they had, but the twinge settled into anxiety that they wouldn't leave. Or that they'd notice her. Or that they'd take a selfie and accidentally catch her in the background.

She headed for the lounge chair farthest from them and stretched out as if she'd come up for some sun. She'd even brought a book in her purse.

Her shopping bag looked strange and conspicuous now, but she hadn't thought that far ahead. She also hadn't thought ahead to the disappointment of the next step. She wasn't betting everything on this. It wasn't even a likelihood, much less a certainty, but she owed Sydney this chance. Her little girl's cursed, criminal birthright.

She took out her book and waited. She checked her phone. Pretended to read again. After a while she gave up and stared out at the mountains.

She hadn't loved him, had she? What kind of person could love a man like that? What kind of desperate fool?

She'd thought him smooth and ambitious, but he'd only been false and greedy. All these luxuries had put him deep into debt. He'd mismanaged his business, and clients had started falling away. He'd failed to pay subcontractors and lost more work. In the end, he'd been limping along with a few big jobs he'd underbid just to hold on.

In August, his bid to build a new outdoor entertainment area for the Holcomb estate hadn't panned out. Someone else had gotten the work, but that August visit had struck Micah with inspiration. All that money. All that land. And all those kids running around on it.

The landscaping meeting was the only connection the police had been able to make, but for Veronica it wasn't theory; it was fact. She could see Micah up there, schmoozing with Hank Holcomb, eyeing the estate, looking down on the whole city of Denver, and wondering why he couldn't have a life like that. He'd planned the kidnapping for weeks or months, he'd pulled her husband into the plan, and Veronica had been there the whole time, helping relax him enough to think clearly. She'd wanted a little piece of Micah's life, and boy, had she gotten it.

The women interrupted her tortured memories by gathering up their things, their words louder and livelier as they planned an evening out.

Veronica waited after they left, giving them time to get on the elevator and then time to come back for anything they'd forgotten. Then she gathered her bags and rushed to the far wall of the rooftop.

There was no hesitation this time. She hopped over the wall and landed with a crunch of gravel. Without Micah's little nest to guide her, she wasn't sure exactly where to look, so she backed up and surveyed the bricks. A half dozen of them looked loose, so she walked a few feet to the left and started there.

For all her planning, she hadn't brought gloves, and the brick scraped at her fingertips as she tried to work it free. It budged once and then refused to move, so she said a quick prayer it was the wrong one and moved on. The second brick came away easily and revealed nothing but a spiderweb in the blank space beyond it.

The third brick was lower, closer to the floor, and she felt a hopeful jolt of recognition as she dug her fingers into the gap. She tugged and pushed and pulled until finally the brick began to slide free. She dropped it on the ground and reached in before she could worry about spiders at all.

And she found something. A pipe. A baggie. She pulled out a bag sprinkled with a few desiccated bits of pot. Her heart dipped a little that it was all she'd found, but she shoved her hand in deep and touched something cool and slick. Plastic. She closed her hand over the thick square and tugged it out, scraping blood from her knuckles in the process. But she didn't care. The find was a heavy weight in her hand as she turned it over, a bundle of plastic wrap and tape. She could just make out a dull-green glint beneath the layers.

She'd forgotten to bring a knife or anything sharp, but it didn't matter. This was either the cash or it wasn't.

Shoving her hand back into the hole, she patted around and found one more tightly wrapped bundle and drew it free as well.

Once the hidey-hole was empty, she tugged all the other loose bricks free as well, but they hid nothing. She placed them all carefully back in their places.

When the wall looked normal again, Veronica shoved her treasure into the empty shoebox in her shopping bag, then popped her head over the wall to make sure the coast was clear. She was alone, so she climbed back to the roof deck, straightened her clothes, and hurried to the elevator.

She worked her bleeding hand into her purse to hide the scrapes when she reached the lobby. No one even glanced at her as she emerged onto the street. She walked fast and then faster, desperate to get to Johnny's truck. Once inside, she dug her keys from the bottom of her purse and stabbed at one of the bundles. As soon as she'd ripped a little of the plastic away, she saw the instantly recognizable ink of US currency and shrieked.

Startled by her own shout, she covered her mouth and looked around. The city moved on, unaware and uncaring. She tugged and tore at a little more of the plastic and saw the number one hundred.

"Holy shit."

Johnny had been paid in twenties, but the police had asked the public to be on the lookout for anyone spending an unusual amount of cash in twenties or hundreds. The Holcombs had accumulated the ransom cash in several different ways, some through the bank and some through personal stashes.

These weren't new bills, either. They were uneven and crinkled. They'd been ordered by Micah to pay in untraceable money in nonsequential bills, and apparently they'd complied.

Still, she'd have to be careful. She'd have to save the money for a very long time. But that wasn't a problem.

Veronica dropped the bills back into the shoebox, then shoved the whole thing under the seat. If they were all hundred-dollar bills, she'd guess she had a hundred thousand now, at least. Not the entire amount, but apparently Micah had spread out his stash. Some had been found in his condo. Some in a safe-deposit box. And some . . . some on the rooftop deck.

Life would be hard for a long while. They'd have to start over. But senior-living facilities were always hiring, and their little apartment in Galveston was cheap. Sydney would recover and make new friends. She'd get better. She'd be happy. She'd have to be at some point. Wouldn't she?

And Micah would start her college fund. He owed Sydney that, at least. He owed her the life he'd stolen from her.

Veronica tugged her wig back into place. She couldn't risk anyone seeing her new appearance before she was out of town. She put her sunglasses and hat on and carefully checked her mirrors before pulling out. From now on she'd be a law-abiding citizen. A paragon of virtue.

The money beneath the seat should glow with accusation, but if it did, Veronica couldn't see it past her shades.

Three hours later, they were loaded up and on the road, Old Man stretched out across the back seat. Sydney had wept as she'd said goodbye to her grandparents, but she was quiet now, worn out from the upheaval.

"We'll stop tonight to get some rest. If you see a spot you like, let me know. Someplace with a pool, maybe."

"Okay." She stared out the window. She was still half an inch below the recommended height, but Veronica let her sit in the front seat now. She'd grown up a lot, after all.

Veronica wanted to give Sydney her new phone, but she hesitated. It felt like too flashy a gift for this moment. It reminded Veronica of her father instead of the steadiness Syd needed right now. So Veronica turned down the music and waited for Syd to look up.

"Grandma put something in the glove box for you."

Sydney's face brightened. "Cookies?"

"No, not cookies. Take a look."

Her daughter reached tentatively for the latch and Veronica tried not to wince. Sydney had never done anything with hesitation before. She opened the glove compartment and saw the red box inside. "What is it?"

"A surprise, silly."

Syd actually giggled at that, and Veronica smiled so hard her cheeks hurt. She hadn't used those muscles often lately.

Sydney popped open the lid of the box and lifted the tissue paper inside to find an envelope. She opened that even more carefully than normal, then drew out a card. Inside was a gift certificate for a meal kit service and a handwritten note: *Let's cook every Sunday and compare notes. I love you, Grandma.*

"Mom! Mom, it's six months' worth of recipe deliveries! Six months!"

"That's so cool! You can cook dinner for us in our new place!"

"Yeah, and maybe Grandma and I can even FaceTime while we cook on Sundays!"

"Grandma would love that. I bet Fitz and Trish can help her set that up. It would be like a little cooking show."

"Yeah!" she squealed. "A cooking show!"

Tears burned Veronica's eyes at the sound. She had to turn her face carefully and stare straight ahead so Syd wouldn't notice.

"Can I call Grandma to say thank you?"

"Of course," she managed to say, picking up her phone from the console to hand it over.

They'd make this work. They'd find a new life together. Somewhere safe and peaceful. Veronica could learn who she was on her own, finally. She'd be better. But she would never truly be free of this. Not really.

But someday . . . someday Sydney would.

ABOUT THE AUTHOR

Victoria Helen Stone, formerly writing as *USA Today* bestselling novelist Victoria Dahl, was born and raised in the flattest parts of the Midwest. Now that she's escaped the plains of her youth, she writes dark suspense from an upstairs office high in the Wasatch Mountains of Utah. She enjoys summer trail hikes with her family almost as much as she enjoys staying inside during the winter. Since leaving the lighter side of fiction, she has written the critically acclaimed, bestselling novels *Evelyn, After*; *Half Past*; and *Jane Doe*. For more on the author and her work, visit www.VictoriaHelenStone.com and www.VictoriaDahl.com.